"DOCTOR? A MOMENT, PLEASE."

Bashir stopped and turned. "Yes, Commander?"

"A word of advice," Vaughn said in low tones. "Don't try to be a hero. Don't think for a moment that you're going to be able to find evidence you can use to expose Thirty-One. Just go in, do the job, and come home. Understand?"

"I understand what you're saying," Bashir said suspiciously, "but not why."

"Because I'd like to see all of you come home alive. Cole needs you to do his dirty work for him, but that's all he's going to allow. Try to go beyond that and I can guarantee there will be unpleasant repercussions." With that, Vaughn turned and walked away.

Bashir stared after the commander for several seconds, wondering not without some smoldering anger what he was supposed to make of all that. The doctor usually enjoyed a good mystery, but this was something else entirely. And as he entered the runabout, Bashir resolved that if and when they returned from Sindorin, he was going to get to the bottom of this particular enigma once and for all.

NJ UNIFORM
CONSTRUCTION
CODE
NJAC 5:23

STAR TREK
DEEP SPACE NINE®

SECTION 31™

ABYSS

DAVID WEDDLE
and
JEFFREY LANG

Based upon STAR TREK®
created by Gene Roddenberry,
and STAR TREK:
DEEP SPACE NINE
created by Rick Berman &
Michael Piller

POCKET BOOKS
New York   London   Toronto   Sydney   Singapore

An *Original* Publication of POCKET BOOKS

POCKET BOOKS, a division of Simon & Schuster, Inc.
1230 Avenue of the Americas, New York, NY 10020

STAR TREK is a Registered Trademark of
Paramount Pictures.

This book is published by Pocket Books, a division of
Simon & Schuster, Inc., under exclusive license from
Paramount Pictures.

ISBN: 0–671–77483-2

First Pocket Books printing July 2001

10 9 8 7 6 5 4 3 2 1

POCKET and colophon are registered trademarks of
Simon & Schuster, Inc.

Printed in the U.S.A.

ACKNOWLEDGMENTS

First and foremost, I'd like to thank Marco Palmieri for thinking of me.

David Weddle's name comes first because he's the guy who came up with the story, but, just as importantly, because he co-wrote "Inquisition," the *Star Trek: Deep Space Nine* episode that introduced Section 31, without which there would be no "Section 31" novel series in the first place. Thanks, David. The *Star Trek* universe is a cooler place for having some dark corners.

Thank you to my beta readers, Heather, Helen, and Katie, for their insightful comments, their unstinting enthusiasm, and their tolerance of periodic anxiety attacks. Additional thanks to Tristan and Joshua, the targets of frequent, unexplained requests for their opinions about things like "What's the difference between a warrior and a soldier?"

Last, hugs and kisses to Katie (the same one as above) for supporting me through this process and to Andy for understanding when Daddy couldn't play because he had to go work on his book.

"For every Julian Bashir that can be created, there's a Khan Singh waiting in the wings."

—STARFLEET REAR ADMIRAL BENNETT

ABYSS

Chapter One

Something was almost ready to come out of warp. Something very big.

It was tripping all of Deep Space 9's proximity alarms, lighting up the sensor board in ways Ensign Thirishar ch'Thane had never seen before. If the readings were accurate—and he was certain they were—a subspace displacement of almost unheard-of proportions was heading directly for the station and playing havoc with the long-range sensor arrays. Shar found himself struggling with his console, fighting back his mounting frustration as each klaxon he muted was quickly replaced by another.

The sudden pins-and-needles sensation in his antennae alerted him to the fact that Commander Vaughn was standing just behind him. Shar tried not to look flustered; the commander had a casual manner about him much of the time, but Vaughn was always an intimidating presence. Most Andorians cultivated a polite, soft-spoken demeanor, even—some might say *espe-*

cially—when they were about to slip daggers between each other's ribs, but Shar was still adapting to Vaughn's habit of shifting back and forth between easygoing civility and Starfleet formality.

"Cardassian control interfaces take some getting used to, don't they?" he asked gently, sipping the noisome beverage Shar had learned was called "twig tea."

"Yes, sir," Shar admitted, thoroughly embarrassed. After six weeks as DS9's science officer, he thought he'd finally mastered the idiosyncrasies of his own console. To have the station's new first officer witness his sudden ineptitude was mortifying.

As if sensing his thoughts, Vaughn leaned over for a better view of the readings. "Relax, Ensign," he said. "Given the circumstances, it's no wonder the arrays are going haywire. Stay with it."

Shar let out a breath and concentrated. As he moved his long fingers over the board again, the klaxons finally began to diminish. When the last of them was silenced, Vaughn patted him on the shoulder. "Good. Whenever operating alien technology, I find it's usually helpful to keep in mind the psychology of the people who created it. In this case, extremely detail-oriented, meticulous, and thorough. Redundancies in the system are a given."

"I'll remember that, sir," Shar said.

"Something coming in?" Shar looked up to see Colonel Kira standing in the open doors of the station commander's office, her voice echoing loudly in the otherwise quiet operations center.

Returning to his position at the central ops table, Vaughn set up an interface with Shar's sensor board. "Certainly looks that way. Something quite large, coming in at low warp."

"Nog?" Kira asked, coming down the stairs to join Vaughn.

"It had better be," the commander said. "If it isn't, we're going to become a multi-gigaton smear of debris across the Denorios Belt."

Kira ignored Vaughn's commentary as she studied the tabletop display. "But no hail?" The question was directed at Shar.

"No, sir," Shar replied, "but we anticipated this. Something this big coming out of warp, when you consider the disruption to subspace, it's to be expected . . ." But Colonel Kira wasn't listening anymore. She was watching the track of blips on the table.

"Does it look to you like he's giving himself enough room to brake?" Kira asked Vaughn.

"It depends on how much momentum it had when Nog took it into warp," Vaughn said. "Let him do his job, Colonel. He seemed to know what he was doing. The kid is smart. And he has style to burn."

"Style," Kira repeated. "Nog?" She seemed to be having trouble forming an association between the two words.

"Sure," Vaughn said. "His little scheme. His solution for . . . all this." Vaughn waved his hand around the dimmer-than-usual operations center. Many of DS9's nonessential systems had been shut off during the ongoing state of emergency. Ever since the colonel had been forced to jettison the station's fusion core, DS9 had been running on a complex network of Starfleet emergency generators. The measure had bought them time, allowing the station to continue functioning, albeit at nearly a third of its normal power consumption. But after two weeks of running at full capacity, the system was showing the strain. In the last few days alone, entire sections of the station had been evacuated and powered down so as not to further overtax the generator network. In fact, with the exception of the scheduled aid convoys to Cardassia Prime and the three Allied ships patrolling space near the wormhole, DS9 was currently turning away all traffic.

The pulse of the station had slowed to a sluggish thud since Kira had ejected its great heart into space. The explosion, according to the Bajoran news feeds, had been visible across most of the planet's nightside, appearing like a new star just as the westernmost cities were slipping into evening and those easternmost were turning off their lights for the night. Young children had run outdoors thinking it was fireworks for a holiday while their grandparents, recalling the arrival of the Cardassian occupation fleet, had fought to keep them inside.

Shar was both intrigued and somewhat perplexed by the behavior of some of his crewmates as conditions aboard the station deteriorated. The more the place began to feel like a frontier outpost, the *happier* some of the old hands seemed to be. Dr. Bashir was practically giddy about it sometimes. Shar had begun to form the opinion that these people were in serious need of some leave time, a *lot* of leave time. *This is what happens,* he told himself, *when you associate with prophets, ghosts, and demons.*

Shar's attention swam back to the conversation between the commander and the colonel. "I admit I've been skeptical about this all along," Kira was saying. "But I hate to discourage Nog's initiative . . ."

". . . and you didn't have any better ideas," Vaughn finished for her.

"Something like that," Kira said. Shar wondered if she minded that the commander finished sentences for her. Then again, he decided, the colonel seemed like the sort who would finish sentences for her commanding officer. He hadn't yet been asked to sit in on a briefing between Kira and her Bajoran superiors. *Now, that would be interesting,* he decided.

So far, there hadn't been any discussion about what would happen if Nog's plan didn't work, but Shar could not find it in himself to be too optimistic about DS9's future. The Cardassian station was thirty years old, and despite all the reengineering that Starfleet had put into it, it had taken quite a beating in recent years. Perhaps it would be a mercy to send the station spinning into Bajor's sun and start over fresh. In such a scenario, considering the strategic importance of the wormhole, it seemed likely that Starfleet would insist on constructing a new starbase, a project that would certainly cause controversy and discord among the Allies, unless Bajor's latest petition for Federation membership were put on a fast track. The Federation was war-weary and its resources were stretched thin. The Council would bend a polite ear to listen to all sides, but when it was done, they would send in the Starfleet Corps of Engineers no matter what anyone said. Shar knew how politics worked. Better, in fact, than he really wanted to know.

"Anything on the short-range sensors, Ensign?" Kira asked.

Shar blinked, then said, "I was told that the short-range array was to be taken offline until further notice. Sir." Shar attempted to project a mental image of Commander Vaughn issuing the order. He knew that Bajorans were no more psionic than most Andorians, but he thought it was worth the attempt.

Vaughn, apparently, had better than average psionic abilities for a human, because he picked up Shar's distress call. "I gave the order, Colonel," he said. "The patrol ships are more than capable of covering our front yard."

"I don't remember authorizing that," Kira said, and Shar felt himself singed by the heat of the glare she focused on Vaughn. He fought the urge to scratch his left antenna.

"You didn't," Vaughn said agreeably. "I decided to shut them down yesterday." He took a sip of tea. "You were busy dealing with the Cardassian liaison at the time. I didn't want to bother you with it. It was an easy choice: short-range sensors or lights."

Shar watched as the colonel held her first officer's gaze for a moment. He knew that Commander Vaughn's job had once been hers. Not long ago, it had been *her* responsibility to know *everything* that happened on the station. Shar had heard that she went through a similar period of adjustment with Vaughn's predecessor, Tiris Jast, and wondered how much Kira still blamed herself for Jast's tragic demise . . . and how much that misplaced guilt played on her natural impulse to micromanage the running of the station. Shar knew enough people with command responsibilities to know that one of the worst things about being promoted was coming to grips with the idea that you had to trust someone else to make some of the decisions.

Kira, it seemed, was still making that adjustment. Her apparent frustration didn't evaporate, but it did recede significantly. "Right," she said. "Lights. Good call, Commander."

Shar felt his own tension diminish just in time to hear Lieutenant Bowers report from tactical that he was receiving warning flashes from all three patrol ships, each going to heightened alert status as the monstrous subspace displacement closed on the Bajoran system. Shar shot a questioning glance toward Kira, and waited for her nod before bringing the short range sensors back online.

He found himself wishing he'd kept them off as he looked at the readings, cursing softly in his native tongue when he saw that the disruption to subspace had intensified markedly. The colonel didn't seem to notice his outburst, more concerned with instructing Bowers to activate the main viewscreen, but Commander Vaughn shot him a warning glance that indicated he might know some Andorii.

The viewscreen came online and Shar tried to divide his attention between the image on it and his console. Space split open with a rapidly dissolving warp field. Time seemed to slow down as the aperture continued to expand, stretching so wide that for a moment, in spite of everything he knew to the contrary about what was unfolding, Shar wondered if DS9 would be pulled inside.

Instead, something emerged. Led by a single runabout, nine assorted Federation starships moving in carefully calculated formation dropped out of warp as one, the bright blue cones of their tractor beams strategically distributed over the tremendous mass of their shared burden. How anyone had talked nine starship captains—not to mention their chief engineers—into even attempting such a thing, Shar couldn't guess. He didn't need to imagine the complex level of calibration and coordination that the operation required, or who was behind it; Nog had transmitted his revised plan before it had been implemented, and everyone but Commander Vaughn had pretty much decided that he was out of his mind. The computer models, not to mention Deep Space 9's increasing desperation, had finally convinced Kira that they had nothing to lose, and Shar privately began to suspect that the colonel shared Vaughn's apparent taste for audacity.

Shar saw the warning signs in the data stream flowing across the board, then looked back up at the viewscreen, expecting to see warp nacelles blowing out, warp cores ejecting, and clouds of white-hot plasma venting . . . but instead he saw something else:

Salvation.

He looked at the colonel. She was smiling—no, grinning—then whooping with triumph as she madly pounded the command station, unleashing the elation of a woman who, he knew, despite everything else she had experienced in her life, never took the miraculous for granted.

Shar looked up at the screen again. It was still there.

Empok Nor, Deep Space 9's long-abandoned twin.

"Colonel, we're receiving a hail from the *Rio Grande,*" Bowers announced.

"It's about time," Kira said, unable to get the smile off her face. "On screen, Lieutenant."

Bowers replaced the exterior scene with the image of Nog at the controls of the runabout. He looked, Shar thought, as though he hadn't slept in days. "Lieutenant Nog reporting in, Colonel."

"Nog, I—" Kira started, then faltered and shook her head, words failing her. Finally she took a breath and tried again. "You realize this is going to ruin my view of the wormhole, don't you?"

Nog almost cracked a smile. "Not for long, Colonel," he assured her. "Once we transfer Empok Nor's lower core to Deep Space 9, we can tow what's left of the station someplace nearby and park it there for the next time we need spare parts."

"How did the station hold up?" Vaughn asked.

"Even better than the simulations projected, Commander," Nog said. "Some minor structural damage to two of the lower pylons, but for a ten-day low-warp journey across three light-years . . . not bad. It's like Chief O'Brien used to say about Deep Space 9: The Cardassians built this place to last."

"You look tired, Nog," Kira said.

Nog shrugged his shoulders, seeming to resist the urge to rub the large black circles under his eyes. "I'm fine, Colonel. Slept three hours last night. I'll be able to start work on the fusion-core transfer just as soon as we've stabilized our orbit."

"No, I don't think so," Vaughn said. "See that Empok Nor is stable, but I want you asleep in your quarters when you're finished." Nog began to protest, but stopped when he saw the tilt of Vaughn's head. "Don't force me to make it an order, Nog."

Nog sagged, then seemed to almost smile gratefully. "Yes, Commander. Thank you, sir. Colonel . . . I want you to know the SCE really came through. This wouldn't have happened without them, or the ships in the convoy."

Kira smiled. "I'll be sure to note that in my report, Nog."

"I also assured the convoy captains you'd be able to arrange shore leave for their crews on Bajor," Nog said, suddenly looking a little worried. "And any maintenance the ships might need . . ."

If Nog expected the colonel to be put out, he was disappointed. "Don't worry, Lieutenant," Kira said, still smiling. "I'll take care of it. And Nog?"

"Colonel?"

"Excellent work."

Nog's face split into a grin. "Thank you, Colonel," he said, and signed off.

Vaughn settled back into a chair and sipped his tea. He looked, Shar thought, as satisfied as he would be if he had just finished pulling the station all the way from the Trivas system himself. "I told you the kid had style."

Chapter Two

It was to be his first vacation in some time, since his trip to Risa with Leeta, Jadzia, Worf, and Quark, before the war. It was also to be his first with Ezri. They were to go back to Earth, back home, so he could show her some bits and pieces of his past, the ones he was willing to share at this early stage in their relationship. And of course, while there, they'd look in on the O'Briens in San Francisco, and drop in on Jake and Joseph Sisko in New Orleans.

But this leave was different for another reason, Bashir reminded himself; Kira had ordered most of the non-techs to clear out, get lost, take a hike. The station needed to be powered down to its lowest threshold before they could transfer Empok Nor's fusion core, as delicate and daunting a bit of surgery as Bashir had ever encountered, and Kira didn't want any unnecessary personnel on board while it was in progress.

"Since when is the chief medical officer considered unnecessary personnel?" Bashir had asked.

"Since now," Kira had replied. "Since I have an Akira-class starship nearby with a fully staffed and fully equipped sickbay."

"But you're letting Quark stay!"

"And there are a lot of people remaining on board who are going to need downtime during the next few days. And much as I hate to admit it, the role Quark plays in the well-being of station crew can't be minimized, especially now. I need him, Julian. I don't need you. Have a nice time."

Bashir shook his head as he recalled the conversation, slipping his toothbrush into the side pocket of his luggage and hefting the bag. Ten kilos, he judged, and smiled in satisfaction. Packing a suitcase had developed into a minor fixation over the years, a game to see if he could pack just the right combination of articles to meet any eventuality during his travels. It sometimes made for an oddly shaped bag and good-natured ridicule from his friends, but sometimes his foresight paid off . . . like the time the *Rio Grande* had lost power near a white dwarf star and Miles had been very glad to see that self-sealing stem bolt. . . .

He placed the bag on the bed. Now to collect Ezri and be on their way to airlock seven before their ride, the civilian transport *Wayfarer,* got under way.

Jadzia, Bashir knew, had been a talented last-minute packer. Worf had mentioned how she once yanked a suitcase out of the closet five minutes before a ship was scheduled to leave and was still the first one to the airlock. It was a gift, Bashir hoped, that Ezri had inherited.

The door to her quarters opened as he approached, the sensors encoded to permit him entry. Either Ezri was expecting him or, more likely, she had forgotten to change the sensor key since the last time he had been invited over. He was pleased to see a travel bag sitting on the floor, though it looked suspiciously deflated. She might be traveling light, but there was a more likely explanation. Bashir picked up the strap with one finger and lifted the bag off the floor. Empty.

He sighed.

"Ezri?" he called.

No answer.

He went into the bedroom, where her uniform jacket had been tossed carelessly over a chair, then followed the sounds of movement into the bathroom. Ezri was sitting on the floor working a blob of clay, pinching and pulling it with her fingers. There were several other blobs on the floor around her. Her red command shirt was caked with the stuff. "I don't know if I'll ever get used to seeing you in that color," he commented.

Ezri looked up and said, "Oh," as if startled. "Hi. What time is it?" There were smears of clay on her chin and cheeks. She scratched her nose and left another blotch.

"Almost thirteen hundred hours," Bashir replied, trying very hard not to sound annoyed. "Our transport is leaving in forty minutes."

"Wow. Later than I thought," Ezri said. "Sorry." She set the object she had been working with down on the floor and carefully studied the mess. "Clay isn't as easy as I thought it would be," she said.

13

"What made you decide to take up sculpture?" Bashir asked. He fought the urge to add, "Especially *now?*"—but lost.

"Well," Ezri said, either missing his exasperation or choosing to overlook it, "I was off duty today and figured that since all I had to do was pack, this would be a good time to work on some of the exercises the Symbiosis Commission recommended."

When they had first become a couple, Bashir and Ezri had lain awake many a night (as new lovers do) discussing their histories, shared and unshared, as well as their similarities and differences. Among the interesting details that had emerged were things like the fact that Bashir liked peanut butter and jelly, but never the two together. Ezri hated yoga and considered lawn bowling a "sport" (it was a family thing). Also, she hated mint chocolate-chip ice cream, which surprised Bashir, because Jadzia had loved it.

They had discussed some more serious things, too, such as how comparable their peculiar situations might be: her joining and his genetic enhancements. Over time, they had come to the conclusion that the circumstances of their transformations were similar only in broad strokes. The change to Bashir's psyche had happened years ago, when he was only a child, and, though frightening, it had been like the thrill one feels emerging from a fog into a clear space with a spectacular view.

Ezri's experience had been almost exactly the opposite in many respects. She had been a mature adult, or, as she conceded, an *adult,* even if not mature on all counts. She had just been coming into a period of her life in which some of its emotional clutter was beginning to sort out, when she was plunged into the mental cacophony of eight other lives.

There had been a time when Julian Bashir had thought that everyone sought out someone like themselves for a partner, someone who would see the world in a similar way. But his relationship with Ezri had changed that, making him realize that he had never needed someone like himself to feel complete. Ezri was someone who could help him bridge the gap between himself and the holes in his experiences.

Dax allowed Bashir to help her up off the floor, then leaned against him for several seconds, steadying herself. Obviously, she had been sitting on the cold, hard tile floor for some time and lost some circulation in her legs. She placed her hands in the middle of her back and stretched, leaving two wet handprints.

Bashir studied the blobs on the floor and saw that they were, in fact, attempts at faces, or, more accurately, masks, since the eyeholes had been left open. He counted eight in all. At least two of them were clearly meant to be males with strong cheekbones and broad brows, while at least three others were definitely women. Bashir recognized one of these, the most clearly defined—with hair pulled back from the forehead and a wide mouth turned up at the corners. Jadzia.

"The previous hosts?" Bashir guessed.

Ezri nodded while looking down at her handiwork, turning her head this way and that. "The idea is *not* to try for something too representational. The exercise is more about impression and emotional response. I think about each host, and the feelings guide my fingers."

"Interesting concept," he said, lightly brushing his

finger across the cheek of one of the male faces, where Ezri had somehow managed to convey an impression of triumph and tragedy at the same time. *Torias?* "But is this the sort of project you want to undertake just before we leave for a vacation?"

Ezri turned to the sink and began to run what Bashir suspected was a large percentage of her daily emergency ration of water into the basin. "Don't try to counsel the counselor, Doctor. Former counselor," she corrected herself. "I know my timing is a little off and I know myself well enough to understand why." Shutting off the flow of water, she immersed her hands and began scrubbing. "I admit it—I'm a little nervous about this trip, about leaving the station right now. I feel like I'm running away just when things are in upheaval."

"You were *ordered* away," Bashir corrected.

"I could make a case for staying if I wanted," she said, hitting the sink's recycle setting. Then she looked up at him and grinned. "But I figure they can get along without me for a while and I really *do* want to go see where you grew up. I'm guessing I'll come away with all sorts of *insights . . .*"

"Oh, lord," Bashir groaned. "Maybe it's not too late to convince Kira to let us stay."

After rubbing the worst of the stains off her hands, she threw the now brown towel into the recycler and refilled the basin. "Ha! No way! Now we have to go. And as long as we're doing some short-term analysis, what's with you not saying anything to anyone about your promotion, Lieutenant Commander? When Nog was promoted, the entire station turned out for the party. Not that I'm jealous on your behalf, but no one has ever accused you of avoiding a celebration."

Bashir shrugged, resisting the sudden impulse to touch the new pip on his collar. "It didn't seem appropriate somehow," he said. "I'm not like Nog. He still needs the recognition, the ego boost . . ."

Ezri was splashing water on her face when she suddenly stopped and looked at him. "*Nog* needs ego boost?"

"My dear ex-counselor," Bashir said, grinning, "I'll have you know that inside that narrow chest beats the heart of a very sensitive young Ferengi."

"Are we talking about the same Nog?" Ezri asked, working the soap into a lather. "The one who watches me every time I walk past?"

"He's just appreciating some of your finer qualities. Again, the mark of a sensitive soul."

Ezri rolled her eyes. Then, she snapped her head around and regarded Bashir carefully. "Hey!" she said. "How did we get off the subject of your promotion?"

"How," Bashir countered, "did we get off the subject of your not being sure you wanted to go on vacation?"

"I'm packing! I'm packing!" Ezri cried, drying her face.

Bashir smiled to himself, then changed the subject again. "I made Nog promise to turn on Vic's again as soon as he's finished."

"You didn't have to do that," Ezri said. Bashir followed her into the bedroom as she pulled off her soiled shirt, remembering to take her rank pips off first, and tossed it in a corner of the room. After donning a fresh one, she began to tear open drawers and toss things onto the bed. "Nog would have done it anyway."

"Vic made *me* promise before we saved his program. I think he was a little worried what would happen if Empok Nor hadn't made it through intact."

"Maybe you should activate him long enough to tell him." She tossed a pile of undergarments onto the bed.

"Just so I can shut him down again until the work's finished?" Bashir asked. "No, it's better this way. And just in case something does go wrong while we're away, I forwarded a copy of his program to Felix."

"Good idea," she said, and to Bashir's abject horror, she gathered the pile of clothes into a ball, obviously intending to carry it out into the living room, where her bag lay. He wondered if this was part of the Jadzia Dax packing technique Worf had never mentioned. "Where's your suitcase?" she asked. "I don't see anything perfect and hermetically sealed lying around here."

"Back in my quarters."

"Well, you'd better go get it if you want to make this flight."

"Yes, ma'am," Bashir said, heading for the door. "And may I say that you've obviously taken well to command." The doors closed behind him before he could hear what Ezri said in reply.

There was a man in Bashir's quarters, gazing out the window.

Standing in the doorway, Bashir felt an absurd desire to say "Excuse me!" and back out of the room before the analytical portion of his brain kicked in. The man was a middle-aged human, medium height and build. He wore a moderately pleasant expression, the kind of bland, neutral smile that Bashir would feel inclined to return while waiting for a turbolift. His dark hair was extremely close-cropped over a well-formed skull. But the man's most noteworthy characteristic was his eyes, which were a startling emerald green.

"Dr. Bashir," the man said. "It's a pleasure to finally meet you."

There was something about the way the man said his name. He continued to collect data—*the movements of his facial muscles, the constant readiness of his seemingly relaxed hands, the way he carries his weight squarely on his pelvis*—parsed it, then drew conclusions.

Section 31.

The doctor slapped his combadge and spoke quickly. "Bashir to ops, intruder alert. Request armed assistance in my quarters immediately."

The man's smile didn't waver. "I'm sorry, Doctor. Your coworkers aren't receiving you at the moment. We really can't afford any interruptions. Lieutenant Dax is still in her quarters and will remain there for at least another twelve minutes or so. She's having trouble finding a padd she wanted to bring with her. Also, the *Wayfarer* is experiencing some minor engine problems. Nothing serious, I assure you." He didn't offer any explanations, but Bashir didn't doubt his word. "Now that you know where things stand, I'd like to introduce myself. Please call me Cole. As you've no doubt already guessed, I'm affiliated with the organization you call Section 31."

"You don't call it that?" Bashir asked.

"I don't call it anything, Doctor. I've found that I rarely need to identify it to anyone who doesn't already know what it is."

Bashir moved to a chair and sat down, realizing he

had no option but to indulge his unwelcome visitor, at least for now. "I can only assume this isn't a social call," he said, trying to maintain the flippant but polite tone.

Cole took a seat opposite Bashir. "Courteous, but direct," he noted pleasantly. "Sloan noted that in his profile. You're exactly what I'm looking for."

"If Sloan mentioned that, then he must have also mentioned that I'm not interested in working with Section 31."

"In fact," Cole replied, "he did mention that. But you might change your mind when you've heard me out."

Bashir rose from his chair, his anger beginning to escape the container of his false civility. He knew Cole was probably armed, probably a trained killer, but he didn't care. All Bashir could think about was lifting the man up by the scruff of his neck and tossing him out of his quarters. Bashir knew it wasn't the most sensible thought he'd ever had, but it was satisfyingly direct.

"Sit down, Doctor," Cole said, not raising his voice. Bashir stopped moving, then found himself settling back into his chair. He realized that his fingers and toes were slightly numb and tingling. "You *will* do me the courtesy of hearing me out."

Against his will, Bashir nodded.

"Good," Cole said, then crossed his arms. "You know, of course," he began, "that you're not the only genetically enhanced human in the Federation. And I don't mean only your little circle of friends—Jack, Lauren, Sarina, Patrick, that lot. There are many others, far more than Starfleet Command knows about . . . or wants to know about, if you want my opinion. One thing I've learned in my line of work, Doctor, is that the best place to hide is where your enemies don't wish to look. Almost four hundred years after the Eugenics Wars, humans are still so terrified of the idea of someone spawning another Khan that they're afraid to admit to themselves that black-market genetic labs exist on dozens of worlds. What do you think of my assessment?"

"I agree," Bashir replied, surprised to hear himself voice the long-held but never-spoken opinion. *Some kind of psychoactive,* he decided. *Not only is it making me compliant, but it's acting as a truth serum.* He quickly reviewed the half-dozen compounds he knew of that would have this effect but would also leave him feeling clearheaded. He decided none of them were likely candidates. *How did he administer the drug? No hypo. He didn't touch me. . . . Aerosol? Yes, that makes sense. Something he sprayed the room with before I got here, something he's immune to.* All of this went on in the analytical portion of his mind while the rest of his attention was fixed on Cole. Despite himself, whatever the drug might be doing, Bashir was interested in what the man was saying.

"And the good news," Cole continued, "from my perspective, at any rate, is that some of these individuals are very happy to have someone acknowledge their existence. One in particular that I came here to discuss with you is Dr. Ethan Locken. Name mean anything to you?"

Bashir shook his head.

"I'm not really surprised. He wasn't in Starfleet, isn't even a researcher despite his astonishing gifts. Doesn't travel in the same rarefied circles as you do, Doctor. He was, I assume, trying to keep a low profile. Sound familiar?"

Unable to fight the impulse, Bashir nodded.

Cole asked, "Do you think it's a coincidence that so many of you—the genetically enhanced, I mean—go into medicine? It really doesn't have anything to do with my . . . my problem, but I'm curious to hear what you think."

"It's not a coincidence," Bashir said. "But don't make too much of it, either. Think about it—anyone who has been genetically enhanced spent a great deal of time around doctors when they were young. Generally, these are favorable impressions, especially if the procedure is successful. If you check the statistics for the general population, I think you'll find that persons who survive a medical crisis when they're young have a predilection for going into the medical sciences."

"Ah," Cole said. "Very well reasoned, Doctor. Excellent point. I can see that I'm going to enjoy many stimulating conversations like this one in the future." He pulled out a compact personal data recorder and made a note. "Very good," he said to himself, then continued, "Where were we?"

"Locken," Bashir replied. He couldn't resist the urge to reply to a direct question.

"Ah, yes. Correct—Dr. Locken. He was a pediatrician. Very popular, I'm told. Very well liked. Had a practice on New Beijing. You've heard of New Beijing, haven't you?"

"Yes," Bashir replied tightly. "Of course I have. *Everyone* has heard of New Beijing. It was a massacre, probably one of the worst of the war, especially when you realize it had no strategic value . . ."

Cole held up a finger, interrupting. "Not exactly correct, Doctor. Terror *always* has a strategic value. Remember that."

Not having been asked a direct question, Bashir could not reply, but he wanted to. Desperately, he wanted to speak, to spew the venom that was clogging his mind and heart.

But Cole wouldn't have been interested. He was already continuing, reciting facts as if he were reading a dossier. "Dr. Locken had no family on New Beijing and his parents were long dead, but he had friends and he had colleagues, and, oh, he had patients. You might have heard the official death toll—five thousand human colonists, all civilians—but it was actually higher than that. Much higher.

"As you might expect, after surviving an ordeal like that, Dr. Locken was somewhat more receptive to our invitation than you've been. He understood the need for an organization like ours in a hostile universe. If only more people possessed his clarity of perception, then perhaps catastrophes like New Beijing might not have occurred."

"Wait," Bashir said, the word ragged, but comprehensible. "I have a question." It was a brutal struggle to speak without being spoken to, but Bashir could feel the effects of the psychoactive beginning to wane.

Cole's eyebrows lifted in surprise. Obviously, he had been expecting the drug to work longer, but he didn't object to Bashir asking his question.

"Did you—did Section 31—know about the plan to attack New Beijing in advance?"

Cole lifted a finger to his upper lip, patted it several times, then said, "You know, Doctor, I'm not sure. I'm afraid none of us knows everything everyone else in the organization knows. Security measure, you understand. It certainly *sounds* like the sort of thing we would hear about long before Starfleet Intelligence. But let's assume we did. What difference would it have made? Enlighten me, sir."

"You could have told someone," Bashir hissed between clenched teeth. "You could have told *me*. . . ."

"And you would have done *what*, precisely? At the height of the Dominion War, would you have tried to convince Captain Sisko or Admiral Ross to have forces reassigned to New Beijing? Say, for example, an Excelsior-class starship and a detachment of Starfleet ground troops? What would that have accomplished? The planet was attacked by two regiments of Jem'Hadar soldiers. The starship would have been destroyed, our troops killed, and all those civilians *would have died anyway*."

Cole leaned forward, warming to his topic. "Oh, and consider this—maybe the Starfleet forces in this hypothetical scenario were needed someplace where they might have done some good, something crucial. Perhaps they'd have been taken from the force that was successfully repelling the attack on Rigel at that time, and perhaps as a consequence the entire Rigel system would have fallen. Think about it, Doctor: Maybe what happened to New Beijing was the best possible outcome that we could have expected."

Bashir's anger was so intense that he wondered why his eyes weren't boiling like two eggs in their sockets. "That," he snapped, "is the most specious, spurious, fatuous sort of sociopathic double-talk I've ever heard! It's exactly that sort of logic that allows people like you to maintain the illusion that what you're doing has some sort of intrinsic value. It's insanity, *Mister* Cole. People *died*—"

Cole rose, a visual cue that had another immediate and involuntary effect on Bashir: he stopped speaking.

"First, *Doctor,*" Cole said in cool and collected tones, "never use the word *'insanity'* unless you know precisely what you're talking about. It's an imprecise word. Second, and I wouldn't have thought you'd need me to tell you this, but *people die all the time.* It's simply a question of how many, who they are, and, sometimes, how they died. That's what my colleagues and I try to do: keep the numbers as small as possible, make sure the right ones don't die, and keep the suffering to a minimum. It isn't easy work, but we do the best we can. You yourself have benefited from some of our efforts, so please be very careful about who you're condemning today."

Bashir's eyes narrowed. *He believes it; he believes every word that he's saying.* And worse, Bashir suspected that what he was saying might even be true.

Cole strolled over to the mantel jutting out of a nearby wall. He bent to study a small hologram of Bashir's parents, then gave a quizzical glance to the larger holo of the Deep Space Niners taken in Quark's bar after their triumphant defeat at the hands of the *T'Kumbra* Logicians. Shaking his head, Cole resumed his tale: "After Dr. Locken agreed to assist us, he underwent training to become an agent. Or, to be more accurate, he indulged us as we took him through our program. Not surprisingly, considering his background, he already knew almost everything we could teach him about how to go unnoticed when he desired. I believe he even taught our trainers a few things." He looked

25

over at Bashir. "You could probably teach them a few things, too, now that I think of it.

"And then, just in the last days of the war, we found him a mission. We flattered ourselves, believing it was the *perfect* mission." Cole grinned once more, but there was no real merriment in it. "So, of course," Cole said, "Locken betrayed us."

Chapter Three

Several seconds ticked past during which, Bashir suspected, he was supposed to offer a comment. He decided to be spiteful, and so, finally, Cole continued. "We discovered a Jem'Hadar hatchery on a planet called Sindorin. Heard of it?"

"No."

"A class-M world in the Badlands. Very unusual for that region with the high concentration of ambient plasma energy. We have no idea when the hatchery was established; not even the Cardassians knew about it. Evidence suggests that the Dominion didn't quite manage to bring it fully online. If they had, that last offensive on Cardassia might have gone a little differently. Something to think about late at night, isn't it, Doctor? Calculate how many more ships and soldiers the Dominion needed to turn the tide of that battle."

"It was Odo who ended the war," Bashir said. "He convinced the Founder that the Federation and its allies weren't a threat to the Dominion. He gave them the cure to your damn virus and prevented the genocide your organization sought to achieve."

"Hm, yes," Cole said. "That's certainly an interesting interpretation of events."

"You have another?"

"We're off topic, Doctor. As I was saying, the hatchery we found was abandoned and undefended. Locken's mission was simplicity itself: Tell us whether the hatchery DNA sequencers could be adjusted so that the Jem'Hadar would be loyal to us."

Bashir said, "You bloody fools."

"A comment, Doctor?" Cole asked. "An imprecation?"

"We just finished fighting a war against a totalitarian power that callously used a genetically engineered army of slave soldiers as cannon fodder. How could you think for even a moment that anyone in the Federation—in the *quadrant*—would tolerate you employing the same methods? It violates every principle that millions of Starfleet officers, Klingons, and Romulans sacrificed their lives to protect."

Cole regarded Bashir for several seconds, then slowly raised his hands and clapped them together half a dozen times. "Bravo, Doctor," he said. "I am impressed. You do have a flair for oratory." Cole folded his arms over his chest. "Now, step down off your soapbox and allow me to guide you through a few possibilities you might not have considered. Give me the benefit of your superior intellect and tell me who you deduce will be the group the Federation will be facing in the next war."

Bashir sighed. He had lain awake many too many nights calculating exactly these variables. "It's difficult to say precisely because of all the factors involved. Unless Chancellor Martok can solidify his power base in the next six months, the peace between the Klingons and Romulans will likely crumble. If they go to war the victor will likely attack the Federation next. The Breen will be watching our borders, too, making raids, checking for vulnerable areas. From the Project Pathfinder database, we know that there are several species in the Delta Quadrant that may be threats in the near future: the Hirogen, Species 8472, the Srivani, the Vaadwaur . . ."

Cole paced the floor, nodding his approval with each of Bashir's observations. "Very good, Doctor. Excellent analysis. I particularly approve of your read of the Delta Quadrant situation. Many potential threats there. You obviously have been keeping up on current events."

"Admiral Ross has been using some of us here as a sounding board," Bashir said dryly.

"Yes," Cole said. "I can see why. You all have lived through unique situations, haven't you? But you're leaving something out, I think, the most obvious . . ."

Bashir was silent for several seconds, but then relented. "The Borg."

"The Borg?" Cole said. "Interesting. We've beaten them, you know? Twice here and at least once in the Delta Quadrant . . . if you believe the Pathfinder reports. But you think the Borg is the number-one threat. Why is that?"

"Because they're relentless," Bashir said. "Because we still don't know how many there are. Because the fact that we beat them makes us all the more interesting to them, that much more worth assimilating. Because I think they recognize something in us that they might have been themselves once and want to exterminate it.

If we survive, if we thrive, it means that some decision they made long, long ago was the wrong one. Because, I think, for all their claims of being emotionless, I think they hate us."

Cole had ceased pacing and was studying Bashir's face carefully, a small, wistful smile playing on his lips. "Thank you, Doctor. Quite excellent. I believe I've learned something important here tonight."

Bashir couldn't resist the urge to ask. "And that would be?"

"You're still a romantic," Cole replied. "We had thought the Dominion War might have burned that out of you, but I see it's still there. That was a marvelously romantic interpretation of the Borg situation, but, I think, essentially correct. They *are* the greatest threat to the security of the Federation, the one we are least able to counter right now. If the Borg attacked *now,* we would be destroyed, even if the Klingons, Romulans, and Breen came to our aid. Computer models don't lie. Oh, and here's another interesting fact that Admiral Ross might not have shared with you: Even if the Dominion were to fight alongside us, we would probably lose. Ironically, the prewar Dominion might have stood a chance against them. If we had allied ourselves with them, but, well . . . never mind *that* option."

Bashir flexed the muscles in his forearms and calves. Yes, definitely some control was returning.

"So," Cole continued, now with a full head of steam, "the question should not be 'How could we contemplate using the despicable methods of our enemy?' but 'What could we learn from our former foes that we might turn to our advantage?' If we continue on our present path, we will not be counting our dead in the millions next time, Doctor, but the *billions*." He stopped pacing and leaned in close to Bashir. "Have you ever seen what the Borg do to a human body? *I* have. Children, pregnant women, the elderly: it doesn't matter; all just grist for the mill. All just *parts*. Don't you think, as a *humanitarian,* that if there's something we can do to prevent that suffering then we should *do* it?"

Bashir stared at the man, aware of a creeping horror sliding up his spine. How many newly made orphans and bereaved parents had he talked to, tried to comfort, ending up feeling utterly ineffectual? Listening to Cole, Bashir felt his head begin to nod, against his will . . . *Almost.*

"How much more sensible," Cole continued, "how much more equitable and humane it would be if the Federation could mass-produce its own army, genetically engineered soldiers who would be happy to sacrifice their lives for their leaders. The citizenry would be liberated from the barbaric practice of war, allowed to enjoy happy, peaceful, long-lasting lives with their loved ones. With the ability to produce unlimited numbers of professional soldiers, we would never again need fear the Borg, the Romulans, or the Klingons. Who could *ever* pose a threat to the Federation again?"

"Let me remind you of something I think you know all too well, but seem to have conveniently forgotten," Bashir replied. "The history of the Federation is steeped in examples of peoples who were able to successfully battle larger, better-equipped, and more advanced aggressors because the citizen-soldier is always going to be more creative and resourceful, better able to adapt to changing conditions on a battlefield. It was an army that fought for a love of freedom, not a love of slaughter, that defeated the Dominion's genetically engineered legions, Mr. Cole."

Cole stared thoughtfully at Bashir and then, for the first time, a troubled expression passed over his features. "You know, Doctor," he finally said, "I wish we'd had this conversation *before* we sent Locken on his mission. As I implied earlier, things didn't go quite according to plan."

"What happened?"

"He left for Sindorin about ten weeks ago, accompanied by a team of specialists. For the first few weeks, he kept in regular contact with us and indicated good progress. Confirmation from his associates showed that Locken was doing exactly what we asked him to do."

"His associates?" Bashir asked. "You mean a spy."

Cole shrugged. "We had to try to protect our investment."

"And then the messages became irregular," Bashir said.

"That's right," Cole said. "And then we stopped hearing from . . . his associates."

"Then they're dead, all of them. Your spies were probably the first to be killed. If Locken is everything you say he is, he probably arranged to have them kill each other."

"Why do you say that?"

"Because if I were Locken, it's what I would have done."

"I recruited some of the agents who went with him," Cole said. "I knew some of them well. They weren't the sort who could be easily deceived."

Bashir shrugged. "Believe whatever you want. It won't bring them back to life. What do you theorize has happened since?"

"We know that he succeeded in bringing some of the

incubators back online and began to grow Jem'Hadar. We can only assume Locken was successful in reprogramming the genetic matrix, and that they're loyal to him."

"Have you done any estimates?"

"We had very little data to work with," Cole said, "but our best guess is between two hundred and a thousand. Worst-case scenario is fifteen hundred. He can't get them all off the planet right now, because he only had one ship, but we think he's found other things for them to do."

"Such as?"

"You've heard about the rumored Breen presence in the Badlands?"

"Yes," Bashir said. "The *Enterprise* investigated and found nothing."

"That's correct. But they couldn't completely rule out that *something* was out there. And since then, a number of ships have gone missing, and at least two former Cardassian holdings have suffered hits by an unidentified attacker . . ."

"They're not 'former Cardassian holdings,' " Bashir said firmly. "They're protectorates. The Federation, the Klingons, and the Romulans set them up to safeguard Cardassian Union territories. They'll be returned when Cardassia is able to resume control of them."

Cole smiled. "Fine, Doctor. Phrase it any way you want. The point is that Locken could make all of this political theorizing moot if he isn't stopped. Perhaps he's planning to use hit-and-run attacks to train his warriors and try to collect usable ships. Perhaps he wants to destabilize the truce between the three powers. Perhaps he's only tweaking them so that they'll discover a genetically engineered human has set himself up as the new Khan. . . . *It doesn't matter.* The only thing that matters is that you stop him as quickly and quietly as possible."

"That *I* stop him?" Bashir asked.

"Of course, Doctor. Who better? Our psych profile indicates that Locken can rationalize his actions because he feels so isolated. Certainly, the trauma of his losses on New Beijing can account for much of this, but our specialists are certain that his psychosis has its roots in his belief that he is fundamentally different from everyone around him, *better* than everyone. In his mind, it doesn't matter what he does to anyone else because, ultimately, it's for their own good. He's a doctor to all humanity."

"To what end?" Bashir asked.

"We don't know," Cole said. "If I had to guess, he's decided that he wants to make the quadrant safe for children and other small things by any means necessary. If you really want to know, *ask* him. We want you to go to Sindorin, establish some sort of rapport, use those forensic skills you just demonstrated, and convince him to turn the hatchery over to us . . ."

"Like hell," Bashir began.

"Or whatever you think is best," Cole continued. "Our goals are the same in this instance. We do *not* want a superhuman launching a jihad with an army of genetically engineered killing machines at his back."

"Especially not a superhuman who knows everything about you," Bashir added.

A tight smile flickered across Cole's lips. "Nobody knows everything about us, Doctor."

"And if I'm not able to persuade him?" Bashir asked.

Cole shrugged. "I very much doubt," he said, "that anyone who could outthink Sloan would have much trouble with a tyro like Locken. He may be . . . enhanced, but he's still quite naive, I think. Almost as naive as you used to be."

Bashir shook his head in disgust. "How could you believe *for a second* that I would buy into this hideous charade? You've managed to mire yourself in a morass of backstabbing and double-dealing and you're expecting *me* to liberate you? Give me *one* good reason why I should."

"Besides the obvious, you mean?" Cole asked. "Besides the fact that the Federation could be torn to pieces if the Romulans and the Klingons discover what's happened?"

Bashir wanted desperately to be able to say, "There are ways around that," but he knew Cole was right. As they had been talking, he had been running simulations and the numbers weren't encouraging. *And that's what it comes down to,* he realized. *Not right and wrong, moral or immoral, but numbers—counting the quick and the dead.* He didn't want to say any of those things because if he did, Cole would know he had prevailed, so, instead, he said, "There are others who can do what you're asking, most of them better than me."

Cole smiled. "Doctor, you underestimate yourself. In fact, there isn't *anyone* better suited. While there are many more enhanced persons out there than the Federation is willing to acknowledge, very few of them are as—how shall we say it?—well socialized as you are. Most of them, in fact, would consider your friend Jack to be a social butterfly. And, speaking of Jack, what do you think would happen to him and his friends if it became known that a genetically enhanced person was responsible for starting a war? How long do you think it would be before Starfleet would disavow them, cast them to the wolves? A week? A *day?*"

"Starfleet would never do that."

"You don't think so? I won't presume to speak for *you*, Doctor, but one of the things *I* learned during the Dominion War is that under the worst circumstances, even among the best and the brightest, morality can sometimes become a pliable thing. If the conditions are right . . . well, I've heard stories even about the late, sainted Captain Sisko."

Bashir glared at Cole from under lowered brows, thinking, feeling like a caged animal inside his own skull.

"Damn you to hell," he said at last, resigned to whatever awaited him on Sindorin. He expected Cole to grin triumphantly, but was surprised to see only a very tired man, a gaunt and bitter man, a man weary unto death.

"Thank you, Doctor," Cole said softly. "When can you leave?"

Bashir shook himself, then said, "I don't know. I have to make some arrangements."

"Of course," Cole said, heading for the door. When he passed Bashir, he dropped the padd he had been holding into the doctor's hands. "Please extend my apologies to Lieutenant Dax for making her miss her vacation. Just out of curiosity—did you *really* want her to go back to Earth with you and visit the old home-stead?"

"Yes, I did," Bashir said. "Very much."

"Really?" Cole said, pausing in front of the open door. "Well, then, it must be love." And then he was gone.

When he was certain Cole wasn't coming back, Bashir stood and walked stiffly across the room to where his med kit rested and opened it. He wanted to get a blood sample before the psychoactive was completely dissipated. As he worked, he took a second to try his combadge. "Bashir to Kira."

"Go ahead," the colonel's voice answered.

"Nerys . . . we need to talk."

Chapter Four

Kira felt a headache building behind her eyes and began to massage the ridges of her nose. "Do we have anything on internal scanners . . . ?"

"Nothing," Vaughn said.

"No surprise there, I guess. I'd have been more shocked if we *had* picked up something."

"So would I," Vaughn agreed. "And then we'd have to worry about why he let us know he was here. No, I think it's better this way. He's gone and we can accept his request at face value."

"It sounded more like a threat than a request," Kira noted. "Or a trap." She looked around the wardroom table and attempted to take everyone's measure.

Bashir was angry, of course. He didn't like being backed into a corner, but then, who did? There was something else going on, but Kira couldn't quite piece it together, not yet. Partly this was because when Julian wanted to conceal something, it stayed concealed. It wasn't so long ago when she had considered the doctor an open book, a man who was all too eager to reveal everything about himself. But now Kira understood that this had been a ruse, a persona created to conceal the "real" Julian Bashir.

Ezri, typically, was wrestling with several emotions simultaneously. Kira read fear (primarily for Julian), anger (mostly at Cole, but with a little reserved for Julian), and an edge of excitement. A quirky smile kept forming at the corners of Ezri's mouth, but she managed to keep it under control. Kira recognized it as the skeleton of the smile Jadzia used to wear when she was undertaking some new challenge or digging into a new mystery. Seeing it made Kira feel at once comforted and disconcerted. *Jadzia is in there somewhere,* she thought. *Listening intently to everything I'm saying.* She knew that wasn't exactly how it worked, but Kira had a hard time shaking the feeling that the ghost of her friend was hovering in the room. She found herself wondering if Benjamin had felt the same way after Jadzia had succeeded Curzon.

Vaughn was harder to read, drinking that damned tea, absorbing everything that was being said, and processing it through his eighty years of Starfleet training. Still, Kira sensed something going on beneath the detached calm, something that felt a great deal like anger, though she was having trouble imagining Vaughn being angry about anything.

But where Vaughn was impenetrable, Ro seemed preoccupied. Maybe it was just the shock of learning about the existence of Section 31. Kira and Sisko had both felt that shock, after Julian had told them about his first encounter with Sloan. Ro, however, seemed to be trying to work through something.

"You have something to contribute, Lieutenant?" Kira asked.

Ro met Kira's gaze, and seemed to reach a decision. "Sindorin," she said. "I know the planet. There was a time when the Maquis considered using it for a base. This was almost three years ago, just before everything fell apart. It would have been a good place to retreat to if we'd had the chance." She indicated the planetological file currently displayed on the wardroom screen.

"It's tropical with about two-thirds of the land surface covered with dense rain forest." Pointing at a subcontinent in the southern hemisphere, Ro continued, "This area was particularly interesting to us because some recent volcanic activity has deposited a rare mineral throughout the water table. The trees draw it up into the canopy and it plays hell with sensors. Anything but the most intense scan bounces right off. The forests are teeming with life, but you wouldn't know it from orbit."

Ro touched the table controls and the holographic image of Sindorin receded. "And here's the other reason we liked the place," Ro said. Red and yellow plasma storms erupted just beyond the edge of the solar system. "It's unusual to find an M-class planet this deep in the Badlands, but, well, not impossible. And, let me tell you, it makes for some pretty amazing aurora effects."

"So why didn't you relocate there?" Dax asked.

"Two reasons," Ro said. "The first was the storms. The shielding on most Maquis ships was never that great. We might not have lost one the first or second time we passed in or out of the system, but, sooner or later, something would have gone disastrously wrong. And, second, like I said, we only found the place a few weeks before the Cardassians joined the Dominion. When that happened, we had bigger problems. . . ."

"Apparently, the Dominion didn't feel the same way," Kira said.

Ro shrugged. "Their ships had better shields."

Kira caused the image to zoom back in on the planet. "So, based on what you've told us, this southern continent is the most likely candidate for a base. Any thoughts on how to narrow that down?"

"It depends. What's needed for a Jem'Hadar hatchery?"

"Genetic material, which the Vorta would have brought with them when they set up the place," Bashir contributed. "They must have abandoned it in quite a hurry to leave some of it behind, perhaps during the final offensive against Cardassia. But they'd have needed water, too. Preferably fresh water."

"It's all rain forest," Ro said, "so there's not a lot of open water. It's all invested in the vegetation. During the rainy season, it rained twice a day, early morning and early evening, so regularly you could set your chrono by it. Would that be sufficient?"

Bashir shook his head. "Probably not. Too dispersed."

Kira watched them talk and noticed how they quickly fell into the easy give-and-take of Starfleet-trained information exchange. It was a skill she had always admired in Sisko, Jadzia, O'Brien, and Julian, but hadn't imagined it extended to *all* Starfleet officers, even former ones like Ro. *Klingons don't do this,* she mused. *Or the Romulans or the Cardassians. They have their own methods, their own martial cultures, but nothing that can compete with this.*

Ro pointed at a large blue splotch near the southern

tip of the subcontinent they had been discussing. "Here, then. This lake. We didn't give it a name. Just called it 'the Big Lake.' It's the only large open body of fresh water on this part of the planet."

Julian leaned in to study the map. "It must be a couple thousand klicks around. Big area to check."

"We'll be able to pick up something once we get in close," Ro said.

"But not *too* close," Julian replied, staring intently at the lake, obviously memorizing the shape of the shoreline.

"Well, that's the trick of it, isn't it?"

"Yes, it is, Lieutenant," Julian said absently. "And thank you for volunteering to come along. It'll be good to have someone there who knows the territory. I have a feeling we'll need every advantage we can get . . . which brings me to my next request. Colonel?"

"Doctor?"

"I'd like to ask Taran'atar to accompany us."

Kira could feel her face knitting into a frown at the suggestion. "You realize that if what Cole told you is true, there's liable to be quite a few Jem'Hadar there."

"Which is precisely why I want one there who's on *our* side," Bashir said. "He'll be able to offer us valuable insights about how they think, their possible responses . . ." He paused, studying Kira's face. "I take it you don't care for the idea."

"I don't. This is getting crazier by the second. You're talking about going to a planet in the Badlands with only one or two other people . . ."

"Possibly three," Ezri chipped in.

"We'll talk about *that* later," Kira snapped. "With

one or two other people, one of them a Jem'Hadar, so that you can confront someone who has set himself up as the local deity. And for what? To save Starfleet some embarrassment . . . ?"

"No, Nerys," Bashir said. "To preserve the peace. To save some lives. I don't like this any better than you, but it's the lesser of two evils."

Kira felt the pressure behind her eyes building. "All right, I'll speak with Taran'atar and see how he feels about this. He might not be able to do this, you know. Odo told him to obey *me*."

"And if you tell him to listen to me, then he will," Bashir said.

"Or any of us, for that matter," Dax added.

"I'm not sure it works that way," Kira said. "Or, if it does, I'm not sure I want it to."

"He's a Jem'Hadar," Bashir said. "He'll do as he's ordered. That's their raison d'être."

"This one might be different," Kira said. "That might be the reason Odo sent him here."

"Or he might be the purest example of the species," Bashir mused. "Maybe Odo wanted us to better understand what we're going to be dealing with the next time we meet the Dominion."

It was an intriguing question and Kira normally would have been happy to debate the topic with her friends and colleagues, but the immediate issue would be what Taran'atar would say about the idea. "Computer, locate Taran'atar."

"Taran'atar is in holosuite one," it intoned.

Curious expressions all around the table.

"How much longer is he scheduled to be there?"

"His session will expire in twenty minutes."

"Then I'd better get down there soon," Kira said. "Julian, I'll call you when I find out what Taran'atar wants to do. Either way, don't slow down your preparations on his account. I'm guessing he's a quick packer."

"I'll have Bowers assign you a runabout," Vaughn said. "Any preferences, Ro?"

"The *Euphrates*," Ro said. "She handles well in turbulent atmosphere. Sindorin has some heavy storms."

"Good choice," Vaughn said. "Six hours from now sound all right?" Ro and Bashir agreed and Vaughn left the room, followed soon after by Ro. Julian had subtly signaled to Dax and Kira to remain for a moment, so they both made a show of stacking padds until the others had left.

"What is it?" Kira asked when the doors had closed behind Ro.

"I just wanted to note," Bashir said, "that the commander didn't seem terribly shocked to learn that there is a secret covert operations group within Starfleet."

"Ro didn't seem surprised, either," Ezri said. "What's your point?"

"I think Ro expects *every* society to have a secret covert operations group," Kira added. "Odo felt the same way. What *is* your point, Julian?"

"I'm not sure that I have one. But Vaughn's service record isn't exactly full of details, is it? I checked, Nerys. For someone who's been in Starfleet as long as he has, you'd think it would contain more than the few meaningless details I found. And he didn't contribute much to our discussion just now."

Kira chose her words very carefully. "Julian, I may not be Starfleet, but Commander Vaughn has proven

44

himself to me, and to this station. If you want to bring his trustworthiness into question—"

"No," Bashir said, as if realizing he'd crossed a line. "I'm sorry. I guess this Section 31 business is making me suspicious of everything. You're right, Colonel. I won't bring it up again." Bashir looked at Ezri. "See you later?"

Ezri nodded. As soon as Julian left the room, Kira said, "I don't like what I just heard."

"Neither do I," Dax said, still watching the door. "But he has a point."

"In what way?"

"Vaughn plays it close to the vest," Ezri said. "He always did. Even when Curzon met him decades ago he was like that. I don't mean he can't be trusted. I think he's basically a good man. Plus, the opinions of Starfleet Command and captains like Jean-Luc Picard count for something, and they obviously have complete confidence in him. But given the strain Julian's under right now, questioning a lack of information—which is what Vaughn represents to him—isn't unreasonable, or unexpected."

Kira could understand that, and wondered if she would eventually have to address the issue with her enigmatic executive officer. First things first, however. "Can Julian do this?" she asked Dax.

"No question," Ezri said. "But he'll need backup he can count on. I think Ro and Taran'atar are a good start, but I want to go, too."

Kira sat down and leaned back, studying Dax carefully. "Do you remember the mission to Soukara?" she said finally.

"Yes, of course," Ezri replied without hesitation. "Jadzia almost died. Worf had to choose between saving her life or meeting with Lasaran. He chose to save me."

"And do you remember what happened next?"

"Benjamin forbade us from ever going on a mission together again."

"And the lesson I should draw from that is . . . what?"

"Colonel," Dax said, straining to sound reasonable, "these are entirely different circumstances."

"Really? Different how? How is this different from the mission to Soukara?"

"Look at it this way. You and Odo together went to the aid of Damar's resistance group while the two of you were in a relationship."

"Odo and I are not you and Worf," Kira said, and as soon as the words were out of her mouth, she knew she was trapped.

"Exactly my point," Ezri agreed. "Odo and Kira are not Jadzia and Worf. Well, Ezri and Julian aren't Jadzia and Worf, either."

Kira sighed. "What if you're wrong, Ezri?"

"I'm *not* wrong and you know it. We'll do this the right way if for no other reason than to prove to you that we can."

"Have you talked to Julian about this? I got the impression he expects you to see him off, not join him."

"Of course we've talked about it. And of course he wants me to come along. He feels exactly the same way I do about this."

"I don't want you to come along," Bashir said.

Ezri, sitting on Bashir's bed, shivered as she watched him repack his travel bag. The station was getting colder and Julian's quarters, which were always a couple of degrees cooler than she liked, were close to unbearable. "You're not being reasonable," she said, then pulled the afghan off the foot of his bed and wrapped it around her shoulders.

Bashir walked over and pulled the afghan more tightly around her. "How am I being unreasonable? I just don't want you to be hurt . . . or worse."

Ezri shrugged his hand away. She wasn't impressed. "Doesn't work," she said. "I don't want you to be hurt or killed either, but I'm not insisting you stay. I know you have to go. It's your duty."

"Yes," Bashir agreed emphatically. "It is . . ."

"And it's mine, too," she said, not letting him finish his thought. "Or do you think you're the only Starfleet officer with a stake in this?"

Bashir sighed, hating the way this was going. "Of course not. But I probably know more about how Locken is likely to react than almost anyone . . ."

"Except for me," Ezri said matter-of-factly.

"You?"

"Me," she repeated. "Julian, you might be an enhanced person, but I, a trained counselor and a lifelong observer of humanoid behavior, live with an enhanced person. Don't you think that counts for something?"

Bashir regarded her without comment for several seconds, obviously looking for a flaw in her argument, and finding none. Finally, he lowered his head in resignation. "Lieutenant, I submit to the overwhelming force of your logic. Obviously, one of the previous hosts spent a great deal of time with Vulcans. You'd better go pack."

"Already did once today," Ezri said, trying not to smile too broadly. "Not everyone is as fussy as you are."

Closing his bag and lifting it from the bed, Bashir pointed at the door. "We'll see what you say about that when we get to Sindorin."

Chapter Five

Ordinarily, Kira wouldn't violate another's privacy by entering a holosuite while a program was running, but she was fairly confident she wasn't walking in on anything the Jem'Hadar would consider embarrassing. As far as she knew, Jem'Hadar couldn't be embarrassed. And even if they could be, it wouldn't have stopped her in this case. Time was a factor.

She entered and found herself looking down a dozen meters into a bowl-shaped pit with a floor of loose soil and walls of broken rock. Below her, Taran'atar was fighting a nightmare.

The creature appeared to be insectile—five meters tall, eight long limbs, each one ending in a two-pronged horny claw. The claws at the end of the foremost limbs were more flexible than the others and were holding heavy clubs that looked like they might have been rubbed or shaped somehow for easier grasping.

The insect aimed one of the clubs at Taran'atar's

head, but the Jem'Hadar sidestepped a half-meter to the left. The club head was momentarily buried in the sandy soil, and Taran'atar leapt up onto the creature's back, then took a swipe with his *kar'takin* at the soft, flexible part where two sections of the insect's chitinous armor overlapped. The blade bit deep and the joint spurted a thick, purplish ichor. The insect made a strange metallic noise, then tore the club out of the soil. Taran'atar backflipped off the creature and landed softly, knees bent, then tumbled to the side as the club descended again.

The creature, which apparently had poor peripheral vision, didn't see where its opponent had gone and issued another piercing cry as the *kar'takin* landed again. It reared, rolling itself up onto only four legs, waving the claws and clubs of its forelimbs but finding no target.

Taran'atar stepped lightly onto the insect's back again, took three quick strides up its dorsal ridge, and landed a heavy blow on the crown of its head. The carapace didn't crack, but what passed for the creature's central nervous system must have been under that part of the shell, because the blow staggered it, its sapling-thick legs buckling beneath it. Taran'atar used the creature's forward momentum to tumble over the top of its head, curled into a shoulder roll, and came to a halt about three meters from where the insect now lay dazed.

Taran'atar rolled nimbly to his feet, then paused, watching the swaying giant. Kira expected him to approach the insect and end the battle, but the Jem'Hadar was obviously waiting for something. Kira wondered distantly if the Jem'Hadar was simply enjoying having the creature at his mercy and wished to prolong the moment as much as possible.

Then, suddenly, the insect's whole body spasmed and it curled into a tight ball, all eight limbs wrapping around its lower abdomen. The edges of the armor plates on its back lifted and stubby, thorny spikes slid out from underneath. Muscles contracted, the creature shuddered again and the spikes shot out in every direction, some embedding themselves in the loose soil, others shattering against the shapely walls. Kira flinched in spite of herself, startled by the simulated carnage.

Taran'atar leapt lightly into the air, correctly judging the trajectory of the half-dozen projectiles that were heading in his direction. He slipped between the two highest-flying spikes, clearing the other four by half a meter, then dropped to the ground directly in front of the bug's great head. He raised his blade high and Kira braced herself for the sight of split carapace or splattered brain matter, but instead heard only "End program."

A momentary shimmer, and Kira suddenly found herself on the same level as Taran'atar, in the otherwise empty holosuite. Taran'atar was leaning on his weapon, gazing at her fixedly, but without concern. "Good day, Colonel," he said, his loose black coverall as clean as it must have been when he started the program. At Kira's request, he had shortly after his arrival on the station stopped wearing his gray Dominion uniform in favor of the less provocative garment.

"Good day, Taran'atar. I hope my presence didn't interrupt your exercise."

"No," he said. Kira had spoken to the Jem'Hadar a number of times since he had come onto the station, but she still had not grown accustomed to his voice. She always expected something on the order of a Worf-like growl, but his tone was higher, richer, more melodious. She wondered if Jem'Hadar ever sang, and, if they did, could they carry a tune?

"But you shut off the program before . . ." She faltered. "You weren't finished."

Taran'atar studied the edge of his blade, then looked up at her. "The battle was won. I would have killed it with the next blow."

"Well, yes, that was obvious," Kira said. "What was that, anyway?"

"On the world where they live, the natives called it something which, translated, means approximately 'Comes-in-the-night-kills-many.' They lived in burrows and would tunnel up underneath their prey, pull them down, and then consume them."

Something suddenly dawned on Kira. Taran'atar had come aboard the station with few possessions, and holoprograms weren't among them. "Did you create that simulation yourself? From memory?"

Taran'atar inclined his head slightly. "I knew the parameters, and was able to encode them onto a data rod preformatted for the holosuite."

A Jem'Hadar of no small talents, Kira mused. Or were they all as capable as this one, and she'd just never known it? One thing was certain, she was never going to underestimate Taran'atar again.

"That one was using weapons. They must possess some sort of rudimentary intelligence."

Taran'atar tilted his head in the Jem'Hadar equivalent of a shrug. "Perhaps. You may be right. It was not my concern. My orders were to kill them, not to study them. They were decimating the population of a settlement the Founders had assigned to grow food crops."

"And you were guarding them, the settlement? That's what you did before you came here?"

"Not before I came here. This was many years ago, long before I became an Elder. The survey team found them before the settlement was established. My unit was assigned to eradicate them."

"Are you telling me you wiped out a native species to establish the farming community?"

Taran'atar nodded. "It is the practice among the Founders to assign peoples who have proven themselves to be superior tillers of the soil to worlds where they may best serve the needs of the Dominion. This group—I do not know what you would call them—was transplanted from another world, one that the Founders had conquered many years earlier. They were a small species, poorly equipped for combat, so my unit was called in to secure the settlement."

"Secure the settlement?" Kira asked. "You mean commit genocide."

Taran'atar took note of her change in demeanor, but didn't hesitate. "Our goal was to completely eradicate the population, yes. This disturbs you?"

"It would disturb any of my people. We ourselves were once enslaved by invaders, too."

"We did not enslave these creatures . . ."

"No, you eradicated them," Kira said. "Can you tell me which is worse?"

Taran'atar asked, "Is it your wish to debate this issue, Colonel?"

Kira felt her jaw tighten. "No, I'm not interested in a debate. That wasn't my intention. In fact, I came here to make a request."

The Jem'Hadar seemed uncertain. "A request?"

"There's something I'd like you to do, but I don't want you to feel *compelled* to do it. You have to decide whether you wish to or not. It is our custom to *ask* our guests for assistance, and to let them make the choice."

Taran'atar clearly wasn't just uncertain now, but agitated and impatient. "I am not your *guest,* Colonel. I am a Jem'Hadar, with a mission to obey, observe, and learn. The Founder . . ."

"Odo," Kira said.

Taran'atar accepted the correction, but his agitation only increased. "*Odo* gave me this task, to serve your will as I would serve his. I still do not understand completely how this can be done, but I took an oath and so I will obey you. But he never said *anything* about making *choices.*" And with this, Taran'atar slammed the head of his *kar'takin* into the holosuite floor. The computer that controlled the room's simulated environments sensed the imminent impact and attempted to generate a cushioning forcefield, but was too slow to block the full force of the blow. The blade bit into the deck and a shower of sparks erupted from a pierced EPS conduit. Safeties kicked in and the sparks stopped.

Kira was too surprised to say anything for several seconds and before she could protest Taran'atar's behavior, the room's com came on and she heard Quark say in diffident tones, "Ah, hey. Hello in there? Maybe you could take it a little easy on my holosuite? No offense, but since Rom stabbed me in the back and took off for Ferenginar, there isn't anyone on the station who knows how to fix the *frinx*ing thing. Okay, Mr. Jem'Hadar? Hello?"

"Everything's fine, Quark," Kira said. "Don't worry about it. I'll have Nog come down and look at it later."

"Oh, Colonel. Heh, well, so you're . . . ah . . . joining

the fun, too. Well, okay. But Commander Vaughn won't let Nog . . ."

"I'll speak to Commander Vaughn," Kira said. "All right?"

"Okay, Colonel. Fine. You two just have fun in there, all right. No problem." He paused. "There isn't any problem, is there?"

"Not unless you don't go away," Kira said.

"Right," Quark said. "Gone."

Kira and Taran'atar stood looking at one another for a moment or two. Then, Kira reached down, tugged the *kar'takin* out of the deck and hefted it in her two hands. It was heavy, heavier even than it looked. "Did you program a replicator to produce this, too?"

"Yes."

Kira nodded, appreciating the balance of the weapon as she scrutinized it. "By the way," she said. "How much did Quark charge you to use the holosuite?"

Taran'atar looked confused again. Kira was momentarily struck by a guilty feeling that she was using up the Jem'Hadar's lifetime supply of confusion. "Charge?" he asked. "When I learned that this facility existed, I told the Ferengi that I would be using it today. He did not mention anything about a charge."

"Yeah," Kira said. "Okay. Never mind. No surprise here. I'll set up an account for you. Try to remember that there are other people on the station who might want to use things and some of them might be in line in front of you." She handed him back the weapon.

The Jem'Hadar accepted it.

"Now, getting back to my request . . ."

"Simply tell me what you want me to do," Taran'atar said.

"I want you to *consider* accompanying Dr. Bashir on a mission to a planet where a human has taken control of a Jem'Hadar hatchery." Briefly, Kira outlined the story of Locken and their guesses about his plans.

Taran'atar listened without comment until she had finished, then said, "It will be as you say. You may consider the Jem'Hadar serving this human already dead."

Kira shook her head. "I'm afraid you aren't getting this. I'm not asking you to go kill all the Jem'-Hadar . . ."

"But there are Jem'Hadar on this planet who have been conditioned to serve this man whom you oppose. Correct?"

"Yes, correct."

"Then I must either kill them or they will kill the doctor and anyone else who accompanies him on his mission."

"Let's get something straight," Kira said. "Your participation in this mission is contingent upon your helping my crew according to their needs. I realize you have a genetic predisposition toward killing your enemies, and use of lethal force may in fact become necessary, but it isn't to be your first option. Am I understood?"

The Jem'Hadar looked down at her. "You wonder at my willingness to kill my own kind. You think because you have fought my species, that you understand what drives it, that it's defined solely by the controlled genetics used to create us. Tell me, Colonel, is that how you feel about Dr. Bashir?"

Kira was taken aback by the question. Taran'atar continued. "You have accepted that he is genetically predisposed to act differently, to think differently, to *feel* differently than you do, even though this disposition was devised by the hand of other beings no greater, no more divine than yourself."

Kira could see where the logic of the argument was headed, but she was helpless to steer a passage around the upcoming rocky shoals. "Yes," she said.

Taran'atar then said, with surprising calm, "Then please extend the same courtesy to *me*."

Kira's eyes narrowed. "You make some very valid points," she said. "But we're still going to do things *my* way. So I'll ask you one more time. Am I understood?"

The silence was deafening and seemed to last for too long for Kira's comfort.

"No," Taran'atar admitted finally. "But it will be as you say."

57

Chapter Six

With less than an hour before the *Euphrates* was to depart, Ro Laren sat in the security office, studying the copious and astonishingly detailed files Odo had left behind.

All but a few of her deputies and supplemental Starfleet personnel were already gone. With so few people on the station, and so much of it currently powered down, onboard security was far less complicated. Ro had decided to use her remaining time to listen to some of Morn's stories, attempt to uncover whatever skullduggery Quark might be engaged in, and read through her predecessor's database. She enjoyed Morn's stories, had managed to quietly sabotage the worst of Quark's indiscretions, and was dutifully amazed at the quantity and quality of Odo's records. There was information buried in the security office that she suspected was unknown even to Starfleet Intelligence.

Shortly after she first came aboard, she had uncovered the first cache of redundantly encrypted files in an innocuous subsector in the office's dedicated mainframe. She wondered if even Kira knew they were there. It had taken Ro five full days of studying the computer system just to figure out what Odo had done to safeguard the hidden files. Then another twelve days to devise a way to access them without tripping the EM pulse that would wipe the data if she'd made a single mistake. Her persistence paid off in the end; the files were hers now, and it was gratifying to know that some of the more subtle skills she'd learned with Starfleet and the Maquis could be combined so effectively.

After she started reading, Ro had been tempted to anonymously contact a couple of the most begrimed individuals mentioned therein and send them a tidbit or two, just to see what would happen. Fortunately, she waited long enough to let the temptation pass. Within a day or two, the wisdom of Odo's designs had become clearer. This wealth of material was meant to be salted away until a moment in the indefinite future—the proverbial rainy day—when it would be most useful. Strangely, that day had apparently never arrived, even in the darkest moments of the Dominion War, but then again, this was not *that* kind of data. It wasn't the sort of information that would save an empire or a world or even an army. It might save one or two lives—special lives, the lives of those who might someday change the luck of armies or worlds or even empires.

If Quark ever learned about this— She smiled at the thought.

Ro noted the time and decided she'd better get to the *Euphrates.* She closed the files and checked the encryption codes again. She'd considered backing up the data, a risky move, but she didn't trust the station core right now for obvious reasons. Instead, she'd taken the precaution of asking Nog to physically retrieve the security datacore in the unlikely event the DS9 had to be abandoned. She was taking a chance trusting Nog, but not, Ro thought, a big chance. Ro liked him. He was an interesting comingling of Federation Boy Scout and scoundrel, both types she understood and whose responses she could predict, which was as close to trust as Ro Laren ever came.

After making sure everything was secure, Ro reached under the desk and pulled out her travel bag. She never had to look inside the bag, because she always knew exactly what was there: a change of clothes; some basic toiletries and first-aid items; enough condensed rations to last three days; a microfilter for water reclamation; a fully charged hand phaser; a tricorder; a small but powerful palm beacon; and, in a concealed compartment, a porcelain fractal-edged knife. If Ro ever found the last item in the possession of any visitor to DS9, she would have confiscated it immediately. It was illegal in the Federation and on numerous independent worlds, Bajor included. Fractal knives had only one use: they were weapons of terror, because their edges were too fragile for anything else. She had taken this particular blade from the body of a Cardassian "information officer" who had used it while interrogating Maquis prisoners. Someone—Ro had never found out who, having arrived on the scene long after the fact—had used the fractal knife on the inquisitor, extensively. She had kept the blade ever since, considering it the ultimate "you never know when you might need it" tool.

She paused at the door and took a last look around at the blank walls. *Was it like this when Odo was here,* she wondered, *or did someone take away his things when he left?* From the little she had heard about the man and, more tellingly, from what she had gleaned from reading between the lines of his reports, Ro guessed that there had never been anything belonging to Odo in this room. Personal effects would have given the criminals he had brought here more information about himself than he would have wanted them to know.

Ro slung her bag over her shoulder, knowing that the walls of her quarters were as blank as these.

Bashir, Ezri, and Ro had assembled in the airlock outside runabout pad C. It was, Bashir noted, only a little more than eight hours since he and Ezri had told the *Wayfarer* to leave for Earth without them. Taran'atar arrived last, carrying only a soft-sided case of suspicious proportions. "Let me guess," Ro said. "Weapons?"

Taran'atar didn't reply, but only laid the pack down on the deck, unfastened a pair of clips, then unrolled it like a sleeping bag. It contained a standard-issue Bajoran hand phaser, with several replacement power packs affixed; what looked like a dozen or so photon grenades; and a sheathed weapon that Bashir guessed was a *kar'takin.*

"What, no throwing knives?" Ro asked.

Taran'atar indicated a small satchel bound into the case's lining.

"Oh, good. Don't want to forget those."

Taran'atar regarded Ro speculatively, but still did not comment. He rolled up the case again with quick, precise movements so that when he was finished it looked exactly the way it had before he had opened it.

Just as Taran'atar was rising, everyone was surprised to see Commander Vaughn emerging from the runabout.

"Sir?" Bashir said. "We didn't expect to find you here."

"Thought I'd save you some time and run through the preflight," Vaughn said. "She's ready, by the way. Try bringing her back in one piece, please. I recently found out what a terrible record this station has when it comes to runabouts."

Bashir almost smiled. "Thank you for seeing us off."

Vaughn nodded. "Colonel Kira intended to be here herself, but she wanted to be on hand when Nog and his crew began detaching Empok Nor's lower core. The operation started about two hours ago. Are you heading directly for Sindorin?"

Bashir shook his head. "Ro and I have been talking. We're going to take a very indirect route, try to look like a survey ship and bore anyone who might be watching. We'll be skirting the edge of the Romulan protectorate, so we're working on the assumption that there are cloaked ships nearby." Ro handed a padd with a copy of their flight plan to Vaughn, who scrutinized it carefully.

"All right," he said finally. "But avoid going into the protectorate if you can help it. And check in periodically before you hit the Badlands. It'll help keep up the pretense that you're surveying."

"Right. And we'd like to know how things are going here," Bashir said. "If it starts to look like Nog is going to blow the place to pieces, could someone please rescue my ficus?"

Vaughn smiled. "I'll see what I can do. Well. Safe journey."

"Thank you, sir," Bashir said, and started to follow the others into the runabout. Vaughn waited until Bashir was just on the threshold before calling, "Doctor? A moment, please."

Bashir stopped and turned. "Yes, Commander?"

"A word of advice," Vaughn said in low tones. "Don't try to be a hero. Don't think for a moment that you're going to be able to find evidence you can use to expose Thirty-One. Just go in, do the job, and come home. Understand?"

"I understand what you're saying," Bashir said suspiciously, "but not why."

"Because I'd like to see all of you come home alive. Cole needs you to do his dirty work for him, but that's all he's going to allow. Try to go beyond that and I can guarantee there will be unpleasant repercussions." With that, Vaughn turned and walked away.

Bashir stared after the commander for several seconds, wondering not without some smoldering anger what he was supposed to make of all that. The doctor usually enjoyed a good mystery, but this was something else entirely. And as he entered the runabout, Bashir resolved that if and when they returned from Sindorin, he was going to get to the bottom of this particular enigma once and for all.

Chapter Seven

"How long is this going to take?" Ezri asked.

"To make it look good, about eighteen hours," Ro said. "Just long enough for everyone—well, almost everyone—to get some sleep, eat a couple meals and get tired of looking at each other."

Ezri, relaxing in the copilot's seat, made a sour face.

Ro caught the look. "Don't take it the wrong way," she said. "I've been on a lot of these kinds of trips. The best thing to do is try to maintain your sense of humor and don't get in anyone else's way." She glanced over her shoulder toward Bashir, who was just going into the aft compartment with a padd in hand. As he disappeared behind the door, Ro added, "Unless you *want* someone to get in your way."

Ezri grinned. "I don't think that's really an option."

"You'd be surprised what you could do on one of these runabouts. When I was in the Maquis, we had ships much less sophisticated than this—basically just big cans with engines mounted on them—and people used to find all sorts of ways to make private space. You had to, especially if you were spending a lot of time together."

"This isn't really like that," Ezri said.

"In fact, it *is*," Ro asserted. "A *lot*. It's surprising how much, in fact. You people on DS9, from what I've seen so far, have a lot more in common with the Maquis than anything I ever saw on a starship."

"*We* people on DS9, you mean," Ezri corrected good-naturedly. "You're one of us now."

Ro shrugged. "Well, yes and no. I'm not old guard— you, Kira, Bashir, Nog. Don't get me wrong: you seem like a good group, but you *are* a little insular. In that respect, you remind me of, well, another crew."

Somehow Ezri knew Ro wasn't thinking about the Maquis anymore. "You're referring to the *Enterprise*, aren't you?" Ezri asked.

Ro snuck a quick look at Ezri, then returned her gaze to the control board. "You're not part Betazoid, are you?"

"No," Ezri said. "Just a counselor. That, and I read your file."

"Ah, yes. My file," she sighed, as if nothing more needed to be said.

Ezri wasn't quite ready to give up, though. "So, what was it like?"

Ro checked their course and submitted a slight correction while she considered her answer. Then, slowly, she reached out and ran her finger along the edge of the viewport. She showed it to Ezri, who saw it was covered with fine gray dust. "It was very clean," Ro said. "Everything. Even the engine room. I've been in a few engine rooms since the *Enterprise* and I know how hard it is to keep one clean. And it was very well lit except, of course, when you wanted the light to be low." Her expression, which had been set in a soft scowl, softened then and she said, "Life on the *Enterprise* was very tidy."

"So you liked it?"

"Did I like it?" she repeated, as if it was the first time she had ever considered the question. "I suppose I did. For a while, anyway. It was so safe, so secure, so invulnerable. But then I came to be reminded about all the people whose lives weren't so safe and secure and I knew I had to make a choice. Follow my orders, or follow my conscience." Ro lapsed into silence again, then noticed the look on Dax's face. "You want to ask me about Picard, don't you? It's all right. Everyone does eventually."

"All right, you got me," Ezri admitted. "I hate to seem predictable, but . . . what was it like serving with Picard?"

Ro smiled, but it seemed to Ezri that the smile was bittersweet. "He was pretty much what you look for in a captain: Tough, but fair. Committed to high ideals. Intelligent, even scholarly, but not stuffy. And he wore a very nice cologne."

Ezri laughed, delighted.

Ro chuckled, too, but tried to keep a straight face. "No, I'm serious. It was very subtle, but distinctive. If you were working on something, head down to the grindstone, and heard a door open behind you, it was always obvious when it was Picard because of this great cologne. And he has a very nice voice. Oh, that's right—and he was a wine snob."

"I think his family owns a vineyard."

"Right. I'd forgotten that. But I'll tell you something

about Picard that you'd never know unless you served with him . . ."

"He's not as tall as he looks in the news feeds?" Ezri asked, remembering the last time she saw him, standing on the Promenade next to Kira only two weeks ago.

Ro shot Ezri a sly glance. "Well, in fact, *no,* he isn't, but that wasn't what I was going to say. It's just that, well . . ." She paused, gathering her thoughts, searching for words. "Maybe the universe seems just as confusing to him as it does to the rest of us. Maybe he feels like it's difficult to decide what he should do, but it never *seemed* that way to the rest of us. He had a gift for looking, sounding, *acting* like whatever he was doing was the exact *right* thing to do . . ." She paused, looked like she was going to continue, then shook her head. "I don't know any other way to put it." Ro looked over at Dax. "Have you ever served with anyone like that? I've heard some stories about your Captain Sisko . . ."

"Benjamin?" Ezri shook her head. "He wasn't that kind of commander, not that kind of man. You know that before I was Jadzia I was Curzon, don't you?"

Ro nodded, watching the controls.

"I knew . . . I've *known* . . . Benjamin for more than twenty years, from the time he was little more than a boy to the day he . . . well, we don't really know with complete certainty what happened to him, do we? You're a Bajoran. What do *you* think?"

"I'm a Bajoran," Ro explained, "but I'm not *that* kind of Bajoran. If you want the religious interpretation, you'll have to ask the colonel. If you want my opinion, I'd say he died in the fire caves."

"If it were anyone else, I suppose I'd agree," Ezri said. "But not Benjamin. Maybe this is all hindsight, but when I look back, I see that Ben's life was like a refiner's fire. Things that would have ground down any other man only made Benjamin stronger and sharper. Hardship *purified* him. He took the heat and he made it his own and at the core of it was the fact that he never ceased questioning his motivations, his desires and fears. He didn't see himself as a prophet or an emissary, not really. But he did what a prophet is supposed to do: he tried to clarify his vision by never allowing himself to think that there was only one path to truth." Ezri stopped speaking, rolling around what she had just said in her head, trying to decide whether she believed it, then finally decided she did. "How does that sound?" she asked.

Ro looked at Ezri and smiled. "Like a hard act to follow."

Back in the runabout's aft compartment, Bashir was removing a bowl of couscous and a cup of broth from the replicator and trying very hard not to let Taran'atar's stony silence unnerve him. Setting the food down on the table, Bashir glanced over at the Jem'Hadar and was surprised to see he was currently showing more interest in the bowl and cup than he had in anything else so far during their trip.

"How's that liquid diet working out?"

Taran'atar looked up. "Adequately."

"I wonder," Bashir said. Shortly after Taran'atar had come to DS9, he'd allowed the doctor to subject him to a complete medical examination. Bashir had put him through a battery of tests, scans, and analyses, in part to verify Taran'atar's claim that he was one of the anomalous Jem'Hadar who wasn't dependent upon ketracel-white for his survival. Withdrawal would never be an issue for him, but without the white to supply all his nutritional needs, Taran'atar needed to eat.

He'd told Bashir that after the Vorta had identified him as having the mutation, they'd devised a liquid diet that would satisfy his nutritional requirements while slowly allowing his digestive system to reassert itself. Taran'atar had committed the formula to memory, and managed to program the station replicators to produce it. Bashir had analyzed a sample of it, and while it was chemically suited to Taran'atar's physiology, he didn't even want to imagine how vile the stuff must be.

"You wonder what?" Taran'atar asked.

"I'm wondering if you're ready to try something other than that concentrated pond water the Vorta gave you," Bashir said with small smile. "How long since you ate last?"

"Six days," the Jem'Hadar said. Because his physiology was so efficient, any food he ingested was completely absorbed and converted to fuel, with no waste. Taran'atar only needed to eat once every four or five days. Six, however, was too long.

"Let me guess: You're finding the Vorta's concoction a little hard to swallow." The doctor pointed his bowl. "Do you want to try some of this?"

Taran'atar hesitated. "I don't know," he said finally. "What is that?"

"This is couscous—grain and spices and beans . . ." He held up the cup. "And this is vegetable broth."

"Humans are omnivores. You do not eat meat?"

"Very rarely," Bashir said. "I never make meat for myself, but I'll eat it if someone else prepares it."

"This is a cultural prohibition?"

Bashir shrugged. "Call it a lifestyle choice."

"Klingons eat a great deal of meat," Taran'atar observed.

"Klingons get diseases of the colon a lot, too," Bashir replied, picking up the cup of broth and carrying it to Taran'atar. "Let's start with something simple. Try this."

Taran'atar took the proffered cup and held it to his nose, sniffing. His face wrinkled and he said, "It has an unpleasant odor."

"Try some anyway," Bashir said, then had another thought. "No, wait, let me check something." He pulled his medical tricorder out of his bag and passed the scanner over Taran'atar a couple of times until he was satisfied. "Go ahead. No allergies."

Taran'atar took a small sip of broth, looked for a moment as though he was going to spit it out, but did not. Finally, he swallowed and appeared to roll the flavor around in his mouth for a moment or two. Then he took another mouthful. Then another. After finishing the broth, he gave the cup back to Bashir. "Thank you. How do you know so much about our biology?"

Bashir handed him the bowl of couscous and the fork. "You aren't the first Jem'Hadar I've examined. Some I've studied quite carefully, in fact. You'll need to chew that, by the way."

"Dissections?"

"I beg your pardon?"

"Did you dissect them?"

Bashir shook his head. "No, of course not."

"Vivisection?"

"*No.*"

"Then I do not understand. How could you know so much about my species?"

Nonplussed, Bashir collected himself for several seconds, then replied, "I . . . we . . . found a Jem'Hadar child several years ago and I was able to observe and record much of its maturation process with my medical scanners. Also . . ." But then he hesitated, uncertain whether to continue. "Well, perhaps I shouldn't be telling you this, but I once tried to help free a group of Jem'Hadar soldiers from their dependency upon the white."

Though his expression didn't change, Bashir sensed a sudden tension in Taran'atar's shoulders and back muscles. In measured tones, he asked, "And did you succeed?"

Bashir shook his head. "The actual situation proved to be not unlike your own: a rare and random mutation."

"How rare?" Taran'atar asked.

"You tell me. Didn't you say the Vorta specifically searched for Jem'Hadar like yourself at Odo's request?"

"Yes, and they found only four of us," Taran'atar said. "Or so they said."

"You sound skeptical."

"The Jem'Hadar understand the Vorta better than the Vorta understand us," Taran'atar said. "We obey them because it is the will of the Founders, but if they did not control the supply of the white, if the white were discovered to be unnecessary or, at the very least, conquerable . . . Most Jem'Hadar go their entire lives without ever seeing a Founder, but the Vorta are there every day—watching, prying, *sneering.* You all look like Vorta to us: humans, Klingons, Romulans, Bajorans, Vulcans—some of the Jem'Hadar who fought in the war said it made killing you more satisfying."

"Charming," Bashir said, deciding he was no longer hungry.

Taran'atar seemed to realize he had caused offense. He felt compelled to explain himself. "The Founder who exil—who *sent* me here told me something I did not understand at the time, but now I'm beginning to see his wisdom. He said, 'Exposure brings understanding.' Then, the Founder laughed aloud and said, 'And just as often, familiarity breeds contempt.' "

Bashir nodded. "That sounds like something Odo would say."

"He also told me to be watchful particularly of the one named Quark. I am not sure why."

Bashir laughed. "I am. But never mind. So, do you actually have any personal feelings about your mission to the Alpha Quadrant?"

"The Founder told me only to obey the colonel as I would obey him. The colonel has told me to obey you. So that," he said, "makes you my Vorta."

"Oh, no," Bashir said. "No, no, no. Not me. I'm the doctor, the man who gives you broth and couscous."

". . . As the Vorta gave me the white."

"Bad comparison. I want you to be well . . ."

". . . So I can fight for you," Taran'atar said. "So I can kill other Jem'Hadar."

Struggling to remain calm, Bashir let out a breath and said, "That's not true. I want you to tell me what the other Jem'Hadar will do so that we can try to find a way to avoid *more* deaths. I'm a doctor. Do you understand what that means in my culture? Our first rule, one of the oldest rules in our recorded history, is 'Do no harm.' It's my role to develop new ways to help, then to teach those ways to others." Then, realizing how pedantic he sounded, Bashir hesitated and tried to shift the conversation back to Taran'atar. "Is there anything analogous to this in the Dominion?"

"There may be," Taran'atar said. "I do not know everything that happens throughout the length and breadth of the Dominion. I am a soldier. *My* role is to defend and, if necessary, to kill. Do you think that makes you superior to me?"

Bashir was surprised by both the question and Taran'atar's matter-of-fact tone. "Better?" he asked. "Well, not better. More tolerant, perhaps. The Federation . . ."

"Not the Federation," Taran'atar interrupted. *"You.* There is something about the way you carry yourself. You wear humility like a shroud. Again, it reminds me of the Vorta."

Bashir knew he was being challenged, that he had to think carefully about what he would say next. There was danger here, but also opportunity. "There were times in the past," he said slowly, "when I felt the need to hide who I was. It's been a hard habit to break. I'm trying to learn new habits."

Taran'atar studied Bashir's face for the space of several heartbeats, then said, "When you think about what you are going to say, you are not nearly so much like a Vorta." He held out the empty bowl. "May I have more?"

Bashir took the bowl. "Yes, of course." Then, he handed Taran'atar a napkin. "Wipe your chin," he said.

Chapter Eight

Bashir's combadge chimed and Ezri called, "Dax to Bashir."

"Go ahead."

"We've found something. You'd better come up here." She paused and Bashir heard Ro speak, though her words were indistinct. Ezri added, "And bring Taran'atar."

Taran'atar followed Bashir into the runabout's cockpit. Ro had dropped out of warp and was using the runabout's thrusters to edge them into the shadow of a large derelict spacecraft. Neither she nor Ezri looked up when they entered, both intent on their instruments. Though they were too close to the spacecraft for Bashir to make out the ship's configuration, Taran'atar announced, "Romulan N'renix-class cruiser. Crew complement: forty-five. Medium shielding, medium weapons, excellent cloaking capability. Maximum speed: warp nine point eight. Can sustain a cruising speed of warp nine point five for over twenty-six hours. Used primarily to transport high-level military personnel and secret technology."

"I've never heard of this class," Bashir said, studying the sensor input. "Has one ever been to the station?"

"No," Ezri said. "This might be one of the classes of ships they didn't want us to know about."

"That is correct," Taran'atar said. "No N'renix-class ship ever left Romulan-controlled space during the war."

"Then how do *you* know about it?" Ro asked, giving the thrusters one more nudge. Bashir looked out the main viewport and saw they were so close to the derelict that he could make out the seams where the hull plates were joined.

"The Dominion's military intelligence on the Alpha Quadrant is extensive," Taran'atar explained. "I made a thorough study of it before embarking on my mission."

"What happened to it?" Bashir asked. "Are there any casualties?"

"It's been hulled in half a dozen places," Ezri said, reading off the sensor log. "No life signs. No energy signature. And the engines are gone."

Bashir winced. "Core failure?"

"No," Ezri said. "I mean the engines are *gone*. Someone removed them. Did a good job, too. Wait, let me check something. . . ." She reset the sensors and did a quick scan. "They took the main disruptor bank, too. Ripped it right out of the belly."

"Are you picking up any third-party engine signatures? Maybe make a guess about how long ago this happened?"

"Long enough," Ezri said. "And, no, nothing."

Taran'atar leaned forward and checked the sensor

readout. He pointed to the pattern of impact marks on the ship's hull. "This is not a Jem'Hadar attack pattern, but it *is* very well placed."

Ro looked over her shoulder at him and asked, "You guys have patterns for weapons-fire attacks?"

"For every class of enemy craft, yes. Each has its unique weaknesses."

"How about Federation runabouts?"

"Aft shield generator."

"I'll remember that."

"That's enough," Bashir snapped. "Can we board her? Is it holding atmosphere?"

"Let me check," Ezri said. She finished her scan and said, "Not in the cargo bays or weapons-control areas, not without EVA equipment. The crew quarters are . . . well, they're gone. Engineering and the bridge are intact, and I think I could reactivate life-support from here, but the corridor linking them is open to space. I could beam over a forcefield generator and plug the hole. Life-support would need maybe an hour to generate enough atmosphere to sustain us. No gravity, though."

Ro groaned. "I hate zero gee."

"That's all right," Bashir said. "We need you to stay here and mind the sensors. Get to work, Ezri. Taran'atar and I will gather our gear."

"On it," Ezri said, and set to her task.

Bashir was struck by a thought and turned back to Ro. "Lieutenant, how far are we from the space lane for this sector?"

"I was just thinking about that myself," she said. "Not far at all. This isn't a heavily trafficked area, but if you were leaving the Romulan-controlled sector of

Cardassian territory, you'd pretty much have to pass by here."

"Could you tell if the ship was towed here?"

"Not unless it was done very recently, but there's one thing that leads me to believe it was."

"And that is?"

"No bodies. If the crew quarters were opened to space, there would be bodies nearby. I don't read any."

Bashir sighed heavily. "Right," he said. "Someone wanted this ship to be found. But why? A scarecrow?"

Taran'atar looked at him quizzically and silently mouthed the word "scarecrow." Then he said, "If I understand the meaning of the word, then, yes, it was meant to incite fear."

"Terror is an effective weapon, Commander," Ro said.

Bashir looked down at Ro, momentarily stunned into silence. Then he laughed disgustedly and said, "I keep hearing that today, so I suppose it must be true. Anything on long-range scanners, Ezri?"

Ezri stopped what she was doing and ran a quick check. "No," she said, "but if a cloaked Romulan ship was approaching, we wouldn't know it anyway."

"Good point. All right, then, we don't have much time to do this. How are you doing with the forcefield?"

"I'd be doing a lot better if you stopped asking me questions," Ezri snapped, but then looked up and added, "sir."

Bashir smiled sheepishly. "Sorry. Come on, Taran'atar, let's go see what Commander Vaughn packed for us."

Ezri waited for Bashir and Taran'atar to leave, then looked over at Ro and said, "He's trying not to show it, but he's enjoying this."

"Yeah, I got that, too."

"He used to play spy on the holodeck."

"Really?" She grimaced. "Never go spying with someone who thinks it's a game."

"I don't think he's played it since he's learned about Section 31. I think it lost its innocence."

"Maybe," Ro said. "Or maybe he lost his."

"The air pressure looks good," Bashir said, checking the sensor readings and closing the front seam of his protective garment. It was a class-B environmental suit—not rated for hard vacuum, but it would be adequate for the conditions aboard the Romulan ship.

"Better than I would have hoped," Ezri said. "We should be all right as long as our air supply holds out." She looked over at Taran'atar, who was checking the charge on his phaser. "What about him? No suit?"

"He doesn't need one," Bashir said. "Jem'Hadar physiology is much better suited for this sort of thing. He'll probably wear eye protection, but not much more."

Confirming Bashir's prediction, Taran'atar pulled a pair of dark goggles out of his equipment belt and slid them down over his eyes. Holding his phaser at combat readiness, he said, "Transport me first in case there is something waiting."

"Sensors say there are no life signs," Ro said.

"Not everything shows up on sensors."

"Good point."

The Jem'Hadar stepped onto the transporter platform. Just before Ro activated it, Taran'atar shrouded, becoming invisible. When the transporter reported that he had successfully beamed over, Dax and Bashir stepped onto the platforms. "Energize," Bashir said.

Materializing in the center of a wide corridor lit only

by emergency lighting, they saw Taran'atar floating a meter off the deck, bracing himself against the ceiling, his phaser at the ready.

"No shroud?" Ezri asked.

"No need," Taran'atar said. "There's no one here."

Bashir checked the status of his and Ezri's e-suits and was satisfied with what he found. Looking back down the corridor, he saw the blue glow of the forcefield generator that was preventing the air from escaping.

"How long will the batteries maintain the field?" he asked Ezri.

"Two hours. Not much more."

"All right, then," he said, pointing up the corridor. "Let's not waste any time. The bridge is in that direction." He had memorized the ship's schematics just before they had left the *Euphrates*. "Taran'atar, would you mind taking point?"

The Jem'Hadar did not reply, but pushed off the bulkhead with an easy, practiced motion and moved silently up the corridor.

Bashir looked uncertain. Dax guessed he didn't have a great deal of zero-gee experience. "Don't worry," she said. "It's rather like swimming. Just don't move too suddenly." She tapped her foot against the bulkhead and drifted forward.

Bashir watched her movements, studied the details of the corridor, and seconds later he was drifting past her easily.

Ezri rolled her eyes. "I bet you were even good at ice-skating the first time you tried it."

"Well, yes," Bashir said, trying to sound humble, but failing. "In fact, I was."

Ezri braced herself against the bulkhead and pushed

Bashir into the center of the corridor as hard as she could. He pirouetted in midflight, landed feet-first against the bulkhead, twisted, pushed off, then sailed after Taran'atar. "I hate you," she called out, grinning. He waved in response, then signaled for her to follow. "No, really," she said. "I do."

The doors to the main bridge were sealed, suggesting that the bridge crew might have had time to erect a barricade before the ship was boarded. When Bashir began scanning the doors for a release frequency, Taran'atar laid his hand over the tricorder display, and then pointed at a pair of small hatches in the walls near the ceiling. "Automatic defenses," he said softly, then quickly sketched out a rectangular area on the floor in front of the doorway. "Kill zone." Bashir passed the information to Ezri, who nodded, drew her phaser, and pushed off to the opposite end of the corridor.

Bashir spoke briefly to Taran'atar, then followed Ezri. As soon as they were at a safe distance, Taran'atar shrouded and Bashir reactivated his tricorder, quickly found the proper frequency, and transmitted it to the doors, which opened without a sound. No illumination spilled out, not even emergency lights.

The hatches near the ceiling remained shut. Bashir and Dax waited.

Twenty seconds later, the Jem'Hadar shimmered back into existence before them. "I've deactivated the defense grid," he said. "It didn't require much effort. There was little power left in the system. The bridge controls are dead."

Bashir nodded toward the bridge. "Is there anyone in there?"

Taran'atar nodded. "If we assume that this vessel was carrying a maximum of forty-five crew members and that between one-third and one-half of them were lost when the hull lost integrity, then *everyone* is in there."

Bashir sighed, then set to work, slowly and methodically preparing himself as if for a minor surgical procedure. He activated the work light on his shoulder mount, then set his tricorder to automatic record and fastened it to the clip in the center of his chest harness. "Will you come?" he asked Ezri, who considered the question only for a second before nodding in assent. "Taran'atar?" he asked.

"I will stay out here and watch. I dislike being in a room with no escape route."

"Ro can transport us out," Ezri said.

"Yes," Taran'atar said. "Assuming she is still there." Then he turned, the air around him seemed to fold, and he disappeared.

Ezri winced, but resisted the urge to tap her combadge. Bashir saw her anxiety and activated his own. "Lieutenant?" he called.

"Ro here."

"Just checking in. Anything out there?"

"Nothing that wasn't half an hour ago. How about in there?"

"Yes," Bashir said. "Something in the bridge. We're going in to check it now."

"I'll resist the urge to say, 'Be careful,' because I hate it when people say that to me, but . . ."

Bashir smiled. "Understood. How's the transporter lock?"

"Solid."

"We're going into the bridge now. If you don't hear

from us in twenty minutes, beam us all out. If you lose the lock, leave. Quickly."

There was only a moment's hesitation, but then Ro said, "Understood. Talk to you in twenty. Ro out."

Bashir looked down at Ezri and asked, "Ready?"

"I think so," she said. Then, incongruously, she laughed. "You know what's strange?"

"No, what?"

She shook her head. "It's just that I know whatever's in there, at some time in one of my lives, I'm sure I've seen something worse. Curzon witnessed the aftermath of half a dozen battles. Tobin saw a woman get shot out an airlock by Romulans. Audrid watched as her husband was killed by some kind of alien parasite. . . . Yet, as much as these were all things that happened to *me*, it's also like something that I've only read about or had described to me in a lecture. . . ."

" 'For now we see through a glass, darkly,' " Bashir said softly.

Ezri hesitated, ran the phrase over her tongue, then said, "I suppose that's it. Yes. What . . . ?"

"It's from the Judeo-Christian Bible," Bashir said, then quoted:

We know in part, and we prophesy in part.

But when that which is perfect is come, then that which is in part shall be done away.

When I was a child, I spoke as a child, I understood as a child, I thought as a child; but when I became a man, I put away childish things.

For now we see through a glass, darkly; but then face to face: now I know in part; but then shall I know even as also I am known.

*And now abideth faith, hope, charity, these
three; but the greatest of these is charity.*

He stared into the middle distance for a moment before shifting his gaze back to Ezri. "When I was a boy,
perhaps a month after the gene resequencing, I found
that passage in a book—not the Bible, but a collection
of essays—and, in that egocentric way children have,
decided it was about *me*." Bashir shook his head and
grinned bemusedly. "Odd," he said. "I haven't thought
about that in years."

Ezri stared at him for several seconds and then, because she could not kiss him through the e-suit, leaned
forward and rubbed her cheek against his. "Every time
I think I know everything about you, Julian Bashir," she
said, "you find some way to surprise me."

Bashir laughed, surprised and delighted. "Well," he
said, "good." Then, he sobered. "But we should go.
Ready?"

"As I'll ever be."

Most of the Romulans had been killed quickly and
cleanly, a disruptor to the back of the head at very
close range. A few, the highest-ranking by what still
remained of their uniforms, had died more slowly.
Two of them—one obviously the ship's captain and
the other an otherwise nondescript woman who Bashir
assumed was a member of the Tal Shiar—had been
killed by degrees. Whoever had done this had partially
melted the walls, then thrust the pair into the molten metal, totally immobilizing them. Bashir guessed
that they had been forced to watch the others being
killed, even as they themselves had died. The burns

would have been fatal, Bashir judged, but not instantaneously.

Bashir could not help but remember the battlefields of the Dominion War, the smell of burned flesh, the sight of bodies pulverized into jelly by concussive sonic blasts. It had been horrible, but there had been something like a reason behind all the terror and death. Here, he judged, there had been no goal except, perhaps, simple sadism, an exercise in power, like a small child who pulls the legs off bugs because no one has told him it's wrong. For the first time, he wanted to leave, to turn his back on the mission and disavow any kinship to the man he suspected was behind it all, though he knew he could not. He wanted, he realized, to be like a child again, and let others make the decisions. ". . . But when I became a man, I put away childish things," he whispered, not even realizing he was speaking aloud.

He was shaken from his reverie when Ezri called, "Julian? Look here." She was scanning the body of the captain, paying particular attention to the man's forehead, which was coated in a crust of blood.

Inspecting the Romulan carefully, Bashir saw that the blood hadn't flowed from a head wound as he had first surmised, but was a scab over a series of shallow cuts. At first, he made as if to scrape the blood away as he might if he were performing an autopsy, but then he felt the weight of death in the room and restrained himself, instead unhooking his tricorder and adjusting it for an epidural scan.

When the image materialized, he cursed, then thrust it at Ezri, who looked at it curiously.

"All right," she said. "I see, but I don't understand. The round figure is the sun?"

"Right."

"And that's a crescent moon superimposed on it?"

"Yes."

She shook her head. "I don't get it. What does it mean?"

Bashir smiled humorlessly. "I'm sorry. Humans *can* be rather self-centered sometimes. We assume everyone in the quadrant knows everything about us, even the things we don't really want them to know. It's an ancient symbol—almost four hundred years old—the sun and the moon together, suggesting totality, everything in the world. It symbolized the rule of Khan Noonien Singh."

"Khan?" Ezri said. "But he's dead. Isn't he?"

Bashir nodded his head. "He is, but apparently his spirit isn't entirely. Locken has appropriated his icon."

"The humans will go mad," Ezri said under her breath. Then, louder, as if remembering that Bashir was human, "Even those who aren't against genetic engineering in principle won't be able to tolerate the idea of a new Khan. It'll send Earth into a frenzy."

"Yes," Bashir agreed. "And frenzied people make rash decisions. Maybe that's what he wants."

"All right," she said, considering. "That fits." She turned away from the victims and began to work the main control panels. "Now let's see what else we can find out about what happened here." She tried to activate the panel, but instead of the control panel lighting up, a prerecorded message began to play on the viewscreen.

There was only a single figure in the recording, a Terran male in his late thirties or early forties. He was neither particularly tall nor physically imposing, though the manner in which he carried himself suggested a feline grace. His hair was red, cut short, and receded into a widow's peak. He wore a simple tunic and a long cloth overcoat, both black, both cut in a fashion like those worn by doctors in civilian hospitals. There was an emblem stitched into the upper left side of the coat front, the same symbol that had been carved into the Romulan's forehead. His eyes, Bashir saw, were a strange color for a man with such a fair complexion, a dark brown, almost black, almost as if his pupils had swallowed his irises.

"My name is Locken," he said, his voice low and reasonable, much more like the family doctor's than a conqueror's. "And you are trespassing. This is the sovereign territory of the New Federation. If you have not come to pay tribute, then leave or be destroyed. There will be no other warning." He paused, still seeming quite reasonable, then added, almost incidentally, "Don't imagine for a moment that you're a match for me. You're not."

Ezri tapped a couple of other controls, but nothing happened. Then she reset her tricorder and performed a quick scan of the ship's computer system. "That's all there is," she said. "The panel was keyed to play this message no matter what we did. Everything else has been deleted." She looked up at the viewscreen and studied the image. "There was something very odd about his manner," she said. "Something . . . inhuman."

"He wasn't addressing equals," Bashir said. "He was talking to lesser beings. Something closer to animals . . ."

"Subjects," Ezri added. "Or slaves."

Bashir's mouth tightened, but then he nodded in agreement. "Or slaves."

"And did you see his eyes? Like two coals. Is that normal?"

Bashir shrugged. "It might be natural coloring. Could be a trait linked to his genetic enhancements. Could be colored contact lenses."

Turning back to the control panel, Ezri asked, "So there's nothing else we can do here?"

"Just one more thing, I think," Bashir said, and tapped his combadge. "Taran'atar, proceed to engineering. Lieutenant Ro, two to beam out."

"Acknowledged," Ro answered.

The Romulan bridge shimmered and disappeared, replaced by the runabout's cockpit. "Why'd you send Taran'atar to engineering?" Ezri asked.

Bashir ignored the question and spoke to Ro. "Lieutenant, please take us out to fifteen hundred kilometers and hold position."

Ro turned around in her seat and looked at them. "What's going on?"

"Before Taran'atar entered the bridge, I asked him to be ready to initiate a warp-core overload on my command."

Dax and Ro exchanged looks. "Do we have authorization to do anything like that?" Ezri asked. "Shouldn't we alert Starfleet and have them contact the Romulans?"

Bashir shook his head. "They'd never believe us. The Romulans would come out here and see that a human had orchestrated that massacre, maybe even find evidence that we'd been aboard and decide that Starfleet was somehow involved. Better to destroy it, and without using weapons that will leave Federation energy signatures."

"You realize, don't you," Dax said, "that this is exactly the sort of thing Section 31 would do. Leave no evidence, clean up the trail so no one will know . . . ? And those people, they had families, friends. Someone should tell them what happened."

"The irony isn't lost on me, Ezri," Bashir snapped. "But I don't think we can take the chance."

Bashir's combadge chirped. "Taran'atar to Bashir."

"Bashir here. Go ahead."

"Ready to beam back."

Ro hit the transporter controls, and Taran'atar materialized behind them. "The task is completed. The overload should occur in six minutes."

Ro wasted no time and gunned the thrusters. "Moving off to fifteen hundred kilometers," she said, then spun the runabout around to face the direction of the Romulan ship, which had dwindled to invisibility. "Anyone want to say anything?"

No one did, and in the silence a few moments later, a brilliant white light erupted outside the viewport, throwing stark shadows into the runabout cockpit before winking out. The instant it was gone, Bashir ordered Ro to proceed on their original course, then turned and stalked into the aft compartment.

Dax realized then that Bashir hadn't needed to stay and watch the explosion, but had forced himself to, making himself face the reality of his decision to employ the methods of his adversaries in order to defeat their purpose—knowing he'd have to live with that decision to the end of his days.

It wasn't the first time he'd felt compelled to make such a choice. He'd done it before, entering the dying mind of Luther Sloan to extract the cure for Section

31's genocidal changeling disease, to save Odo's life. Part of Julian had died that day, and Ezri knew she'd just witnessed another part of him die now.

The thought made her ache inside. No, this wasn't the first time he'd made such a choice. And she feared for him that it wouldn't be the last.

Chapter Nine

It was hours later that Taran'atar, watching sensors, announced, "Something on long-range."

"Jem'Hadar?" Ro asked.

"No. Engine signature is wrong. Something Federation, possibly Vulcan."

"Probably a survey ship. The Federation hasn't been able to get into this sector without a lot of trouble for the past couple of decades. The Romulans probably don't like them being here, but they can hardly chase them out."

Dax had come up next to Taran'atar to examine the readings herself. "So, nothing to worry about?"

"No, it's something to worry about. We don't want *anyone* knowing we've been here, least of all a bunch of Vulcans. If the Romulans ask them later, 'Did you spot a Federation runabout in the area . . . ?' "

"They'll say, 'Yes,' " Dax said.

"Right." Ro signaled Bashir.

"Yes?" came the curt reply.

"We've got company, Doctor. I'm changing course. Heading for the Badlands now. The ride will probably get a little bumpy then. The plasma storms cause a lot of turbulence, sometimes long before you actually see one."

"Will it damage the runabout?"

"Not if I'm doing my job right."

"All right," Bashir said. "Understood." And then he signed off.

Ro, concerned about Bashir's abrupt tone, looked at Dax, cocking her head toward the aft compartment. "Was it bad?"

"Bad enough," Dax said, understanding that Ro was asking about the Romulan ship. She slipped into the seat next to Ro and started working her panel. "I'm used to the idea of the Jem'Hadar being ruthless and efficient, but this was worse somehow. This was . . . sadism or something calculated to look very much like it."

"Why do you say that?"

Dax considered the question, then said, "Everything was very . . . orchestrated for effect. It was almost like being in a holonovel—all very ominous, but also very structured. The only thing missing was the music."

Ro grinned sardonically. "You'll forgive me for saying this, but *that* sounds a little calculated, too. Situations like this, everyone writes a little narrative in their head as they go along, the story they'll tell when they get back."

"*If* they get back," Dax said.

"No, not *if*," Ro corrected. "Once you start thinking about dying, you don't write the story in your head. As soon as you find you're not writing the story anymore, it's time to start worrying."

"You forget," Dax said. "I've already written eight stories. I *know* what it's like to die."

"Sorry, but I don't think that's true," Ro said. "You know what it's like for a life to *end*. That's not the same thing as dying. If any of the previous hosts had died before Dax had been transplanted, we wouldn't be having this conversation."

Dax turned to look at Ro. Coolly, she asked, "So what's your point?"

"That you should never say 'if,' " Ro said, "if you plan to live."

Dax accepted what Ro told her, but seemed preoccupied. "Something else on your mind?"

Dax hesitated. "We got a look at Locken—a recording he left—and what I saw didn't jibe with the carnage."

"Maybe he's lost control of the Jem'Hadar."

"Maybe . . . But, no, I don't think so. He told them what to do. Might have even been there to stage-manage it. He wanted the scene set exactly, precisely *right*. He wanted it to have an impact and knew what to do to achieve it."

"Doesn't make it any less horrifying," Ro said.

"No," Dax replied. "*More* horrifying. I think that's part of the reason Julian is so angry. I think he feels like it's his fault, that he should have done something. Maybe made an effort to find Locken before something like this could have happened."

"Meaning what? He's responsible for the actions of every genetically enhanced person in the quadrant? That's rather a big load. I'm not sure I'm comfortable sharing a mission with a martyr. I've dealt with them before—the Maquis was full of them—and you know what?"

"What?"

"They always get what they want: they always die."

Dax shook her head. "Julian's not a martyr. He just wants the universe to be a just place."

"Oh, great," Ro said. "So he's not a martyr, he's just crazy. And what about you, the Trill with a half-dozen lives behind you?"

"Eight," Dax corrected.

"Eight, then. What do you want?"

"I just want everyone to come home safe," Dax said.

Ro nodded. "All right, then," she said. "We do agree on something after all."

After four hours, Ro dropped out of warp and they hit the first wave of turbulence. She turned over the pilot's chair to Dax and went aft for some sleep.

It was, Dax thought, like sailing through rough seas: not life-threatening, but requiring a pilot's undivided attention. Dax tried to smooth out the bumps, but the inertial dampers couldn't compensate for the irregular chop generated by the plasma waves. Twenty minutes later, they hit a high-pressure ridge that tossed Ro out of her bunk. She rolled onto all fours, then ran into the cockpit even as Dax was calling, "Ro!"

"Here," Ro said, sliding into her seat.

"Shields are on full and I'm down to one-quarter impulse."

"Give it a little more than that or we'll be tossed."

Dax did as she was ordered and the surges seemed to

even out. After she switched control to Ro's board, she took a second to sneak a look through the viewscreen and saw a huge plasma plume swirl into a funnel, a red-gold streamer bursting from its center.

"Wow," Dax said, a second before the wave of turbulence struck them broadside. She would have, she knew, been thrown from her chair if she hadn't been strapped in. Behind her, Bashir cursed as both he and Taran'atar belted themselves to their chairs.

"Hang on to your stomach," Ro said. "Here comes another one." The runabout pitched and yawed while all around them plasma streamers erupted, flared, then faded, leaving red and green afterimages dancing on Dax's retinas.

"What's our course?" Dax asked, trying to wrestle some usable data off her console.

"Just turn the sensors off," Ro said, blinking, trying to clear her vision. "They're not going to be much use now."

The runabout was swept into a maelstrom of light and energy. Ro did not so much pilot the ship as goad it from side to side, avoiding globes of coruscating energy and ribbons of supercharged plasma. The inertial dampeners were almost worthless and anyone who wasn't strapped in would have been pummeled into unconsciousness in seconds.

Dax stubbornly kept checking the sensor feed, apparently more out of need to keep busy than out of a belief that she would be able to see anything. She was, therefore, able to exclaim triumphantly, "Starboard, fifteen mark seven." Ro had spotted it almost at the same instant and no sooner were the words out of Dax's mouth than the runabout was slipping into calm, open space.

Turning to survey her comrades, Ro asked, "Everyone still here?"

Taran'atar, leaning forward in his seat, was ignoring her, straining against the harness to look out the viewport, obviously preparing himself for whatever threat might be approaching. Dax was mussed, but looked excited. Ro recalled someone telling her that Ezri was prone to space-sickness, but she showed no sign of it now. In fact, she seemed to be actually relishing the rough ride. Conversely, Bashir's complexion was waxy and nearly green. He was holding a full hypo in his shaking hand and now, slowly, carefully, pressed it to his exposed forearm. "I've been trying to do that for half an hour," he said. Then, he looked at Ro. "And the Maquis used to hide in here all the time?"

"Well, yes," Ro said, and was tempted to leave it at that. Having a reputation for reckless courage was occasionally a useful thing. On the other hand, having a reputation for insanity was not. "But I've never been through anything like *that*. Our ships wouldn't have held together. Whatever else Locken has done to his Jem'Hadar, he's bred them to have strong stomachs."

After checking her sensors, Ro fired the maneuvering thrusters and pointed the bow of the runabout toward Sindorin to give everyone a good look. It was a small world, closer in size to Mars than to Earth, a blue-green orb dappled and streaked with gray-white cloud. They were parked over the northern ice cap, which was tiny, no more than the faintest hint of a white bull's-eye in an otherwise blue dartboard.

"What's our approach vector?" Bashir asked, checking the sensor feed.

"The landmass we're looking for is in the southern hemisphere, so we can't see it from here. Hopefully, they can't see us, either. I'm going to go in fast over the ice cap, try to stay low and approach near sea level. Everyone okay with that?"

"You're the pilot," Bashir said.

"That's right," Ro said.

Less than two minutes later, Dax announced, "Something decloaking on the port side. Two hundred meters. It's big. Oh, hell, it's a Cardassian weapons platform." Ro hit the port thrusters and the runabout lurched to starboard. Behind her, she heard Bashir groan. "It's trying to get a lock on us. Shields are up, but . . ."

The runabout bucked and slid to port, the inertial dampeners pushed beyond their ability to compensate. Ro tried to coax the ship back into a semblance of level flight, but the bow kept sliding away underneath her feet, slicing through the atmosphere at a steep angle.

"That was a direct hit on our aft power coupling," Dax yelled over the noise of rushing air. "We've lost deflectors, tractors, environmental . . . everything. Somebody find some power."

Bashir, working the engineering board, yelled, "On it!" Seconds later, Ro's board lit green and she fed as much power as she dared into the shields and stabilizers. The nose lifted, the bumps smoothed, and the air circulators began to clear the air.

Another bolt of energy sizzled into their stern, and the runabout staggered, but did not tumble. "We're out of range," Ro announced. "Where the hell did they get a Cardassian weapons platform?"

"If the damage to the Romulan ship was any indication," Bashir said, "Locken has been pirating whatever technology he can. It wouldn't surprise me if he salvaged that platform from the aftermath of a battle somewhere at the edge of Cardassian space."

"Great," Ro replied. "But they know we're here now. Do we abort?"

"Not an option," Bashir yelled, pointing out the bow viewport.

Three ships were flying in formation up out of a gray cloudbank, weapons firing. In the split second before she threw the runabout into a roll, Ro saw that Bashir's guess must be right. None of the ships had a familiar configuration, but all had familiar elements. One had the hull of a Jem'Hadar fighter, but was armed with Romulan disruptors half-surrounded by a Breen impeller wing. Another was a wingless Klingon bird-of-prey, outfitted with Federation warp nacelles. The third was composed of so many different bits and pieces that Ro couldn't even guess where it all came from. *They shouldn't be able to fly. How could they make all those systems compatible?* Ro dumped all their reserve power into the engines and redlined the thrusters, pressing her back into her seat.

The patchwork fighters' first shot cut through the shields as if they were gauze. Seconds before her control board overloaded and died, Ro set the stabilizers for glide and locked them into position. "Everyone out!" she cried, unlocked her harness, and reached under her seat for her bag even as the runabout's belly slapped into the first layer of cloud cover.

Taran'atar was already standing on a pad, his weapons satchel slung over his shoulder, when Ro took the three steps from the pilot's chair to the transporter. She pulled a med kit from a storage locker and hooked it to her belt, then turned to look for Bashir. It was more important that the doctor get off than anyone else, and Ro wasn't sure that the batteries held a big enough charge for two transports. But Bashir hadn't moved from the engineering board and was only able to stop working long enough to make a second's eye contact. "Go!" he shouted. "The presets are gone. I have to stabilize power to the inertial dampeners and the transporter's compensators or you're going to end up as a couple of smears spread across twenty kilometers of terrain."

"But you should go!"

Bashir only shook his head and manipulated the controls, his hands moving faster than Ro could follow. "You couldn't do this," he said.

"We're closing on the shoreline," Dax said, not looking up from her board, obviously trusting Bashir to do whatever had to be done. "We're almost in range. Get on the pads!"

Ro hissed a curse, then stepped onto the pad next to Taran'atar. "Don't be long!" she shouted. Bashir waved reassuringly; then the cabin disappeared in a haze of silver sparkles. Seconds later, they materialized in a barren patch on a low hilltop surrounded by a ring of tropical vegetation.

As soon as she felt the ground beneath her feet, Ro craned her neck back, scanning the sky for signs of the plummeting runabout. The sun was sinking into the western sea, streaking the sky with bands of ochre, orange, and crimson. Directly overhead, the heavens were already almost black, and though she knew to expect it, Ro was still rattled by the paucity of stars. This deep in the Badlands, only the brightest lights could cut through the thick curtains of plasma particles.

Taran'atar tapped Ro on the shoulder and pointed to the east at a thin streak of silver light. "The runabout," Ro said, then began to count in her head. When she reached sixty, she looked around the clearing for a pair of silver columns forming out of thin air. When nothing appeared, she counted to sixty again. Nothing happened. She tapped her combadge and called, "Team one to team two. Team one to team two. Please respond."

Nothing.

She kept the channel open, losing hope of a reply as each second passed, but unwilling to give up. Just before the streak disappeared over the edge of the eastern horizon, Ro unslung her tricorder, checked their coordinates, and read them off into her combadge.

Taran'atar hissed, "No," threw Ro down onto the spongy ground, and covered her mouth with his hand. When he turned her head to the side, Ro thought he might be about to twist it off, but he was only trying to point out a patch of foliage at the bottom of the hill, barely visible in the deepening gloom. Leaves stirred where there was no wind and Ro thought she detected the barest glimmer of shimmering air.

Taran'atar released his hold on her mouth and Ro whispered, "Did they see us?"

Taran'atar shook his head once, then pointed at a stand of trees out of the line of sight of their pursuers. Taran'atar shrouded and disappeared. Ro sighed, unholstered her phaser, and started for the trees, staying as close to the ground as she could.

Behind her, over the ridge of the hill and far to the west, Sindorin's sun sank below the horizon and was swallowed by the sea. Night came on, moonless and with few stars to light the way.

Chapter Ten

Ezri shouted "They're down!" almost at the exact moment the runabout was slammed by another disruptor bolt. Her stomach dropped as the ship began to roll to starboard, but Julian managed to redirect power from somewhere and stabilized the craft before its descent became too steep.

Ezri checked the sensors again, hoping she could direct the transporter to beam them to within a couple of klicks of Taran'atar and Ro and found . . . nothing. "Sensors are gone," she shouted over the rising shriek of reentry.

"So is the transporter," Julian yelled back. "Get in the pilot's seat. Controlled reentry."

She did as ordered, pausing only long enough to buckle the crash harness and say a prayer. Seconds later, the pilot board flickered on, darkened, then flickered on again. Somehow, Bashir had rerouted all the remaining battery power to one of the only systems that seemed to be fully functional—the runabout's antigravs, usually used only for liftoff and landing. They weren't in free fall anymore—not exactly—but it was a stretch of the imagination to call what they were doing "flying." The problem was that the antigravs couldn't take this kind of abuse over any period of time. They would blow out if Julian kept feeding them power at the current rate and they were still almost ten kilometers up, moving much too fast.

The solution, she realized, was simple, but it made her heart freeze in her chest. "Do you see what I'm going to do?" Julian called over his shoulder.

"Yes."

"Can you handle it?"

Ezri couldn't answer immediately. He was, she saw, going to shut off power to the antigravs—and everything else in the runabout—and they were going to drop like a rock until the antigrav coils cooled off and recharged. Then Julian would fire up the engines again, just long enough to slow their descent to a survivable rate.

"How many times will you have to shut off power?" she called, trying to memorize the panels while she could.

"Three. The last drop should put us about one hundred meters above the canopy."

She closed her eyes then and almost turned to Julian to say, "I'm not a pilot." But something made her stop. Ezri looked down at her hands and saw that she was manipulating the controls, resetting couplings and bypassing presets.

Yes, I am, she thought, *because Torias and Jadzia both were.* Their knowledge, their skills, were *hers.* All she had to provide was her own force of will.

"Ready," she said.

"Good," Julian said, and she could hear the relief in his voice. "When I cut power, count to ten and then fire the antigravs again. Try to keep the nose up . . ."

"Make sure you distribute the power evenly or we'll go into a tumble."

Julian laughed mirthlessly. "You're the pilot. Get ready. Here we go."

The lights went out. Suddenly, there was only the rush of atmosphere around the runabout's hull.

1 . . . 2 . . . 3 . . .

She had never before realized how many different noises runabouts made—the hiss of the air circulators, the ping of the sensor grids, the thrum of the engines—and now there was only this, the sound of gravity doing its job.

. . . 4 . . . 5 . . . 6 . . .

If the antigravs didn't come back on and they reached terminal velocity, at their present height, it would take them about seventy-five seconds before they hit the ground. *Why am I thinking about this?*

The power came back on and Ezri reengaged the antigravs. Her head snapped forward and she felt a shooting pain down her left side. Lights came on and the runabout bucked beneath her.

Lights out. Count. The runabout was sliding to port. *Must be encountering some strong turbulence.* Made sense. It was a tropical area at sunset. Masses of air moving back and forth as the landmass cooled . . .

. . . 7 . . . 8 . . . 9 . . .

Lights on. The shock wasn't so abrupt this time, so they must be moving slower. Either that, or she was ready for it. She fed as much power as she dared into the antigravs and waited for the lights to go out again.

Once they were out, she knew it would only be two or three seconds before they hit the canopy and then it would all be luck, a matter of what was underneath them. Ezri wiped something out of her eyes, then realized it was warm and sticky. *Blood?* she wondered. *Why is there blood on me?*

The antigravs died. Ezri looked over at Bashir, whose hands were still racing over the engineering panel . . .

And then the lights went out for the last time.

The station moaned and rumbled beneath Kira's feet. Far below the Promenade, Nog was tearing something loose, something serious enough to vibrate through the station's vast superstructure. She looked around the dimmed Promenade, half-expecting the walls to tumble in. Kira sometimes imagined that there was a nerve running from her inner ear, down through the soles of her feet, and deep into the bowels of the station; it often seemed as if she was more sensitive to the sounds of Deep Space 9 than anyone else aboard.

Shar had just reported that work on installing the new core was going well. Structural connections ruined by the breakaway of the old core were being cut free and replaced in preparation for the new one.

Viewed from the observation port in lower pylon two, the core detachment from Empok Nor had been a sight to behold, as engineering crews in EVA suits and work bees carried out the complex task of freeing the massive lower-core assembly from its station. The runabouts *Rio Grande* and *Sungari* then gently towed the core right past her, into position for Phase Three of the transfer. She remembered that Dr. Tarses had likened it to a heart transplant, which, she supposed, was as apt a way of looking at it as any . . . especially since it was she who had created DS9's great gaping wound.

Walking toward her, emerging from the shadows of the closed Klingon restaurant, one of Ro's deputies who had remained aboard with the skeleton crew was patrolling the Promenade. She nodded to him, recognizing him as someone she'd seen regularly at temple services, but he'd already looked away, carefully avoiding any obvious display of disrespect as he passed her.

It's there, though, Kira thought, involuntarily reaching up to and feeling bare skin where her earring used to be. *This stops now.* She halted in the middle of the main floor and turned around. "Do you have a problem, Corporal?" she called out, her stern voice booming through the mostly empty Promenade.

The deputy froze in his tracks, startled into an about-face, and came to attention. "No, sir," he responded, still carefully avoiding eye contact with the colonel.

Not good enough. "I thought perhaps you'd forgotten how to show proper respect to your commanding officer."

The corporal flinched almost imperceptibly as her voice blasted him. "Sir! No, sir!"

"Because if there's something causing you to forget who commands this station, I'm quite certain I can find someone else to do your job."

The corporal swallowed visibly. "That won't be necessary, sir!"

She let him suffer under her scrutiny for nearly a full minute more before she spoke again, her voice closer to normal. "Carry on."

"Yes, sir! Thank you, Colonel." The corporal turned on his heel and hurried off.

Damn Yevir and the Vedek Assembly anyway, she

thought, resuming her stroll in the other direction. Kira's banishment from the Bajoran spiritual community had effectively made her a pariah among many of the faithful, even those who served under her. She still had all the authority of a colonel in the Militia, her orders obeyed and her command unquestioned . . . but her bond to the people was gone. Not one of them spoke to her when not on duty, and all of them avoided eye contact unless necessary. And civilians made no pretense at all of hiding their disdain, nor vedeks and monks their open scorn. Even Vedek Capril could no longer bring himself to look upon her. To him, to all of them, she was *Attainted.*

Except Ro, she thought. Ro, who, while faithless, seemed to understand better than anyone what being Attainted had done to Kira, although she freely admitted she couldn't understand why the colonel had accepted Yevir's judgment. Kira wasn't surprised. Ro was an outsider to their people by choice, her contrariness and defiance of Bajoran faith something to be worn like a badge of honor, like her improperly worn earring.

But Kira wasn't Ro. She couldn't defy the Vedek Assembly's judgment of her, even though she knew the actions that led to it had been the right ones to take, and proven so. To Kira, being part of a community of faith meant being true to it, even if that same community cast her out. She would accept its judgment; she would put her earring away and stay out of the temples, she would close her books of prophecy and stay away from the Orbs.

Yevir can take it all away, and I'll accept it . . . because I still have my faith.

"Evening, Colonel."

Kira looked up and saw another member of Ro's security staff patrolling the level-two balcony. Even in the gloom, Kira recognized the man. He was Sergeant Shul Torem, one of the first men Odo had taken on after the Occupation. A gruff, solitary man, Shul always seemed happiest working the late hours, when few people walked the Promenade. Odo had always spoken highly of him, mostly, she had suspected, because Shul hadn't given a damn whether Odo liked him or not. She stopped and smiled. "Good evening, Shul."

Shul leaned on the railing and nodded. "Thought that was you I heard."

Kira laughed. "How could you tell?"

Shul smiled back. "Sorry about Corporal Hava back there. I'll give him a stern talking-to."

Kira nodded. "I'd appreciate that. Quiet tonight, otherwise?"

"When they're not down there bangin' away on whatever it is they're bangin' on."

The corner of Kira's mouth crooked up. *So, it's not just me after all,* she thought. She said, "They should be done soon. Then we'll be busy again."

The watchman shrugged. "It could stay this way from the start of one week to the end of the next and that would be all right with me. Fewer people, fewer problems."

Can't argue with that. "If you feel that way, why don't you stay down on Bajor? I'm sure there are lots of places you could work where you wouldn't have to see . . . well, anyone. A farm, for instance."

Shul turned his head from side to side, stretching his neck, apparently trying to restore circulation to tired muscles. "I've done my share of farming, thanks.

Besides, Colonel, if I lived down there, I'd always have to be travelin' back and forth to see the old woman and I'm not really much of one for space-flight."

"The old woman?"

"My wife."

"Oh," Kira said. "You're married?" She didn't mean it to come out as a question, but there was no concealing she was surprised. Shul didn't seem like the marrying sort.

"Thirty-two years," Shul said. "Last month."

"Oh," Kira said. "Well, congratulations."

He shrugged again. "Doesn't take much skill to stay married. Just some patience and the common sense to know when to shut up and listen."

Kira laughed, delighted. "I'll have to remember that. So your wife works here on the station? What does she do?"

Shul seemed surprised by the question. "She's over at the temple, Colonel. You know her: Aba. Cleans up after the services, keeps the candles lit. Cooks breakfast and lunch for the vedeks."

"Sure," Kira said, picturing a red-faced, jolly woman. "I know her." She held her hand up to the height of her own nose. "About this tall. Laughs a lot."

"That's her," Shul said, nodding, practically smiling.

Kira was having trouble imagining these two people together. As she recalled, Aba would typically talk a blue streak to anyone who came within striking range, though on the couple of occasions when she had been sucked in, Kira had realized that Aba wasn't so much speaking to *her* as continuing a conversational thread that had unraveled when her last victim had moved out of range. "Well," Kira said, "please give her my regards when you see her."

Shul nodded, but there was something about the way his face didn't move that made it clear he wouldn't be passing along Kira's greeting. Aba was one of the faithful.

"Well, good evening then," Kira said, and made as if to continue her walk. Before she moved three paces, she turned and looked up again and was not at all surprised to see that Shul had not moved from the spot by the railing. "You know that I've been Attainted?" she asked flatly.

Shul nodded, then seemed to decide that wasn't enough and said, "Yes, Colonel."

"Aba wouldn't like it if she knew you were talking to me."

"Well," Shul said, "I won't mention it to her if you don't."

"But it doesn't bother you?"

He frowned. "Bother me?' 'Course it bothers me. Seems that vedeks sometimes use an awfully big stick to try to keep people in line. Doesn't seem very prudent to me. When I was a boy, I used to help take care of a herd of *batos*. You know *batos?* Big, smelly creatures, you know?"

Kira nodded. "Sure. I know *batos*."

"They're the kinda animals that you have to poke along to keep 'em moving. I found out something funny about 'em when I was around seven. If you hit them too hard, they seem to sort of wake up, like they're not so much dumb as they're thinking about something else and weren't really paying attention to you. That's when you're in a lot of trouble, you know?"

Kira nodded again, wondering where this was going.

"I don't think too many vedeks have herded *batos,*
Colonel. In my opinion, what they did to you was
pretty much the same thing as hitting a *batos* too hard.
Maybe not hard enough to wake it up, make it stop
thinking about whatever else was on its mind, but almost. You understand what I mean?"

Smiling, grateful in a manner she scarcely understood herself, Kira said, "Yes, I think I do. Thank you,
Shul. It's been a pleasure."

"Pleasure's mine, Colonel. Oh . . . the word around
the station is that you heard from the constable not too
long ago. Is that right?"

Odo's message, given her by Taran'atar. "Yes," she
said. "Yes, I did, Shul."

"If you don't mind my asking . . . is he well?"

"I think so."

"If you see him again . . . please say hello for me."

Kira smiled. "Sure thing."

Shul nodded once more and went about his business.

Kira went on, thinking she might drop in at Quark's,
when her combadge signaled. "Ops to Colonel Kira."

Doesn't anyone see the 'Closed for repairs' sign?
She tapped her badge. "Go ahead, Shar."

Shar said, "I have First Minister Shakaar on subspace, waiting to speak with you, Colonel."

Kira closed her eyes and groaned inwardly. When
Shakaar hadn't contacted her immediately after the Dominion and Avatar crises had been resolved she knew it
was a bad sign. That the first minister had been touring
key Federation planets on Bajor's behalf for the last
month certainly explained it, up to a point . . . but not
completely. The more time that went by without con-

tact from him, the more she knew she'd regret his call when it finally came.

Shar's exact choice of words bore out her expectations. Shakaar wasn't "asking to speak with you," or even "requesting the pleasure of speaking with you," but "waiting to speak with you." *Three years certainly have changed a lot of things, haven't they, Edon?* she thought, remembering the days when a call from Shakaar would have created a thrill of excitement and not a wave of anxiety.

"Route the call to my office," Kira said. "Advise him that with the turbolifts offline, it'll take me a few minutes to get there."

"Yes, Colonel. Shar out."

Kira reached her office in just over a minute, some of her tension pleasantly released by her rapid ascent up the emergency stairs. She sat down behind her desk and immediately keyed open the standby channel. "First Minister," she said, trying to sound accommodating. "Thank you for waiting. My apologies, but we're experiencing some technical difficulties until the station's new core is online."

Shakaar looked up from a padd that he'd been studying while waiting for her. Judging from the furnishings she could see behind him, Kira guessed he was calling from his ship of state, the *Li Nalas*. "Hello, Nerys," he said, ignoring her use of his title. "Yes, I know all about your core. I've been receiving regular reports from my staff on Bajor." He picked up another padd and glanced at it. "By the way, that young officer who put me through . . . Ensign ch'Thane, was it?"

"That's right."

"Ah," Shakaar said. He made a note, then looked up again. "I met some Andorians while I was at the Federation Council. Interesting people. Very . . . political. I think your officer may be related to their senior representative."

That's old news, Kira thought. Word of Shar's parentage had already gotten around the station, as did his apparent unease with having it brought up.

"I'm on my way back from there to Bajor even as we speak," Shakaar went on.

"That's good news, sir," Kira said, wondering when Shakaar was going to get to the point. "I trust your tour went well."

"I think I made a good case to have Bajor's application for Federation membership revisited. We should hopefully know something in the coming days. Although between you and me, all this politicking gives me a headache."

Kira smiled despite herself. She knew Shakaar would much rather be tilling earth than giving speeches and attending diplomatic functions.

"And, speaking of politics, how is the Jem'Hadar ambassador?"

Ambassador? Kira thought, but decided this wasn't the right time to explain what was wrong with that title. "He's fine, First Minister." *I just sent him on a secret mission that he may not survive, but otherwise, he's fine.*

"What's he like?"

Kira was taken off guard by the question. "He's . . . old. At least, by Jem'Hadar standards. I suppose you could even say that he's wise after a fashion." *That sounds good,* she decided, then surprised herself by feeling as if it might also be true.

"Well," Shakaar said, "perhaps I'll get to meet him before too long."

Kira felt the tension returning, wondering how much longer they were going to engage in chitchat before he came out and told her what he wanted. She knew Shakaar well enough to know that he wanted her off-balance before striking.

"So," Shakaar said, "the situation with Vedek Yevir went badly, don't you think?"

Ah, Kira thought. *Here we go.* She said, "I suppose that depends upon your point of view."

"Nerys," Shakaar said, his voice warming with sympathy. "This is me, Edon. You don't need to play these games with me."

Oh, but you can play games with me? "It's my problem, First Minister. I'll deal with it."

"I'm afraid I disagree, Nerys. This isn't just *your* problem. This will affect how every Bajoran on and off the station will deal with you in the future."

Not every Bajoran, Kira reminded herself, thinking of Ro and Shul. "I think I've earned the right to work this out for myself, First Minister," Kira said.

"Earned?" Shakaar asked, his voice rising sharply and, Kira thought, somewhat artificially. "This has nothing to do with what you've earned, Colonel. This has to do with what you *owe.* This is about what you should be doing to bring the continuing chaos on Deep Space 9 back under some kind of control."

Chaos? Kira thought, wondering who might be writing the reports Shakaar had been reading. "First Minister," Kira said, struggling to remain calm. "My station was attacked two weeks ago by rogue Jem'Hadar who managed to destroy a Nebula-class starship and sabotage the station's power core. Since then, we've spent twenty-six hours a day, every day, working to restore the station to full operation. And, against all hope, I think we may have found a solution—"

"This attack, Colonel," Shakaar interrupted, consulting his padd. "Isn't it true that during it your first officer, close to seventy station personnel and residents, and over nine hundred crew members aboard the *U.S.S. Aldebaran* were killed, due in large part to your allowing your upgrade schedule to fall behind, leaving DS9 vulnerable?"

"We were understaffed and inadequately protected. Neither Starfleet nor the Militia took my complaints seriously—"

"—And afterward, no fewer than five Jem'Hadar soldiers successfully infiltrated the station. Correct?"

"Jem'Hadar are difficult to detect while shrouded—"

"—But not impossible. And you *had* just been attacked by them. Surely infiltration was foreseeable?"

"Their ships were all destroyed, even the one that tried to help us. There was too much damage to our—"

"And just prior to the attack, a prylar was murdered on the Promenade."

"She was *assassinated*—"

"—After which, your people discovered and withheld a priceless historical document containing, at minimum, potentially explosive information—"

"—evidence in my security officer's investigation of the murder—"

"—which you uploaded to the Bajoran comnet on your own authority—"

"—because the Vedek Assembly was acting to suppress—"

"—And meanwhile, the one Jem'Hadar you detected successfully escaped custody and sabotaged the fusion reactors. And your solution was to eject your entire lower core, a decision which led directly to the station's current woes. Am I up to speed, Colonel?"

Part of Kira wanted desperately to slug Shakaar right through the screen. "Your information seems decidedly one-sided, First Minister," she said coldly. "Tell me, those reports you've been getting from your staff, were any of them from me, or anyone else from DS9 who actually witnessed those events? If not, may I respectfully request that you, your ministers, and the Vedek Assembly all just *keep your comments to yourself.*"

Shakaar wasn't even slightly impressed or intimidated. "Do you understand now why this isn't just your problem, Nerys?" he asked gently. "You're right about the reports. They *are* one-sided. And not one report from the station in the last two weeks has found its way to me. Do you think I'm an idiot that I don't see that? I'm trying to show you what a dangerous situation you've gotten yourself into. You've made enemies, Nerys, in the Vedek Assembly, in the Militia, and inside my own government. Enemies who will keep doing whatever they can to destroy you, especially now that you've been . . ."

"Attainted," Kira finished quietly, when it was clear that Shakaar could not. "You can say it, First Minister. I've been Attainted." It shocked her to see Shakaar hesitate like that. To some extent, even he thought she'd become a pariah.

Shakaar took a deep breath, then asked the Question Direct. "Do you feel that you're still capable of commanding the station, Colonel? Not *your* station, but *the* station. The *Bajoran people's* station?"

"Yes, First Minister," she said. "I believe I'm still capable."

"Because," Shakaar continued, "I spoke with an admiral at Starfleet Command who seemed to think there was a captain available who might be the perfect candidate for such a posting. He made a good case for why it might be a good idea to return the station to its previous command structure . . ."

"*First Minister,*" Kira said through gritted teeth. "I'm fine. Everything is under control. Please don't expend any more energy worrying about us."

"I'm not 'worried,' Colonel. I'm planning for the future. My job is to be thinking ahead, to see what Bajor might need over the course of the next year, the next five years, the next millennium. Bajor *needs* Deep Space 9, Colonel. Bajor might *not* need you in command of Deep Space 9. Do I make myself clear?"

"Yes, First Minister."

"I would rather keep you there, Nerys," Shakaar said, once again switching tones, switching tactics. "You know the job. You know the people, but you could stand to learn some lessons in diplomacy. As I said, you have a tendency to make powerful enemies—"

"Are you one of them, Edon?"

Shakaar looked stung. "I don't know if you realize how hard some people are working against you, Nerys," he said finally. "This is just the beginning. I can ignore it up to a point, hope that it'll eventually die down and wither on its own. But if it doesn't . . ."

"If it doesn't?" Kira demanded.

"This a very delicate time for me, politically, Nerys, and for all of Bajor. Everything we've been working toward is coming to a head, but it won't take much to make it all unravel, especially if your enemies decide I'm on your side. Do you understand what I'm saying?"

"Yes," Kira said. "I think I do." *You want my resignation. That would solve this particular political dilemma quite neatly, wouldn't it? Well, I'm not going to make it that easy for you, Edon.*

"It's been an honor and privilege to hear from you, as always, First Minister," she said formally. "Will there be anything else?"

Shakaar could no longer hide his frustration. "Why do you always have to be so damned impossible?"

"I'm the commanding officer of Deep Space 9," Kira said forcefully, enunciating each word so he'd know she would never go quietly. "It comes with the job."

They held each other's gaze for a long moment before either of them spoke again. Then Kira repeated her earlier question, "Will that be all, First Minister?"

Shakaar continued to study her face for several seconds; then he actually smiled, not politically this time, but the way she remembered, as if he was satisfied to know that she hadn't lost any of her edge. "Yes, that'll be all. Be well, Nerys. We'll talk again soon." He signed off, and the screen went to standby mode.

It took Kira several seconds to realize that Shakaar hadn't relieved her of her command, that he never intended to. He was simply warning her, in his own very effective way, that there were rough seas ahead, and if she couldn't weather them on her own, she'd lose everything.

In other words, business as usual. Kira pushed her chair away from her desk. Rubbing her eyes, she realized how tired she was, but couldn't remember exactly when she had gotten up that morning. With so many of the station's lights shut down, her internal clock was thrown off. Even the chronometer on her desktop console was wrong, the power having been interrupted so many times in the past two weeks. She could think of only one person who might know exactly what time it was. Kira reactivated her companel and said, "Kira to Quark."

"Yes, Colonel. Lovely to hear from you. What can I do for you today?"

"What time is it, Quark?"

"Why, Colonel," Quark said, "it's Happy Hour."

Kira smiled. "Of course it is," she said, and signed off. Then, speaking to an empty office, she repeated, "Of course it is."

Chapter Eleven

"Have I mentioned," Ro asked, wiping water from her eyes, "how very much I hate being wet?"

"Yes," Taran'atar grunted. "You have. Several times. Please don't do it again."

Ten minutes after the sun had set, clouds had rolled in off the sea and unleashed a torrential downpour. Ro remembered the predawn and post-dusk rains from her previous visit to Sindorin, but, she decided, it must have been the dry season—or the *drier* season, at any rate—because she hadn't experienced anything like *this*. The good news was that the deluge was so intense that their trail had been rendered untraceable to anything but the most sensitive short-range sensors.

The bad news was that they were now soaked to the bone in a dark rain forest that was inhabited, Ro knew, by several creatures that could be quite deadly to most humanoids, even, she suspected, a Jem'Hadar. A fire would improve their chances (assuming, of course, that they could light one), but if Locken's Jem'Hadar were still on the prowl, it would be as good as sending up a flare.

Good news and bad news aside, they couldn't move now. Rain was sluicing down off the treetops, transforming game trails into narrow, rushing streams. Ro suspected that Taran'atar might be able to keep his footing, but she knew just as well that she would have her feet swept out from under her before she could take three steps. They weren't going anywhere.

A bolt of lightning crackled across the sky and Ro tried to use the split second of light to get a look at the surroundings, but all she ended up with was a silhouette of drooping, waterlogged vegetation and streaks of gushing water. The crack of thunder crashing down on the heels of the lightning bolt made her teeth rattle and her empty stomach reverberate like a kettledrum.

"Can you see anything?" she asked Taran'atar. She suspected Jem'Hadar had better night vision than Bajorans.

"Yes."

"What?"

"I see rain."

"And what else?"

"Trees. Many trees. Also undergrowth. More importantly, I see no Jem'Hadar. Otherwise, if you mean 'Can you see anything useful?' then the answer is no."

Ro didn't reply.

She kept expecting the storm to reach its climax, for a pause between flash and crash, but the pause never arrived. A hundred meters to the west, a treetop exploded into flames and then was quickly quenched by the downpour. *That could have been this tree,* she thought, *and we could be two tiny little piles of ash being washed down a hillside.* Before the flames died away completely, she glanced over at Taran'atar, who scuttled closer and, through clenched teeth, asked, "When can we move?"

"Soon. As soon as the rain stops. For a half hour after it ends, nothing moves. Except, of course, for the Jem'Hadar."

Taran'atar nodded in agreement. "If they are still out here, we will elude them. They may be Jem'Hadar by birth, but they have not received proper training. Did you see how they pursued us before the rain began?"

"No," Ro said. "I mean, I might have seen a few strands of grass swaying back and forth when we ran through a field . . ."

"Pathetic." Taran'atar said. "And their uniforms. Did you see them?"

"Maybe for a second when they unshrouded. Were they wearing red, some silver trim?"

"Vanity."

Ro was tempted to laugh, but she sensed it would not be well received.

Then, as suddenly as it had begun, the rain stopped. Dark clouds scudded and Ro felt the hairs on the back of her head stiffen when the breeze picked up. Auroral displays from the plasma storms were already becoming evident to the south. Taran'atar stood up. "I'll return," he said, and shrouded. Not a single leaf stirred, nor did a drop of water fall that could not be accounted for by wind or gravity. It was as if he had never been there.

Several minutes passed. Ro shivered in her wet uniform as the breeze picked up. She stood up slowly and tried to peer through the foliage, but the auroral light did nothing to illuminate the terrain. *"Taran'atar,"* Ro whispered, then shivered again. "Where are you, dammit?"

And then his disembodied voice was in her ear: "Someone is out there."

Ro's heart jumped and she almost fired her phaser. She wanted to yell "Don't *do* that!" but refrained. Instead, she opened her pack, pulled out the fractal knife and clipped it to her belt, then checked the charge on her phaser. *"Who's* out there?" she whispered softly. "Jem'Hadar?"

"No," Taran'atar said softly. "Whoever they are, they move more swiftly and make better use of the cover. They know this forest."

Ro felt hope rise within her. "But you didn't get a good look at them?"

"No," Taran'atar replied, now somewhere to her right. "They are ahead of us, moving in the same direction. I came back to warn you. If you draw their attention, I'm certain I could kill them all."

"No!" Ro said, too loudly. "Wait! I mean . . . they might not be enemies."

Taran'atar unshrouded directly in front of her, and Ro suddenly found herself staring into the eyes of a very suspicious Jem'Hadar. "What do you mean?" he asked. "I thought everyone on this planet was an enemy. What has the doctor not told me?"

"Nothing," Ro said quickly. "He told you everything he knew. . . . It's difficult to explain. I was hoping this wouldn't even come up. . . . Damn." She pulled her tricorder out and checked for life signs. As she expected, Sindorin's environment made the readings intermittent and imprecise, but not useless. Pointing to the southwest, she said, "They're about a hundred meters that way."

"There is a game trail leading in their direction," Taran'atar informed her. "If you are careful, you will not make much noise." He was obviously not pleased that she was withholding information, but was still willing to follow her lead for the present.

"Don't get too close," Ro said, rising and stretching cramped muscles. "And try to stay downwind. Their sense of smell is extraordinarily acute. And stay unshrouded. This is going to be hard enough to explain without having you appear out of thin air." She checked the directional reading one more time. "You're sure there are no Jem'Hadar nearby?"

"Considering how loudly you talk, if there were you would be dead by now."

"Fine, I'll be quiet," Ro said. "Let's go."

Taran'atar turned and headed down the slope, walking quickly, but silently. Ro tried to stay right behind him, but slipped before she had gone ten meters. She managed to stay on her feet, but only by grabbing an overhanging branch, which brought a cascade of rain down on their heads. "Wonderful," she sputtered. "From now on, I'm volunteering for *all* the missions."

The slope soon leveled out and they had only traveled a couple of hundred meters before they were in deep forest. It didn't start to rain again, but Ro could hear the breeze whispering through the treetops, shaking the canopy and occasionally loosing sprinkles of fat drops. It was dark, much too dark to see where she was stepping, and Ro had to pull out her beacon, set it on low, and keep it pointed at the ground. If anyone saw the light, she was dead, but it was either use it or wait until morning. Neither was an attractive alternative and Ro worried that Taran'atar would leave without her if she tried to stop. It was wearisome, nerve-racking work, slogging through the muddy undergrowth, every second wondering when the crack of weapons fire would break the nearly silent night.

Two hours later, just as Ro was beginning to feel that the only way she would get any rest was to throw herself down on the ground and pretend she had fallen, Taran'atar stopped to examine an ancient tree. Training her lamp light on the trunk, Ro saw that someone had burned away a meter-wide strip of bark using what looked to her like some kind of energy weapon. The tree was already dead, held upright only by the web of vines and branches connecting its crown to its neighbors'.

"Who did this?" Taran'atar asked. "The ones we follow?"

Ro shook her head. "They don't have energy weapons," she said. "What do you think?"

Taran'atar leaned forward and examined the burns more carefully, then put his nose against the dead wood and inhaled deeply. A large burrowing insect popped out from under a dangling piece of bark and scurried up the side of the trunk. The Jem'Hadar watched it go, but did not otherwise react.

"Romulan disruptors," he said, then looked around at the other trees in the small grove. About half of them, Ro saw, had suffered the same fate. Taran'atar pointed at specific burns. "Breen. Federation phasers. If we assume that the enemy human is pirating much of his equipment, he would arm his Jem'Hadar similarly." There were also large holes in the soil. Someone had obviously expended a lot of energy trying to destroy root systems. "But what were they firing at?" he asked.

"About another half hour and all will be clear," Ro said. "That is, assuming they haven't all been killed."

"No," Taran'atar said. "Someone has been through this grove recently. They stopped for several minutes, too, though I cannot tell why."

Ro looked up at the dead trees, each of them gigantic and probably ancient beyond telling, each now its own grave marker. "I know why," she said. "To pay homage. To remember."

Taran'atar stared at Ro, waiting for her to elaborate. When she didn't, Ro let him walk away while she stood silently for half a minute, listening for voices she knew she'd never again hear among the treetops. Then, dry-eyed and without comment, she followed her companion deeper into the forest.

Ro didn't have to look at her tricorder when they found the next grove of ancient trees, because she knew she was in the right place. Here the trees were unscarred, the root systems undamaged, but in every other important particular, this place was identical with the one they had left behind forty-five minutes ago.

"Come stand near me," Ro said to Taran'atar. "And lower your weapon."

Taran'atar regarded her skeptically, but Ro persisted.

"Look," she said. "You know and I know that you could probably wipe out the whole lot of them with your bare hands. It's not going to make much difference to you if you point your phaser at that ground for five seconds."

He was staring at her again. Ro wondered how long she could continue to press her luck with him. A younger Jem'Hadar would doubtless have killed her by now. But she supposed that was part of Odo's point in selecting *this* one. Having survived years longer than most of his kind, maybe Taran'atar had learned patience, and was less quick to jump to conclusions. After a moment, he did as she bade him.

Ro holstered her phaser, then cupped her hands around her mouth and bellowed a low, staccato, hooting call that echoed strangely under the canopy. There was no reply, but the forest, which had been alive with small, rustling noises, suddenly grew still. Ro turned to the east and called once more. Again, there was no reply, so she turned to the south, inhaled deeply, and lifted her hands. Before she could call again, a high-pitched voice called out, "Why are you here? Why is *he* here?" The voice came from directly overhead. There was no question who the voice was referring to when it said "he."

"He's my companion," Ro said. "He won't hurt you."

The speaker, now higher up and to her left, made a noise, an *ack-ack-ack* sound that Ro recognized as laughter, though there was no humor in it. Ro heard another noise, a deep inhaling sound, and only recognized it for what it was when a glob of phlegm dropped from the canopy and landed at her feet. She decided to ignore it.

"Do you remember me?" she asked. "Is there anyone here who knows me?"

"Yes," the voice said, now lower down again and behind her. She began to wish that at least one person she spoke to that night would stay in one spot for more than ten seconds. "I remember you. That is why I was told to come speak with you. You might not remember me because I was a young man when you were here last and now I am very old."

Ro was confused. "It's been less than three years," she said.

"It has been a *lifetime*," the voice said. The branches overhead rustled and something suddenly dropped to the ground in front of them. Taran'atar crouched, his phaser up and aimed—

Suddenly Ro was in his way. "Put it *down*," she hissed.

Taran'atar's eyes narrowed, the weapon inches from her abdomen. Ro had no doubt that it wasn't set for stun, but she didn't budge. Taran'atar finally lowered his phaser.

She turned around slowly to face their host, who was obviously shaking with terror. The figure crouched in the shadows, small and unthreatening.

"I apologize for my companion, and our intrusion," Ro said. "We'll leave if you wish. We didn't come here to bring you more trouble . . ."

"But you already have," the figure said. "The Jem'Hadar are moving about in the forest, obviously looking for something. It's not—they think we're all dead. They've gone for a while because they don't like the rain, but they'll be back."

Behind her, Taran'atar seemed to be grinding his teeth together. Obviously, he didn't think much of Jem'Hadar who didn't like to get wet.

"Again I ask: Why are you here?" the figure repeated. "And why did you bring *him?*" He raised an arm and pointed a long-fingered hand at Taran'atar. "He wishes to kill us. They all do."

"No, he doesn't. He isn't like the others, I swear it. He simply doesn't yet understand that you aren't a threat to him. It's a complicated story," Ro said, dropping down on her haunches so she was as low to the ground as the other. "I'll be glad to tell you the whole thing, but I don't think we should do it here. Is there anyplace safe we can go?"

Again, the humorless *ack-ack-ack*. "Safe?" the figure asked. "This is Sindorin. No place is safe, not anymore. But perhaps we can find someplace a little more sheltered." He casually scratched the back of his head. "And there are others who will want to hear what you say." He stopped scratching and stood a little straighter. "Wait here until I come back."

From his crouched position, the figure leaped straight up into the air, easily clearing four meters, and grasped a low-hanging vine. Soundlessly, he pulled himself up, hand over hand, into the canopy. Ro listened carefully to see if she could tell which way he was going, but she heard nothing. Then, she turned slowly and walked to where Taran'atar was standing. "Can you tell where he went?" she asked.

Taran'atar nodded to his right. "He went south by southwest about two hundred meters. He is speaking to three others like himself. Who is he?"

"Him, personally? I don't know his name. But he's an Ingavi."

The Jem'Hadar shook his head. "The name means nothing to me. I was under the impression this planet was not populated by any sentient species."

"No *indigenous* sentients, no," Ro said. "Listen, I want to thank you for your forbearance, and your trust in me. I realize it can't be an easy thing for you."

Taran'atar inclined his head, accepting her statement. "You live dangerously," he noted, "but not recklessly. I will not challenge your authority. However, if you wish to avoid any further . . . misunderstandings, you would do well to brief me now on everything you have been withholding about this planet." Ro was surprised to realize that she felt no sense of threat. Taran'atar was not trying to intimidate her; he was attempting to gather information, though how he might use that information was another issue entirely.

"Here's what I know," she said. "The creatures, the Ingavi, were native to one of the worlds that fell under Cardassian control about seventy-five years ago, just as the Cardassian Union was beginning the same wave of expansion that eventually swallowed up Bajor. The Ingavi were still a young warp culture—they'd only had it for about fifty years—and a group of about two thousand fled before the Cardassians could completely annex their planet. They were forced into the Badlands to avoid pursuit, lost their primary drive, and were lucky enough to make it here relatively unscathed. They made a controlled reentry—barely—and managed to unload a few bare necessities before the ship sank in the ocean.

"The Ingavi family I stayed with the last time I was here said about twelve hundred refugees survived the first month after the crash, but after the initial shock wore off, they realized just how lucky they were. Sindorin is similar enough to their own world and many of the survivors decided there was an almost mystical connection between them and their new planet."

"So," Taran'atar asked, "they came here from a moderately sophisticated world?"

Ro nodded. "Tech-wise, Ingav was a lot like Bajor had been when the Cardassians arrived. But Ingav's occupation never ended. More than that, I don't really know. I haven't had the chance to do any research about their homeworld."

"But the being we spoke with did not smell like he comes from a technological society," Taran'atar commented.

Ro, impressed by the observation, said, "He doesn't. They aren't technological. Not anymore. From what I could piece together, the survivors decided to abandon as much technology as possible when they integrated themselves into the environment. They knew certain technological emissions were detectable from a distance; it was how the Cardassians found them. By then they'd become obsessed with avoiding detection, concealing themselves from outsiders. And as I've already explained, conditions on Sindorin make it damn hard to find anything or anybody most of the time."

Taran'atar furrowed his brow. "They gave up technology out of fear."

"It's understandable," Ro said, "They'd been through a lot. The ship they arrived in crashed off shore. They probably got some basic supplies off before it sank, but not much. And these people were in shock—first they were forced off their planet and then crashed on an uncharted world. The wonder is that they didn't sink into barbarism. From what I saw, in the seventy-five years they've been here, the Ingavi have devised a very stable, very balanced civilization. They have some technology, but they use it judiciously. As you saw, they're arboreal; they cultivate fruit- and grain-producing vines in the canopy, and rarely come down to the ground."

"And these circles of large trees?" Taran'atar asked.

"They tend to build settlements in them. The older trees are more stable, less likely to fall over if struck by lightning or die if there's a ground fire."

"That is why the Jem'Hadar destroy them." It was a statement, not a question. "Target practice."

Ro said nothing.

"But this still does not explain how you know so much about them," Taran'atar said, looking around at the clearing.

"I'll get to that," Ro said, then looked back over her shoulder. "Are they still up there?"

Taran'atar shook his great horned head. *He must look gigantic to the Ingavi,* she thought.

"They've moved farther away. I cannot hear them now. They move quickly through the treetops. I do not think even a well-trained Jem'Hadar could keep up with them."

"That explains why there are some still alive."

"Yes," he said, and turned back to look at her. "Continue."

"Right," Ro sighed. "Most of what I said was true: The Maquis were looking for a new base and we thought Sindorin looked like a good candidate, so I came here with two others and we did a survey. The part I left out was the mudslide. They have a lot of those here. The heavy rains and loose soil can be treacherous. My two companions were killed—suffocated or drowned, whatever you call what happens in a mudslide—and I was in pretty bad shape. The Ingavi found me, took me back to their village, and nursed me back to health. I stayed with them for about three weeks until I was strong enough to find my ship." Ro sighed and craned her head back to look up at where the canopy would be, though she could see almost nothing more than a few feet away from the beam of her light. "I learned a lot about them during my convalescence, and I promised them I would never reveal to

131

anyone that I had discovered them." She paused, shaking her head bitterly. "Problem was, the Dominion came anyway. Then Section 31. I kept my silence to protect them, and it didn't matter. It didn't matter."

Taran'atar tilted his head. "I don't understand. They were weaker than the Maquis, surely. What did it matter what they wanted?"

"What are you saying? We should have killed them or conquered them, is that what you're suggesting?" Ro asked coldly.

"But the Maquis were at war, and had need of this place."

"That's not good enough," Ro snapped. "I wasn't going to do to them what the Cardassians did to Ingav, or to Bajor. They've suffered enough."

"Yes. We have," said a familiar voice from directly overhead. Ro shined her lamp straight up, directly into the large round eyes of the Ingavi they had been talking to earlier. Hanging head-down, he flinched away from the light, then released the vine he was clinging to and dropped lightly to the ground at Ro's feet. This time, he did not stay crouching, but drew himself up to his full height—about the center of Ro's breastbone—then swept one arm forward in what she interpreted to be a courtly bow.

"My name is Kel. I am to serve as your guide while you are here. Those among us who remember Ro Laren speak of you with honor and affection. The heads of the families say you owe us an explanation as to why you are here, but we've decided to believe you mean no harm."

Then he turned to Taran'atar and said, "On the other hand, they all wanted to kill you, but I told them that you heeded Ro Laren when she asked you to lower your weapon. They have decided this means I have spoken for you, Jem'Hadar. So, if this is a trick and you plan to kill us all, kill me first. Otherwise, I could not bear the shame."

Taran'atar listened attentively, then nodded once.

Ro took the opportunity to take a closer look at Kel and found that she did not, in fact, recognize him. Like the rest of his kind, his head, arms, and legs were covered in short, coarse green hair—not their natural coloring, but the result of a colonial microorganism that clung to Ingavi fur, a harmless parasite that helped to camouflage them in the forest. He wore mottled green shorts, a close-fitting vest of the same color that had many sealed pockets of several different sizes down the front, but no shoes because the Ingavi used their long, prehensile toes while climbing as much as they used their hands.

Like most of the Ingavi males she'd seen during her previous visit, Kel had large eyes, a flat nose, and a wide, down-turned mouth. There was, to Ro's eyes, something about their habitual expression that made her think of a perpetually put-upon civil servant and, as far as she could tell, there was nothing about Kel's personality that would dispel that illusion.

Lifting one long arm, Kel pointed into the forest and said, "We have a shelter in this direction. Some of my friends are attempting to distract the Jem'Hadar—the *other* Jem'Hadar—who are searching the forest for you, so we must hurry."

Taran'atar looked back over his shoulder as though he was thinking about going back to face the other Jem'Hadar, but shook it off and returned his attention to Kel. "Lead on."

The Ingavi turned to Ro and said, "Talk to me while we walk. I will have to explain to the others why you are here when we arrive." He glanced at Taran'atar. "And why we should believe that this one is different from the others."

"Taran'atar isn't one of those who have been menacing you," Ro said. "He . . . works with me, and accompanied me in returning to Sindorin because what threatens you now also threatens our worlds." Ro told Kel an abbreviated version of the tale that brought her to Sindorin.

When she was finished, Kel asked, "So do you think your comrades perished?"

Ro puffed as they climbed a long, steep slope, but managed to say, "There's no way to know. It's possible, though I doubt it. There was no explosion when our ship went down, as far as I could tell. And Bashir and Dax, they seem a resourceful pair."

"That's not a reason," Taran'atar commented, chugging steadily up the hill. "It's an opinion."

"I agree," Kel said, loping along at an easy pace, "but I hope you are right, Ro. If this madman, this Locken, is the one responsible for these latest atrocities, then I hope your friend finds him and stops him."

"I think he could," Ro said, stopping to catch her breath when they reached the crest of the hill. Dawn was beginning to turn the sky to the east pink. "Or, anyway, he stands a better chance than anyone else. And Taran'atar and I will do whatever we can. It's the least we can do."

"The least you could do," Kel corrected, "is nothing, so anything you will do is welcome."

"But now you tell me of your fortunes, Kel," Ro said. "How have the Ingavi fared since I was last here?"

Kel looked up at her from under lowered brows. "Very little has occurred that I would call fortune, Ro. We have endured, but little else, though my wife tells me I am inclined to take the dark view. Now, come," he said, pointing the way down the hillside. "It's best not to be above ground when the sun rises."

There were caves where there should not have been any. Ro knew a little bit about geology, enough to know that the loose, shallow topsoil usually associated with rain forests could not support a system of caves as extensive as those the Ingavi refugees were hiding in. A surreptitious check with her tricorder revealed the truth: they were not in a cave at all, but inside the hollowed-out remains of a massive petrified root system. Sometime in Sindorin's distant past, its ecosystem must have supported the existence of gargantuan trees, plants so immense that they would have cast a shadow over half the area now covered by the Ingavi's rain forest. Ro didn't feel like she knew enough about botany to be sure of her idea, but she felt the blood rush in her veins at the thought of bringing a Starfleet survey team back to the planet to confirm the finding.

And then Ro felt ashamed. *Another* disturbance, *another* group of outsiders to harass the Ingavi? It wasn't right. She'd restrain herself, though she was surprised to find that the urge to explore—something she thought had atrophied forever when she had fled the *Enterprise*—was still there. How odd.

Kel introduced Ro to his extended family, most of whom seemed to already know who she was. Then, he grudgingly indicated Taran'atar, who took this as a signal to glide into a corner, where he hunkered down to watch the door, apparently making a sincere effort to appear as harmless as possible, although the Ingavi all jumped nervously whenever he shifted his weight or moved his hands. It was painful for Ro to watch, not in the least because the Ingavi had to know there was nothing they could do if Taran'atar took it into his head to open fire.

There were about twenty Ingavi in the bunker, and though it appeared to Ro that they had made themselves as comfortable as possible, it was clear they were miserable. They wanted to be swaying under the treetops, but here they were in these dank, dark, windless holes.

"How long have you been down here?" Ro asked, taking the small bowl of food Kel's wife, Matasa, offered. It looked like grubworms mixed with sawdust, but Ro ate it gratefully. She knew from her previous visit that she could digest Ingavi food (indeed, their digestion was considerably more delicate than the average Bajoran's) and that what she had been given was a generous portion by their standards. Ingavi ate many small meals every day and eating was usually an invitation to talk.

"One dry season and most of this rainy season," Kel said.

The better part of a year, Ro translated. "And before these Jem'Hadar, there were others?" she guessed.

Kel nodded. "The others were worse in many ways. They looked, acted, more like him." He pointed at Taran'atar, who was, Ro saw, silently declining the bowl he'd been offered.

Kel's family finished their meal, then invited Ro and Taran'atar into a small circular chamber where the air was fresher. Ro inspected the ceiling and saw that the Ingavi had inserted into the loose soil some kind of long, narrow tube that was drawing down air. Someone lit a small oil lamp and Ro turned her lamp off. Something shifted at the edge of the room and Ro realized there was an elderly Ingavi sitting there, wrapped in a heavy cloth. He had almost no hair left on his head, very little on his forearms or legs, and Ro noticed a milky white film over his eyes—cataracts, a severe handicap in an arboreal species.

"Hello, Ro," the old Ingavi said. "I hope the years have been kind to you."

Ro was surprised and delighted to realize she recognized the voice. "Hello, Tan Mulla," she said, bowing at the waist. "Passably kind, sir, and the same to you. I'm sorry we meet again under such circumstances." She turned to Taran'atar and explained that the Tan was one of the Ingavi who had rescued her after the mudslide.

"Yes, I was," Tan Mulla agreed. "And it is an action I have never regretted, though I confess I came close to despair today when I heard you had returned accompanied by a Jem'Hadar. But my nephew"—he nodded at Kel—"says you vouch for him."

"I do," Ro said, trying to sound certain. "We have a common goal. These other Jem'Hadar are not like him and he has been ordered by our leader to help us fight them." *Close enough to the truth without getting complicated.*

"I think we understand," the Tan said, but shook his head in mild disbelief. "You'll forgive us if we are suspicious. Not long after you left came the first Jem'Hadar, they and the pale ones who speak so well but smell so bad."

"Vorta," Taran'atar offered, the sound of his voice causing several nearby Ingavi to flinch.

"Yes," the Tan agreed. "Them. We did not like them,

but they assured us they meant no harm and we believed them . . . for a time. Then they began to tell us, 'No, don't go there,' and 'Not allowed here,' all the time explaining why it was for our own good. We tried to respect their wishes as best we could, but then they began to harm the trees." He paused and inhaled deeply and let out a long wheeze. The air underground obviously did not agree with him. "We knew this did not bode well, so we ran and hid."

"We saw some of those trees," Ro said.

"There are worse areas, places where the forest floor is open to the sky for as far as I could see," Tan Mulla said, then pointed to his eyes. "When I could still see, that is. They built a very large structure and ringed it round with fences. Then, when they were secure, they came into the forest and hunted us. My family—those you see around me—once numbered in the dozens. Now, we are no more than those you see here. It is the same for all the other families, if not worse. We were fortunate to find this place. The Jem'Hadar never discovered that we hid underground."

Ro asked, "And then the Jem'Hadar left?"

"Yes, very suddenly. But their stronghold did not stay empty for long. Others came, men and women not unlike yourself, but with smoother noses. They began to create new Jem'Hadar, but these new ones seemed . . . less efficient than the previous ones. More brutal. I would even say clumsier, in some ways."

"Do you know how many there are?" Taran'atar asked softly.

"We think perhaps ten score now. But their creator, whom they call the Khan, is making more. We have done our best to stay hidden from them. Although there are many among us who would prefer to fight, even if it means we will die, because our lives now have become unbearable."

"I understand," Ro said sincerely. "As I told you when we first traded stories, my world was once occupied by the same aliens who conquered Ingav. I knew the anguish you felt then, and I know it now."

"I remember. You said then that you were fighting the Cardassians. Did you win?"

"No," Ro admitted. "I lost."

"What happened?"

"The Cardassians allied themselves with the Jem'Hadar, and together they waged a war against the entire quadrant. They eventually were defeated, in part because they turned against each other. But many died on all sides of the conflict, and my original cause was made moot. By the end, the Cardassians themselves suffered the most." She wondered if this news would come as some comfort to the Ingavi. She doubted it.

"But if there is peace now," Kel asked, "why has this horror come to Sindorin. Did you break your vow of silence?"

"No!" Ro said. "The people who started breeding these Jem'Hadar are renegades and opportunists. What they're doing violates the laws where I come from, threatening many beyond Sindorin. We've come to stop them, to rid this place of them. I'm just sorry, so very sorry that you found yourself trapped between all these forces. It's not right . . ." But she found that she didn't have words, couldn't find a way to define her anguish.

Beside her, Taran'atar uttered a word that Ro could only assume was a curse, then stood and marched out of the chamber. The startled Ingavi watched him leave, but no one questioned where he was going. Ro found herself compelled to make excuses and follow the Jem'Hadar, both worried and not a little curious about what had disturbed him. She found Taran'atar standing in the next chamber near the exit. He had opened his weapons satchel and was inspecting its contents.

"What's wrong?" Ro asked.

Taran'atar did not reply, but began checking the charge on his phaser.

"Taran'atar?"

"Nothing," he snarled. "Nothing is wrong." The power pack was fully charged, so he checked the edges on his throwing knives. Not looking up at her, he continued, "And everything is wrong. *You* are wrong. All this is wrong. The Founder—how can I say this?—he must be ill, possibly deranged from living among you for so long. Or a deviant. Why am I here? Why should I care about these . . ." and he said a word that Ro could not understand, the same word he had uttered in the small chamber. "Why do *you* care about them? They are weak. If they die now, *what does it matter?*"

Ro knew the philosophical gulf between them was too vast to bridge in one conversation, so she didn't try. Instead, she kept it as simple as possible. "They want to live."

"As do I," Taran'atar said. "As do all things. But what has any of this to do with our task here?" Taran'atar rose and slung his weapons onto his back. "If we die fighting Locken, then we die. I do not regret giving my life for my duty, Lieutenant, but I still do not understand what my duty here is."

"We're here to stop Locken."

"Then let us be about it!" Taran'atar hissed.

Ro sighed. "All right then. Let me put the question to you. What can we do in our present circumstances? What would you want to do to stop Locken?"

Taran'atar's shoulders relaxed and he seemed to give the question serious consideration. "A campaign?"

"Call it what you will."

"If I am to wage a campaign, I need supplies and troops."

"I can get you troops, I think. The Ingavi will fight. And not for us. They'll fight to win back their world."

"These creatures are no match for the Jem'Hadar," Taran'atar stated flatly. "Not even *these* Jem'Hadar."

"Neither were humans," Ro pointed out. "Or Bajorans. Or Klingons. Or Romulans. Or anyone else in the Alpha Quadrant. That *was* what the Dominion once believed, wasn't it?"

Taran'atar stared back at her, his pebbled brow knotted in turmoil. Finally he sat on the ground cross-legged, elbows on his knees, palms spread. He looked, Ro thought, strangely like a Bajoran monk in meditation. "We will need more supplies," he said. "And weapons. I do not have enough here to outfit an army . . . not even *this* army."

"Then, we'll have to find some more," Ro said, feeling hope rise in her for the first time since they beamed down to the planet's surface . . . how many hours ago? She had lost track of time.

"What about the ship?" Taran'atar asked.

"What about it?"

"You yourself thought it unlikely the runabout was destroyed, and I tend to agree. I've been considering the matter since you first brought it up. The runabout was little more than a conveyance, not a real threat, even to the limited forces at Locken's command. And those forces *are* limited. Especially if he must resort to gathering wreckage for his spacecraft."

Ro was following Taran'atar's train of thought. "Locken wasn't trying to destroy the runabout," she realized. "He just wanted to disable it so he could salvage it for himself."

"Precisely," said Taran'atar. "And if he hasn't yet recovered it—"

"He has not," a voice said. Kel again, standing in the opening between the root chambers. He had, she realized, been standing there for some time, listening to her debate with Taran'atar. "I believe," he said, "that there may still be time to find your ship. And we can help."

Chapter Twelve

"How many crash landings is that for you now?" Ezri asked.

Bashir rolled to the edge of his bunk and looked down at Ezri who was stretched out on hers a meter below. He thought for a moment, then said, "Four."

"Only four?" Ezri asked, surprised. "I would have thought it was more than that."

"Actual contact between a ship and a planet's surface? No, just four: the *Yangtzee Kiang;* the *Rubicon;* the time in the stolen Jem'Hadar ship; and now."

"Huh. I guess I thought it was more than that, you being such an adventurous fellow."

"I'm adventurous," Bashir replied, "but careful."

"Ah. Well, that must make all the difference." She climbed out of her bunk and stretched, rolling her shoulders from side to side.

"How's your collarbone?" Bashir asked.

"A little stiff, but all right." She had cracked it in the

crash, the worst of their combined injuries. He had been permitted to treat the break as well as various cuts and bruises, but then the Jem'Hadar had relieved him of his equipment—communicator, medical tricorder, hypo, and all the medication—and he felt slightly naked without them. "How are you?" she asked.

Bashir sighed, then sat up, almost hitting his head against the ceiling. "Annoyed. Angry. Fearful for . . ." He almost said "Ro and Taran'atar," but changed it to "the future." There was no sense in openly discussing their comrades since, in all likelihood, the cell was being monitored. A small black dome in the center of the ceiling was obviously the decoy, with the real surveillance device probably hidden among the needlessly complex-looking lighting fixture in the corner of the room opposite the bunks. Bashir made sure to act as if he didn't care whether the cell had cameras or not, scrutinizing every part of the room with equal emphasis. It wasn't bad as cells went, he decided. Hot and cold running water. Even a small screen around the toilet for privacy's sake.

The Jem'Hadar had left them alone since they had been brought in and Bashir suspected their jailers were attempting to unnerve them, make them anxious about when Locken might arrive. Pitching his voice low, he asked, "Did you ever find your combadge?" When the Jem'Hadar had searched them, Ezri's had been missing.

"No," she said ruefully. "It must have fallen off during one of the bumps."

"Too bad. Did you have a chance to check the status of the runabout before they beamed in?" This was a safe topic since their captors undoubtedly knew more about the current condition of their craft than they did.

"Not really," Ezri said. "I think the fuselage was intact and I didn't hear any warning alarms from either the warp nacelles or the coolant system, so there weren't any leaks. Other than that, the only thing I remember is my board giving a funny little burp just before we crashed—some kind of power surge through the system just before the emergency shutdown. Did you see that?"

Bashir shook his head. "No, sorry. Missed that. Any idea what it was?"

She shrugged. "Can't say. Wasn't consistent with a burned-out system, though."

Bashir was struck by a suspicion, but he decided not to voice it just then. Changing the subject, he asked, "Did you get a chance to look out the viewports before the Jem'Hadar beamed in? Any idea about the crash site?"

Ezri opened her mouth to reply, but was interrupted before she could speak by a calm, clear, reasonable voice. "You were," it said, "extraordinarily lucky." Dr. Ethan Locken was standing in the cell door, beaming rapturously. He was wearing the same coat and smock they had seen him in on the Romulan ship, though in every other regard he appeared much less threatening than he had in the recording. Indeed, he seemed nervous and was unconsciously picking at the cuticle of his left thumb with his right one. "Dr. Julian Bashir," he said with undisguised admiration. "I can't tell you how delighted I am to finally meet you. Never in my wildest imaginings did I think Section 31 would be stupid enough to send you after me."

Bashir stood up. "Why stupid?"

"Because you're probably the one person who will truly understand what I'm trying to do here."

"And that is . . . ?"

"Save lives," Locken said simply, his cheerful smile never wavering.

"You said we were lucky," Dax said suddenly, before Bashir could inquire further. "In what way?"

"There's a salt marsh about a hundred meters to the north of where you crashed," Locken said, still addressing Bashir. "If you had gone down there, you would have sunk. Even assuming you didn't have any hull breaches, it would have been hard to get you out. To the north and west, there were much larger, much stronger trees. You would have dashed yourself to pieces against those. The grove you landed in, the trees are all young and much more flexible. They acted as a kind of crash net. Now there's an ancient word for you: 'crash net.' Do you know what I mean?"

Bashir nodded. "We used them on the station, in case the tractor beams failed when a ship was coming in hot. Our former chief of operations installed them."

"Yes, of course," Locken said. "O'Brien liked his low-tech solutions, didn't he?"

Bashir felt himself visibly start at the mention of his old friend's name and saw by the expression on Locken's face that he knew he had scored a direct hit.

"Don't worry, Doctor. Nothing sinister. I made it my business to keep tabs on you. Someday soon we *must* discuss your little obsession with the Alamo."

Ezri almost smiled despite herself.

"You might be interested to hear," Locken continued, "that I have a similar fascination with the Battle of Thermopylae."

"The three hundred Spartans against the army of the Persian Empire," Bashir recalled.

"Very good, Doctor," Locken said, smiling. "It's always a pleasant surprise to meet a well-rounded scholar. Is it only me, or have you also found that most people in the medical profession aren't really interested in the liberal arts?" He spread his arms expansively and exulted, "This is already better than I'd hoped. I feel like I know you, that we are simpatico."

"Except, of course," Ezri interjected, "that we're in a cell and you aren't."

Locken did not respond to the barb, but only walked away from the frame of the cell door. Seconds later, the forcefield was deactivated and Locken stepped into the cell. Sketching a quick bow, he asked, "Would you please accompany me to my chambers? I've prepared a light supper."

"Good," Ezri said, heading for the door. "I'm starving." For a second, Bashir thought that Locken hadn't planned on including her in the invitation, but then their "host" nodded and lifted his hand, giving her permission to pass. Ezri smiled ever so slightly, then waited for the two doctors in the corridor.

Bashir saw only a single Jem'Hadar posted at one end of the hall. There were no other obvious surveillance devices in sight, suggesting that Locken's resources were limited, and that he hadn't yet been able to begin full-scale production of his troops.

Though the place had a very "Dominion standard" look to it, Bashir couldn't overlook that the walls were all hung with paintings and art in other media, all obviously executed by the same hand: Locken's. There was a pair of gigantic, but well-balanced and aesthetically pleasing, pots standing guard beside the door to Locken's quarters. When Bashir stopped to admire them, Locken smiled and said, "Don't touch, Julian. The glaze isn't quite dry."

Bashir was surprised. He knew a little about pottery, enough to know how difficult it was to throw such large pieces. He had assumed they were replicated. "You did these?"

"Oh, yes. A hobby."

"I'm impressed." *A little fine art, a little galactic oppression,* Bashir thought. *When does he find time to sleep?* But then he considered his own all-too-frequent bouts of insomnia and realized that the answer to the question was *He doesn't,* and filed the fact away for later consideration.

Locken's private rooms were an understated mix of opulence and functionality. The living area was large, almost fifteen meters on a side, and Bashir assumed it had once been the compound's communal area, the place first the Vorta, then the Section 31 agents, had gathered to work as a group whenever necessary. There were no groups now—only Locken—so he had taken over the entire space.

One wall was dominated by a large computer workstation, probably the primary link to the computer core. Bashir made a mental note of this. On the wall opposite the door was a small but apparently well-equipped kitchen flanked by a large dining table set for one. *No replicators.* Bashir didn't see anything in the room that stamped its occupant as a megalomaniacal dictator, no life-size portraits or graven images. In fact, the room's most notable feature was its lack of personal touches, except for a small end table that displayed a selection of artwork created by children of different ages, from preschool to prepubescent, most of it addressed to

"Doctor Ethan." Most of the pictures were either water-damaged or charred, and, Bashir realized with a small shudder, most of the children were probably dead, killed on New Beijing.

Amid the children's artwork, Bashir found a single holo, a group of men and women, all wearing lab coats, all smiling nervously. Locken was easy to pick out in the group. Next to Locken stood a blond-haired gentleman who had a very paternalistic arm around his shoulder. "Nice holo," Bashir said. "Was this the staff at your clinic?"

Locken's overly alert and attentive gaze relaxed into a genuine smile. "Yes," he said. "My colleagues."

"Obviously you were good friends with this gentleman," Bashir said, pointing at the blond man.

"Dr. Murdoch," Locken replied. "He was my closest friend, my . . . my mentor. I knew the *techniques*. It was all up here. . . ." He tapped his forehead. "But I didn't know how to treat patients. The children, a lot of them were afraid of me somehow, but Murdoch showed me how to set them at ease."

"It's a difficult skill to master," Bashir said. "Especially with children."

"I expect you two never met," Locken said, a questioning note in his voice.

Bashir shook his head. "No, never."

Awkwardly, as if he didn't know precisely how to continue the conversation, Locken pulled out a small control unit something like a tricorder and said, "But I promised dinner, didn't I?" He tapped a couple of keys and the lamp over the dining room table lit up. A moment later, an automated trolley covered with a selection of covered dishes trundled in and stopped before the table.

"I've prepared several things," Locken said shyly, indicating where Bashir and Dax should sit, then realized that there were no place settings. "I'll get you some tableware and napkins from the kitchen," he said apologetically, and ducked into the kitchen. When he returned, he continued, "Just take whatever you want from the trolley. No serving staff, I'm afraid. Even I wouldn't dream of using Jem'Hadar as domestics."

"But you're a god, aren't you?" Ezri asked, peeking under covers. She settled on a small salad and some rolls. "Doesn't that mean they'd wear an apron if you asked them?"

"I've never asked," Locken said. "You're a vegetarian, aren't you, Julian?"

"More or less," Bashir said, lifting the cover off a small bowl. He sniffed the contents. "*Plomeek* soup?"

"Yes," Locken said, taking the cover off what looked like a plate of lamb chops.

"Replicated or homemade?"

"Oh, homemade, of course," Locken said, returning to the table. "It's awful if you replicate it. The herbs just don't come out right."

"Yes, I know," Bashir said. "I've tried. This smells . . . good."

"Thank you. It's taken me a lot of years to perfect the recipe. A Vulcan colleague in my postgrad days said mine was superior to her mother's."

"You must have been so proud," Ezri said, sitting down at the table.

Locken did not respond, but as Bashir sat down beside Ezri, he saw the corner of Locken's eye twitch.

The soup was sublime. Locken ate at a stately pace and seemed to prefer to keep his peace, which surprised Bashir. In his experience, people who typically ate alone usually ate too quickly and tended to prattle on when they had company. That role, unfortunately, fell to Ezri, who seemed prepared to hold up the conversation for the entire table, gabbering merrily as a magpie about whatever entered her head.

When Locken carried the dishes into the kitchen, Bashir asked her, "What are you doing?"

"What do you mean?"

"The way you're acting—the nonstop talking. Why are you doing that?"

"To keep him off balance," Ezri explained. "To keep him from engaging you in conversation. He wants to win you over."

Bashir shook his head in consternation. "He's not going to 'win me over.' I'm not that easily persuaded, Ezri."

"He's very charming," Ezri said. "You have a weak spot for charm, Julian."

Bashir was stung by the observation and said, more sharply than he intended, "You obviously don't know me as well as you think you do."

"I still remember when you first met Garak . . ."

"Garak?" Bashir said. "I always thought of Garak as more mysterious than *charming.*"

"He was both. It's a potent combination—charm and mystery—particularly for you. . . ."

"That's beside the point," Bashir interrupted. "And not true, either, but we'll discuss that later. The impor-

tant thing is I want *him* to talk. I'm supposed to be trying to *understand* him. How can I empathize with the
man if you won't be quiet?"

"What are you saying?" Ezri asked, narrowing her
eyes. "I'm a trained counselor . . ."

". . . Which would be fine *if* we're dealing with
someone who needs help getting over a nasty breakup,
but this is an entirely different order of being."

"Oh, of course, Julian," Ezri said icily. *"He's just
like you."*

Bashir was staring at her openmouthed, stung by the
retort, when Locken returned from the kitchen carrying
a bowl of fruit. "Something wrong?" he asked. "I don't
want to interrupt . . ."

"No," Bashir said, "nothing serious. A difference of
opinion."

"Well, that happens," Locken said, picking up a pear-
shaped fruit with a mottled purple skin. "Even with
people who have a lot in common." He smiled at
Bashir, then began to tear at the fruit's rind with his
thumbs. "Try some of this," he said. "It's wonderful. I
found a grove of them out behind the compound."

Bashir accepted the section of fruit, trying to imagine the neo-Khan picking fruit after disposing of the
Section 31 agents. Locken was right. The fruit was de-
licious: lively and tart. Ezri refused any, claiming she
had lost her appetite. When they were finished, Locken
wiped his hands on a napkin and said, "I guess it's time
for the tour now. What's the fun of having a secret base
if you can't show it off?"

Locken looked at them both, obviously waiting for a
smile. "You Starfleet types don't have much of a sense
of humor, do you?"

Against his will, Bashir felt the corner of his mouth curl up. Ezri was right: charm and mystery *were* a potent combination.

Locken took a delightful pride in his complex, and, Bashir thought, justifiably so, it being both elegantly refurbished and well maintained. As they walked, Locken pointed out areas of special interest or pieces of art he had created. As they talked, Bashir and Locken played at a subtle cat-and-mouse game, each of them attempting to draw information out of the other without revealing too much about himself. Ezri walked half a step behind the two men.

"You've always been interested in the arts?" Bashir asked.

"Interested? Well, yes, I suppose, ever since the enhancement procedure, though I've only recently put my hand to anything. I was always afraid of drawing too much attention to myself. Being too good at too many things . . . it seemed dangerous. It was all right to be a good doctor, but only because I always tried to look like I was working very hard at it. Do you know what I mean?"

Bashir nodded, remembering the nights in the medschool library when he had to pretend to read the same page over and over again even after he had memorized an entire textbook.

"I suppose," Locken continued, "if I had received some encouragement from my parents, it might have been different, but they were always so concerned about my keeping the treatments a secret. It was difficult; they were so frightened of what might happen to *them*, though they never seemed to think very much about what I might be going through."

Bashir paused to take a closer look at a holographic sculpture, though it wasn't long before he realized he wasn't really seeing it. Instead, he was thinking about a lecture he had received from his father when he was thirteen about letting the other boys win in games sometimes, about the need to give the wrong answers on tests sometimes, about *not letting anyone know*. "The Secret Life of Jules Bashir," he had come to label it in his own head. And now here he was speaking to someone who understood, *really* understood.

"But I decided," Locken said, "to try to make the best of things, to create a meaningful life for myself. After I finished medical school, I accepted a position at the New Beijing Pediatric Center. They were doing some very interesting work in correcting prenatal microcellular damage. Did you ever read any of it?"

Bashir nodded absently. "A little," he said. "But I don't have much use for obstetrics on DS9. It isn't that kind of place."

Locken smiled as if he knew better. "I'm sure Colonel Kira and Captain Yates would beg to differ. Oh, and let's not forget Lieutenant Vilix'pran. No matter what else I accomplish here, I can safely say that the best work I ever did was back on New Beijing. We helped mothers bring new lives into the world . . ."

Bashir glanced at Ezri and watched her roll her eyes.

Locken had not missed it, either. "Mock if you will, Lieutenant," he said. "But one of the reasons settlers came to New Beijing was because of the work we did at the center. I treated more than a couple of Trill there, which means I have to ask myself why they didn't find what they needed at home. Do *you* know?"

Ezri didn't respond.

"I thought so," he said, and Bashir had to wonder at the change in his tone. Perhaps the shyness and humility were a little more calculated than he had thought. Or perhaps the differences in his personality existed side by side . . . ?

"And I'd still be there," Locken continued, his voice rising. "If it weren't for the damned war. *Starfleet's* war."

"Starfleet didn't start the war," Ezri retorted.

"Or the Dominion's war," Locken countered. "Or the Romulans' war or the Breen's war. It doesn't matter. The only thing that matters is it came to New Beijing and we didn't want it. We didn't *deserve* it, but there it was."

"Do you know *why* the Dominion invaded New Beijing?" Bashir asked, trying to break some of the tension, but keep Locken talking. "Starfleet could never make sense of it."

"Why?" Locken repeated, his bitterness growing. "Apparently it was all a mistake. They'd been misinformed."

Bashir frowned. "What do you mean?"

"I mean the Dominion apparently had erroneous intelligence that we were developing biogenic weapons on New Beijing. At one point while I was hiding from them, I managed to capture one of their Vorta. We . . . *spoke,* and he explained that they had learned we were developing a pathogen that would be effective against the Jem'Hadar. I didn't know this at the time, but I could tell them today that the idea is ludicrous. Any pathogen potent enough to kill a Jem'Hadar couldn't be released into a planetary environment without killing anything else it came into contact with."

"I agree," Bashir said.

"Ah, yes," Locken replied. "You know whereof I speak, don't you? You were able to observe a

Jem'Hadar go from newborn to full adult a few years back, so you have a fairly complete genetic sample, don't you? Impressive, isn't it?"

"The Founders are extraordinary genetic engineers," Bashir said, but thought, *He doesn't know about Taran'atar. That means he and Ro are still free.*

Locken went on, "Remind me to show you some notes I've been developing for a paper suggesting the possibility that the Founders were once solids themselves and their current state is the result of genetic engineering."

"I'd like to see that," Bashir said. "Later. Continue with your story."

Locken stopped in front of a large window and stared out unseeingly into the night. They were on the second or third story, Bashir saw, overlooking a short, muddy lawn, and the lights in the corridor were low, so most of the illumination came from a pair of lampposts outside at the perimeter of the fence. "It was a nightmare," Locken said, his voice coming harsh and raspy. "The colony's automatic defenses went down and Starfleet was spread too thin. They couldn't—or wouldn't—send anyone."

"If they could have, they would have," Bashir said. "You must realize that."

Locken sneered, but did not respond to Bashir's claim. "And then the Jem'Hadar began beaming down," he continued. "They were everywhere—in homes, offices, clinics, parks, in the children's ward. . . . There was no warning, no request for surrender. They weren't an occupying army—they were *butchers*. Have you ever seen Jem'Hadar in combat? I don't mean against Starfleet or Klingon troops. Have you ever seen them tear into a civilian population?"

"No," Bashir said, his voice catching in his throat. "No, I haven't. And I never want to."

"No," Locken agreed, shaking his head. "You never do. And if I have my way, you never will. Not you or anyone else."

"How did you survive?" Dax asked.

Locken turned toward her, seemingly surprised to find she was still there. After a lingering pause, he answered, "I kept my head, Lieutenant. I hid when I could hide, fought when I had to fight."

"Against Jem'Hadar?"

"Jem'Hadar are mortal. They can be killed if you know where to strike them. One of the things I learned on New Beijing is that I can deal death quite efficiently when I must."

I know that feeling too, Bashir thought.

"But you weren't able to help any of the others?" Ezri asked. "Your colleagues? Your patients?"

Cocking his head to one side, Locken stroked his eyebrow thoughtfully and said in his mildest tone, "You know, Lieutenant, it strikes me that you've been attempting to sow some sort of discord. I wish you'd stop. It's really rather annoying and stands no chance of succeeding. But to answer your question, by the time I had recovered from the shock of the initial attack, my patients and my colleagues were all dead. They had a weapons platform in orbit."

"Like the one that shot us down," Bashir observed.

"Yes," Locken said. "Like that one. By the way, you wouldn't have had a problem approaching Sindorin if you had only announced yourselves sooner. You *were* planning on announcing yourselves, weren't you?"

"Right after we fired the quantum torpedoes," she said.

"*Ezri,*" Bashir said through gritted teeth. "I think that's enough for now." She didn't respond out loud, only glared at him.

"Yes, I quite agree," Locken said. "Would you like to see the rest of the facility?"

"All right," Bashir said. "And I'd like to hear some more about how Section 31 approached you. I have to confess I'm a little surprised you cooperated with them as long as you did."

"I cooperated with them as long as it suited me," Locken said, turning down a short corridor to stop before a pair of large, utilitarian double doors. "This leads to the Jem'Hadar barracks," he explained, laying his palm on an identity reader. "They won't be able to see us where we'll be, but try not to make too much noise anyway. There are some young ones in here and they tend to be . . . irritable." The ID reader pinged and the doors swung open slowly, revealing a long dark corridor. Bashir glanced at Ezri, but she wouldn't meet his eyes.

"I'll keep that in mind," Bashir said. "You were saying about Section 31—"

"I wasn't," Locken replied, "but since you seem to want to hear anyway . . ." He waited for the doors to close, then pulled out his control unit again and pointed it at a row of black glass panels that made up one long wall of the corridor. At his touch, the entire wall lightened to transparency. "After the Dominion forces left New Beijing," Locken explained, "Federation relief teams arrived to help the survivors, to scrape dirt over the wreckage and to bury the dead. When they realized who I was, they asked me to stay on and help." He shrugged. "What could I say? Part of me desperately wanted to leave, but it was my home, so I stayed. I became friends with another one of the workers, a woman named Merra. We often found ourselves working on the same teams. Somewhere along the line, I realized she had been arranging that."

"She was a Section 31 agent," Bashir said.

"Of course," Locken agreed. "But she was also my friend. I still miss her."

"What happened then?"

"Sometime after the last of the dead were interred, Merra told me about Section 31—her version of what it was, at least—and told me that they had asked her to watch me, to learn about me. Merra was, I think, a true acolyte. She fervently believed in Section 31's mission and her superiors must have thought she could transfer her faith to me."

"Did she?"

Locken smiled. "I agreed," he said slowly, "that there needs to be a single, intelligent, unifying force organizing the quadrant. Section 31, by its very nature, cannot be that force, but I admire the organization, their ability to muster resources. I learned a lot from them."

"I've been meaning to ask you," Bashir said. "Where are the agents who accompanied you here? I haven't seen any other humans."

"My former colleagues are now my guests," he said. "If you'd like to meet them later, I'd be happy to arrange it. I'm not a murderer, Julian."

"Not a murderer?" Ezri flared. "What about the crew of that Romulan ship? That wasn't murder?"

Locken turned on her, his face flushed. "That was war, Lieutenant," he said. "The first volley in a new war that will bring about a permanent peace."

"That wasn't war," Ezri hissed. "In war, the victor

takes prisoners when they've defeated an enemy. What I saw was a total and complete disregard for any universally recognized rules and conventions. What I saw was *sadism*."

"Those are *your* rules and conventions, Lieutenant," Locken said. "Your limited concept of right and wrong. I've moved beyond your outmoded ethics. I see the universe as it really is and I see my place in it. Being the limited creature you are, you couldn't comprehend what I'm saying, but Julian understands." He spun back to face Bashir. "Don't you, Julian?"

Bashir was shocked by the transformation he had just witnessed. Until now, Locken had come across as traumatized, even deluded, but now here was the spark of megalomania that lay at the core of the neo-Khan's recent actions. Locken and Ezri stared at him as if he were about to judge the value of their arguments. The pulse of the world seemed to slow as the seconds ticked past, until Bashir finally said, "I think I'd like to see the rest of the facility." Dax just stared at him. And Locken, once again full of courtesy and goodwill, gestured toward the observation windows.

"Take a look," he said. "I think you'll enjoy this."

They were looking down through the transparent ceiling into a series of large chambers. In the room immediately below them, a trio of adult Jem'Hadar was drilling a group of youngsters in weaponry. "I like to keep the birth groups together whenever possible," Locken explained. "It promotes unity."

The youths appeared to be about twelve or thirteen, which meant, Bashir knew, that they were probably not more than two days old. Within the week, they would be adults, battle-ready and disciplined. That was not quite the case today, however; when one of the instructors handed a student a short sword, the boy lifted it over his head and would have brought it crashing down on the head of his "brother" if the instructor had not cuffed him in the mouth.

"You haven't begun to give those six ketracel-white yet, have you?" Bashir asked.

"No, not yet," Locken said. "My experiments show that if you give it to them too soon, it makes them harder to handle. Too late and they sometimes develop a histochemical response, and die."

"An allergic reaction?" Bashir asked, interested despite himself.

"A protein-inhibitor reaction. I suspect it has something to do with my formula for ketracel-white. The only sample I had to work with when I was duplicating the biochemistry was a little old, so I suspect something degraded. I'll show you my data logs later. You've done some work in that, haven't you?"

"Yes. Well, no. Not the real thing." Bashir was impressed. Locken had just casually—perhaps *too* casually—revealed that he had learned to synthesize ketracel-white, a problem that had eluded some of the best minds in the Federation.

"Another peculiarity: My Jem'Hadar go through white much faster the the Dominion's Jem'Hadar did," Locken continued. "They need to replenish as often as six times a day. Naturally I've dispensed with ritualizing the administration of white. I let my troops control their own intake. Pipes from the distillery actually lead directly to dispensers in the barracks.

"At first, I wasn't sure I understood why the Founders decided to create a species with a biochemical dependence. It seemed counterintuitive, especially since the Jem'Hadar were genetically programmed to think of them as akin to gods. But then, I began to see the sense of it. In addition to nourishing them, the ketracel-white also relieves them of any unnecessary concepts of guilt or innocence. In their view, there is only order or disorder. It is a very ... liberating perspective."

"I'd imagine it is," Dax remarked, unable to help herself. "It enables one to justify almost anything."

Locken ignored the gibe, indicating with a wave of his hand that they were to continue down the narrow corridor. The second chamber, much larger than the first, was a shipbuilding bay and contained the fully functional composite ships that had attacked the runabout, plus four others in various stages of construction.

"We've turned necessity into a virtue," Locken said, indicating the ships. "When we began, all I had was the ship we came here in. I used it to salvage wrecks littering the area, then studied the components until I was able to piece together a working fighter craft."

"You assembled a high-performance fighter by *studying* the components?" Bashir asked, impressed despite himself. "But none of the ships had the same computer systems, or structural systems, or anything. Something like that shouldn't have been possible."

Locken gave a not entirely convincing shrug. "It was an interesting challenge, I'll admit that. But once I devised the proper algorithms, well, not so much a problem."

More of the false modesty, Bashir thought. *I begin to perceive a pattern.*

"You didn't have any use for our runabout?" Dax asked pointedly, noticing that it wasn't in the bay.

"Oh, I plan to put it to excellent use, Lieutenant," Locken said, favoring her with a supremely confident smile. "In time. But there's no hurry. It'll keep very nicely where you set it down until I'm ready to get to it. Besides, I didn't want it close enough to serve as a temptation for either of you."

The next chamber, smaller than the previous two, was a dimly lit lab. The doorframe, Bashir noted, glowed faintly blue in the low light. "This is where I manufacture my ketracel-white."

"A forcefield on the doors," Ezri said. She had evidently noticed the blue glow, too. "You don't trust in your own godhead?"

"I'm a very cautious individual," said Locken, "and though I don't think my Jem'Hadar would ever succumb to the temptation to break in, better to be safe than sorry. But this is a very dull stop on the tour. Come see the last chamber. This is where things get interesting."

Looking down into the chamber, Bashir felt his gorge rise and his stomach drop. There was nothing at all interesting about what was below them unless you could consider hell an interesting place.

It was a Jem'Hadar factory.

Bashir knew that he should use the word "hatchery" or "crèche" or something that could justifiably be applied to living organisms, but there was nothing about the place that hinted at anything resembling an organic process. It was a production line. At the center of the room was a machine that vaguely resembled the incubation chamber Quark had discovered among some ship wreckage he'd purchased several years ago, except much, much larger. Perhaps the unit Bashir had studied back on the station had once been part of a larger machine, or, just as likely, Locken had improved on the Dominion design.

"Look over there," Locken said, proudly pointing at a large translucent tube attached to the underside of the incubator. "There's a pupa coming through now."

Bashir watched as an oblong blob about the size of a soccer ball slid into the tube. Then, the tube contracted spasmodically, each convulsion pushing the shadow a little farther along. When the small bundle reached the end of the tube, it slipped out into a netted bag, still steaming from the warmth of the incubator, a thin stream of ooze dripping through the mesh.

"A pupa?" Ezri asked. "You call them pupa?"

"It isn't really in the mature form yet," Locken explained. "There's a short gestation period and then it enters the larval stage and begins to grow very rapidly."

"You mean it's a baby," Ezri said.

Locken began to laugh, giddy with delight. "That's wonderful, Lieutenant. Really. Never lose that sense of humor and you'll be fine, but also be sure you don't confuse it with unnecessary sentimentality. The Jem'Hadar don't care."

A pair of robotic arms yanked the netting tightly around the infant, then lifted it high and carried it away deeper into the factory. Bashir guessed it was placed in some sort of feeding chamber where it was maintained until it entered the "larval" stage.

"How quickly can you produce them?" Bashir asked, struggling to keep his voice steady.

"Not as fast as I'd like," Locken said. "I've improved

the process to the point where a new batch—usually a couple of dozen—is produced every week."

Bashir watched Ezri flinch at the use of the words "process," "batch," and "produced," but he felt he was getting valuable information and he didn't want Locken to stop talking. "Usually?" he asked. "But not always?"

"There are problems sometimes," Locken explained. "We do a quality-control check just before the incubation period ends and I've found that the reengineering I've worked into the genetic code doesn't always take. It's strange—it's almost as if the Founders knew someone would try this someday and configured the code to fight off any restructuring."

"You're talking about the sequence that makes the Jem'Hadar obey you?" Bashir asked.

"Yes. It's the main sequence I check, but not the only one," Locken said. "Have you seen any information about transcription error rate in the Dominion? I imagine Starfleet would be very interested in something like that."

Bashir said no, and began to ramble on about Starfleet attempts to get information out of Vorta while simultaneously calculating how many Jem'Hadar Locken could have produced in the weeks since he took over Sindorin. "So you have, what, two hundred adult Jem'Hadar now?"

"One hundred eighty-two," Locken corrected. "And about fifty immature units. The incubator is very, well, I guess 'fussy' is the word, and I haven't been able to train the Jem'Hadar to tend it. It's not the sort of thing they excel at. But that will be changing soon. I've been distracted by other problems, but it won't be much longer before I go into full production. Soon, there will be more Jem'Hadar here than I'll know what to do with. Though, naturally, I know *exactly* what I'll do with them." He glanced at Ezri and asked, "What's wrong, Lieutenant? No pithy comments about not counting my Jem'Hadar before they're hatched?"

Ezri, who was still staring into the first chamber, trying to see where the robot had taken the unborn Jem'Hadar, turned to Locken and stared at him, her face locked into a rictus of loathing. Her mouth opened and she struggled to speak, but, finally, all she could do was turn her back to the incubation chambers, her shoulders hunched, her arms wrapped around herself.

Locken followed without comment, stopping only to glance at Bashir with an expression that said, *What shall we do about her?* "She doesn't understand," Locken said, amused by Ezri's revulsion. "She thinks genetic engineering is perverse, unnatural. Yet, I would be willing to wager she doesn't have any problem with traveling the cosmos in a faster-than-light ship or using medical technology to cure diseases or correct birth defects." He raised his voice to make sure Ezri could hear him. "But let me ask you both this: Does anyone in your immediate family have an artificial limb or organ? Perhaps a device that augments their hearing or vision? How about something as basic as a heart monitor?"

Ezri said nothing, but Bashir could tell that Locken had her attention.

"But genetic engineering—what is that? Isn't it just another advance in technology? We'll use it on plants. We'll even use it on animals, the lower-order animals at any rate. Am I wrong or don't many terraformers use algae ponds filled with genetically enhanced microorganisms that hyperproduce oxygen? Aren't there a million similar examples of controlled genetics throughout the Federation?"

Ezri turned, but her face was set, implacable.

"Everything changes, Lieutenant, everything evolves," Locken said, his voice calm and even, as if he were lecturing a slow, disobedient child. "Sometimes, we need to give evolution a boost, a little tweak and most of the time we decide that's fine—unless it's ourselves we're doing it to. Then, it's unnatural and immoral. Do you know what I think, Lieutenant? I think the *laws* that govern these areas are unnatural and immoral, not to mention hypocritical and absurd. What is it they call these laws, Julian? A 'firewall'? What an evocative word that is. Fairly enflames the senses, doesn't it? And do you know what I see going up in flames?"

Bashir, as if caught in a hypnotic spell, could not resist answering. "No," he said. "What?"

"Our genetic potential," Locken said softly. "We *could* be better than we are, but only if we're not afraid. The Federation has grown feeble, its strength sapped by weak-willed politicians who are too concerned with public opinion to make the tough decisions. The Klingons, the Romulans, the Breen—they can all smell the Federation's fear, taste its weakness. It's only a matter of time before the barbarians descend on the Federation and tear it apart like the Huns overriding Ancient Rome. It *will* happen. It's only a matter of time—and afterward it's only a matter of who's left to pick up the pieces."

Locken turned to look down into the chambers beneath his feet, then pressed his hands and face against the glass. "Plato had the right idea. You've read *The Republic*. The Federation—or this miserable rabble that the Federation has become—needs us, Julian. It needs philosopher kings—enlightened men and women who will rule wisely, but with courage and daring.

" 'Philosopher kings'?" Ezri asked mockingly. " '*Enlightened* men and women'? Like Khan, you mean, and his genetically engineered elite. Right—*there* was an enlightened group. I've seen the two-dees, read the histories: the food riots, the 'genetic cleansings,' the camps. Do you *really* think . . . ?"

"Winners write history, Lieutenant," Locken interrupted, pitching his voice low and cutting through Ezri's vehemence. "I thought you knew that. And no one knows anything with absolute certainty about that era. Yes, Khan made some mistakes, but think about what he might have accomplished *if* he'd had a chance. Think about what might be different today."

"Like *what?*" Ezri asked, exasperated. "Precisely *what* would be different?"

Locken's face flushed a deep scarlet. He clenched his teeth and Bashir saw tears spring into his eyes. Locken turned away and took several deep, shuddering breaths. When he turned around, Bashir saw no sign of emotion in his face. The rage or sorrow or regret—whatever it had been—was gone, replaced by a pure, crystalline light. "Like what, Lieutenant? How about all the lives that would have been saved if Julian and I were the norm and not the exception?" He faced Bashir, making his case directly. "Think about all the human lives that have been lost since Khan's time in battles with the Romulans, the Klingons, the Cardassians, the Tzenkethi, *the Borg*. If Khan had won, the Federation would be much more powerful today, the Dominion would never have stood a chance, *and New Beijing would never have happened.*"

Ezri flashed Bashir a look that said more than words ever could. If she had been holding a phaser, Bashir suspected, she would have shot him on the spot. Not for personal reasons, not for the sake of vengeance or hatred, but for the same reason anyone would kill a diseased wild animal that had found its way into a nursery school: because it was the only thing to do.

Locken was still looking at Bashir. "It isn't too late, though. That's my point in all this. We can't fix the past, but we can learn from it to shape the future. We could do it together, Julian. You and I together could recreate humanity in our image."

Bashir felt something rise up within himself, and was as surprised as Locken when it expressed itself in an incredulous laugh. "You can't be serious," he said. "That's the most ridiculous thing I've ever heard. You're just mouthing words. You sound just like the villain in every bad adventure serial ever written. Why would I ever consider helping you in this *insane* scheme? What could you possibly have to offer humanity that would make them want to follow you? Some vague promises of genetic improvement? Of invincibility?" He shook his head. "It's not that simple, you know. You want to offer people some hope that genetic manipulation might improve their lives or the lives of their children? They have that now; the people of the Federation have those options available to them, but they've chosen not to take them. Perhaps the rest of humanity doesn't have our lightning-quick minds or our sharp reflexes, but they *do* possess the ability to make moral decisions—and this is the decision they've made."

Locken's expression didn't change as Bashir spoke,

not a blink or a wince showing that the man had heard or understood a word he had spoken. But then he shook himself, strode forward, and brushed past Bashir. "Follow me," he said. At the very end of the corridor, he pulled the control unit from inside his coat and pressed it into a recessed panel on the wall. After keying in a code sequence, a section of wall slid open and Locken beckoned for Bashir to look inside.

"You said that I had nothing of value to give to humanity," he said proudly. "How do you think humanity would respond to *this?*" He must have activated another key on his control unit, because the lights came on and Bashir suddenly found himself facing a duplicate Locken.

He was standing, or rather floating, in a large transparent tube. There was a breathing mask over his face and several monitoring devices were stuck to his arms, chest, and groin, but there was no mistaking the red hair and the dark eyes, despite the fact that the eyes were empty of intelligence. Then he stepped to the side and saw behind the first tube another just like it with another floating body. And behind that tube was another and behind that another. He could not see to the back of the room, but there could be no doubt that Locken had been busy.

"Clones?" Bashir asked. "Have you lost your mind, Locken? *Clones?* Who cares? Cloning technology has also been available for hundreds of years. It doesn't mean anything if you can't transfer the intelligence, and that sort of engrammatic work is . . ." He hesitated, then, in hushed tones, said, "You've figured it out."

Locken grinned. "Almost," he said. "I have the theory worked out. The Dominion left behind traces of the technology they use to copy Vorta minds into their clones, but Vorta and humans—the physiology is very different. It almost looks like their brains were designed to facilitate the transfer process, but I think I know what needs to be done. The work you did with the Klingon—Kurn, I think his name was—that might be key."

Bashir's mind began to race. It was a fascinating concept and he could see exactly how his work on Worf's brother would be useful. Against his will, Bashir began to ponder the possibilities. What wouldn't humanity agree to in exchange for the promise of immortality?

And then there was a stir behind him as Ezri stepped forward, her gaze locked on the tube, her jaw clenched. "He'll never help you," she said, turning the full force of her disdain on Locken. "He'd never set himself apart like you have and try to tell humanity that he knows what's best for it. And he'd *never* engineer a race of beings to worship him like a god. You obviously don't know *anything* about him." She turned to look at Bashir, obviously expecting a cocky grin, a thumbs-up, or some other mark of solidarity . . . and found herself instead seeing the last thing she expected.

Uncertainty.

Locken, amused and triumphant, said only, "Obviously, Lieutenant, you don't know him as well as you thought you did."

"Oh, gods . . ." Dax whispered, then spun on her heel and ran down the corridor.

"Don't worry," Locken told Bashir. "She can't go far. I locked the other door."

"I wasn't . . . worried," Bashir mumbled. "I . . . I'm just very tired now."

"I understand," Locken said gently. "It's been an eventful day and you obviously have a lot to think about. Sleep on it and we'll see how things look in the morning."

Bashir listened to the sound of Ezri's footsteps echoing down the corridor. He knew he should run after her, confront her, try to explain what had happened, but all he could think about was how weary he was of always having to explain *everything* and how it seemed it always took so long for everyone to understand even the simplest things. And now, a new sound: Ezri pounding on the door. She wanted out. She wanted to go away. She didn't want to listen. He couldn't see her at the other end of the dark corridor, but he could feel her anger, her frustration, her fear.

He felt something inside him begin to slip loose, to tumble forward, to slide into the dark expanse. "Yes," Bashir said, staring into the abyss. "I guess we'll see how things look in the morning."

Chapter Thirteen

"What is this place?" Ro called up to Kel. "It seems familiar."

The Ingavi released his grip on the branch he was dangling from and dropped headfirst ten meters, snagging another branch a mere two meters above the ground and swinging himself up into a seated position. "Do not speak too loudly," Kel said. "The Jem'Hadar have claimed this area for their own and though they do not come here every day, they come often enough."

The sun would rise soon, Ro knew, and soon they would have to make a decision: stay under cover until nightfall and rest or continue to the spot where the Ingavi thought the runabout had gone down. Kel said it was still a few hours' hike, and while it seemed sensible to stop and rest, part of her wanted to press on.

"If the Jem'Hadar come here, why are we going this way?" Taran'atar asked, stepping into the clearing and

173

dropping his shroud. He had been slipping away about once an hour—"reconnaissance," he said, though Ro wondered what he could be finding out that their arboreal spies could not.

And spies they had—in abundance. Kel had been true to his word; he had found them an army, though there was still a question about how effectively Ro and Taran'atar could use them. In the end, they could end up being nothing more than cannon fodder and that thought tore at Ro. What right did she have to ask these people to die? Certainly, they seemed willing enough to fight, but could they truly understand what they were about to face? She shook her head and tried to focus.

"There is something here," Kel said, "that you need to see."

"Quickly," Taran'atar snapped. Kel dropped to the ground and bounded up the trail a couple of dozen meters, then suddenly veered to the right. Above them, in the highest branches of the canopy, Ro heard their Ingavi army take a collective breath, then release it in low, grunting hoots that reverberated in the branches and seemed to shake dew from the leaves.

They walked through the dense brush over uneven terrain for several minutes, Kel first, followed by Taran'atar, then Ro last. Even in the dim predawn light, she saw signs that this narrow trail had once been well traveled by the standards of the forest. There was something familiar about the place, too; she had been here before, on her previous visit, though there was something dreamlike about the memory.

The trail opened out into yet another grove of huge trees. There must have been a cold spring nearby, because a heavy mist clung to the place, cloaking the ground up to the height of two meters. The fog didn't drift, but seemed only to ripple in the breeze like heavy gray curtains.

"Do you recognize this place now, Ro?" Kel asked softly.

"Yes," she said. "I remember now. I was brought here once. This is the oldest grove, the place where your people first settled when you came here." She explained to Taran'atar: "The Ingavi chose to live in the kinds of groves we saw earlier because they felt they were all connected to this spot."

"Physically or spiritually?" Taran'atar asked.

Ro was surprised by the question, but decided not to comment. Also, she didn't know the answer. "I don't know," she said. "I was never clear on that. All I know is that this is an important place for them, the forest at the heart of the forest."

"I understand," Taran'atar said. He turned to Kel and asked, "Why did you bring us here?"

In response, Kel only lifted his arm and pointed into the mist, directing Ro and the Jem'Hadar to enter.

"You won't come with us?" Ro asked. "Show us what you want us to see?"

"My people do not enter this place anymore." It was all he would say.

"Let us get this over with so we can continue our journey," Taran'atar said.

"He wouldn't lead us into danger," Ro said.

"Not intentionally, no." It was, Ro realized, almost a compliment coming from the Jem'Hadar. She wondered if Kel would care.

They strode into the mist and Ro quickly felt herself grow disoriented. The trees were closer together than they seemed from a distance and loomed up out of the fog, massive and somber.

"When you were here before," Taran'atar asked, "was this place tended?"

"Yes," Ro said. "They treated it like, well, a public garden, if you know what that is."

Taran'atar nodded.

"Any group that passed near here would stop and groom it, keep it tidy."

"But not anymore," Taran'atar observed.

"Yes," Ro said. "I see what you mean." Dead branches and leaf litter crackled under her feet and the sound—or possibly the mist—gave her a chill.

They stopped, each realizing that they were near the center of the place, and looked around at the trees. The canopy overhead was so dense that Ro sensed it would be dim in here even at high noon, but enough predawn light was filtering through the branches that she was now able to make out a few details. Something at eye level winked, but then was gone. *An insect?* she wondered.

Ro peered closer and saw it again—a faint glimmer. Reaching out, she touched a tree trunk, brushing away a piece of loose soil or moss, and found what she had seen from the corner of her eye: the flat head of a nail. Now that she knew what she was looking at, she saw another, perhaps a meter to the left of the first. A small, pale stick was wedged between the nail's head and the tree trunk. She reached up, touched it with the tip of her finger, then pulled back, shaken.

It wasn't a stick.

Ro knelt down and turned on her palm beacon. Here were more, many more, a jumble of tiny bones. They were too small to have been an adult's. Ro felt the bile at the back of her throat, but she willed it back down. She would not further dishonor this place.

She stood, a little light-headed, and walked around the tree, studying it carefully. Yes, there were more nails, most in sets of two, some high, some low. Here and there bits of bone and fur clung, and Ro tried not to think about the bit of moss she had brushed away earlier.

Moving faster, willing herself to be calm, she walked from tree to tree and studied each, wanting to check them all, but desperately wanting each one to be the last. There were more nails, many more. Most of the bones were small, but not all. It quickly became obvious that not all the victims had been brought here at the same time. The atrocities that had been committed in the grove had happened over the course of many weeks, possibly even months. The insects, the molds, and the elements had done their work; they had reclaimed the raw materials for another cycle of life, but not all the evidence had been erased yet.

It didn't occur to her until she reached the spot where they had come into the grove that she hadn't seen or heard Taran'atar since they'd entered the grove.

"Taran'atar?" she whispered.

He shimmered into view halfway down the trail. "Are you finished?" he asked.

"Finished?" she asked irritably. "Yes. I've seen what he wanted us to see. What about you?"

"What about me?" he asked as she fell into step behind him.

"Did you see?"

"I did not have to see anything," Taran'atar said. "I could smell it."

"What? Smell what?"

"Fear," Taran'atar said. "Uncomprehending dread. An echo of horror. The trees are saturated with it."

"They were children," Ro said. "Most of them. Why would they do that to children?"

" 'They'?" Taran'atar repeated.

"The Jem'Hadar."

"Jem'Hadar did not do this," Taran'atar said. "Or if they did, they were very poorly trained Jem'Hadar. It was not . . . orderly."

"Then who?" Ro asked. "The Section 31 agents? If so, why? What would it prove?"

"Isn't it obvious, Ro?" Kel called from a branch overhead. They had reached the spot where they had turned off the main trail. "It was him, the one you are here to find: Locken. The Khan."

"Locken?" Ro asked incredulously. This did not fit the mental picture she had formed of the man. He was ruthless, but she hadn't imagined him capable of such casual brutality. "But why? It makes no sense. He was . . . he was a pediatrician. He treated children, all kinds, from every species in the Federation . . . I don't understand."

"What don't you understand?" Kel asked. "Why he would order his Jem'Hadar to kill the adults, the parents, but would tell them to save the children and bring them here? Why he would press their limbs against the trees and then . . ." But it was more than he could stand.

Kel cupped his hands over his eyes and lowered his head. Above them, invisible, dozens of voices hooted and cursed. "And then," Kel finished, "he would sit on the ground and watch them. For hours sometime. However long it would take and sometimes it would take so very, very long. We tried to save them, every one of them, but the Jem'Hadar . . ." Here his voice cracked and he stared at Taran'atar. "They ringed the place around, faces pointed outward, not hearing the cries of parents or children."

Kel fell silent and Ro waited for him to speak again, but it was clear he had no words for what he was feeling, not even an inarticulate cry of rage.

"But why?" Ro asked again.

"Why?" Taran'atar asked. "Isn't it obvious? *Because he could.* Because he knew that whatever he once had been, he was no longer. Because there was no one who could tell him he may not. Because it is what unchecked power will always do."

There was something about the way Taran'atar said these words—so knowing, so serene—that rankled Ro. "You would know, wouldn't you?" she asked. "Isn't that what the Dominion is all about? Don't the Founders do pretty much whatever they want? Isn't that what they wanted to do to the Alpha Quadrant? Nail us all up to a tree?"

Taran'atar stared at her impassively, then slowly shook his head. "You don't understand," he said. "You obviously know nothing of the Founders. They . . ." But he checked himself. "This is not the place or the time. We have much to do still, if we can do anything at all." He looked up at Kel. "We have seen what you wanted us to see. Now, lead on."

Kel nodded and leaped up onto a higher branch, then swung forward, moving gracefully, almost carelessly. It was a breathtaking display of athleticism and Ro could not help but admire it for its simple beauty. When she looked around, she found that Taran'atar was also gone, having either shrouded or slipped away into the jungle unnoticed. For all Ro could tell, she was alone in the forest, the only humanoid creature for hectares around. The wind shifted and something fell rattling through the branches to the ground. Readjusting the straps of her pack and setting off down the trail, Ro tried not to think of bones.

"Commander, a call for you. Colonel Kira."

Vaughn, sitting in the center seat and studying a padd with the specs for the command/control module, looked over at Bowers and said, "Put it through, Lieutenant."

"You'll have to use the controls on the arm of your chair, Commander. I can still only transmit text from this console."

Vaughn looked down at the armrests and cursed under his breath. Whoever it was who designed these things never seemed to be content to follow the layout of the previous generation.

"Com channel three-eight-five, sir."

Vaughn found the contact, pressed it, and said, "Vaughn here." No response. "Nothing's happening," he told Bowers.

"You have to hold it down until the connection is made, sir."

Vaughn pressed hard on the contact with three fingers. "We're going to do something about this later," he said ominously to the entire bridge, but before anyone could respond the main viewscreen lit up.

"Do something about what?" Kira asked.

"About the whole ship, Colonel," Vaughn replied. "I'm beginning to think it doesn't care much for me."

Plainly amused, Kira shrugged. "Sorry to hear that. I hope you both can work it out. I'd hate to have to choose between the two of you."

"Ouch," Vaughn said. "Noted."

"I imagine the *Defiant* isn't much like the last few ships you served on, is she?"

"Not very," Vaughn said, smiling. "She reminds me of the ships of my younger days—all engine and weapons, halls too narrow to walk two abreast, and junior officers sleeping two or three to a room." He inhaled deeply, smelled burning insulation and lubricant, grateful that the *Defiant*'s bridge did *not* remind him of a hotel lobby.

"Those were the days, eh, Commander?" Kira said. "So how's it coming? Admiral Ross is expecting a progress report."

Vaughn found the proper contact on his left armrest, calling up a status screen and dropping the data as an inset in one corner of the viewscreen, which would be duplicated on the colonel's own monitor. "Fairly well," he said. "All things considered. What I should have said earlier was that the *Defiant* seems to occasionally resist refitting. She warmed right up to the new biochem lab, but she's being positively cranky about the new stellar-cartography equipment. Shar thinks he has the problem sorted out, although we blew a main when we tried to reroute power for the new navigational controls earlier today. How's that coming, Tenmei?"

Prynn Tenmei, the conn officer, checked her status

board and replied, "Repair team estimates three hours fifty minutes, sir."

"It'll be fixed by the end of the day, Colonel. And we've swapped out one of the old short-range probe launchers for a long-range tube. That seems to have gone all right. No worries on the weapons systems, of course. And where are we with the upgrades to the conn, Ensign?"

"Module one has arrived and is being unpacked, sir," Tenmei said. "Module two failed the primary test cycle and we're checking it for bugs. Anticipate completion at twenty-thirty hours tomorrow."

"Did you catch that, Colonel?"

"Yes, Commander. You should also know we received a revised ETA for the new warhead module. The *U.S.S. Gryphon* should be arriving with it in tow inside of seventy-eight hours."

"Thank you, Colonel, that's excellent news."

Kira nodded. "Oh, and Ensign? I've manned that station. Be good to her."

Tenmei grinned at Kira. "Of course, Colonel." She stroked the main panel of the conn and said, "Though we're still in the 'getting acquainted' stage."

"Maybe you should give the commander a lesson when you have a minute. He seems to make a bad first impression."

Tenmei's face snapped shut. "Yes, Colonel," she said curtly, but would say no more. There was an uncomfortable pause as Kira tried to figure out what she had done wrong, but Vaughn rescued her.

"Anything else, Colonel?" he asked.

"No, that's fine. Admiral Ross should be satisfied, thank you."

"Any word from our friends?"

Kira shook her head. "Not since yesterday." She didn't need to add *since they signaled they were about to enter the Badlands*. Vaughn could read the concern on her face. "Are you coming back to ops?"

"Later," he replied. "After I finish here, I'm going to get some dinner. Are you free?"

Kira considered, then said, "No, not tonight. I don't think I'd be very good company. Tomorrow?"

Vaughn nodded. "Tomorrow." Kira signed off and Vaughn absently stared at the blank screen for several seconds.

"Commander," Bowers called, crawling out from under the aft tactical console. "I've gotten as far as I can with this until the new units arrive. If you've no objection, I'm going below to check the installation of the industrial replicator."

Vaughn rubbed his temples, then felt his stomach rumble. "No, let's call it a day. We're making good time. Go relax, Sam. You can check the IR system tomorrow."

"Thank you, sir," Bowers said, "I'll be sure to get on it first thing." The lieutenant packed up his tools and exited the bridge, leaving only Vaughn and Tenmei. The ensign was struggling to lift the faulty conn module out of the panel.

"Can I help you there, Ensign?"

"No, sir," Tenmei said, without looking up. "Thank you, sir."

Vaughn stood and walked around to the front of the conn. "No, really. That looks heavy."

"It's not, sir. I'm fine." She had poked the tips of her fingers under the lip of the module and Vaughn could see that the weight had turned them deep purple.

"Are you sure? If you need help . . ."

"I'm *fine,* Commander," Tenmei said icily. *"Thank you."* She yanked her fingers out and the module clacked back into its grooves. "Dammit," she whispered, sucking on her fingers.

"Are you hurt?" Vaughn asked, holding his hand out, beckoning her to show him her fingers.

"No," Tenmei said. "I'm fine. I don't need any help." She refused to look up at him, but when he looked at her more closely, he saw there were tears in the corners of her eyes.

"Ensign," Vaughn said, employing his command tone. "Show me your fingers."

Tenmei reluctantly pulled her fingers out of her mouth and held them out for Vaughn's inspection. They were bruised from the weight of the module and there was blood oozing out from under three of the nails.

Vaughn scowled. "Report to the infirmary, Ensign."

"Yes, Commander," Tenmei said and walked stiffly to the exit. The doors opened as she approached, but before she stepped through, Vaughn decided to take a chance. "Prynn?"

Tenmei stopped, but refused to turn around. "Yes, Commander?"

"Would you care to have dinner with me?"

Tenmei's head snapped around, the look of cold fury on her overwise lovely face painful to see. She held his gaze as she spoke. "Permission to speak freely, sir?"

"By all means," Vaughn said quietly.

"I accept the reality that you're my CO on this ship, and the first officer of the station. I respect and honor your rank, and I'll follow your orders without question. I'll even carry on the pretense in mixed company that I can stomach being in the same room with you. But beyond that . . . you can go to hell. *Sir.*"

Tenmei turned and stalked out, the doors snapping closed in her wake, leaving Vaughn alone on the bridge of his ship.

"I'll take that," he said, "as a no."

Chapter Fourteen

Ro had carefully crawled up the side of the fallen tree trunk and peered out into the clearing. The runabout was nestled snugly in a small grove of crushed saplings about eighty meters dead ahead. It had looked surprisingly intact, and it appeared that Taran'atar had guessed right. But it only made her wonder why Locken had made no move as yet to transport the craft to his base. *Maybe those patchwork ships of his aren't good for surface-to-air towing. Maybe he thinks he can take his time, because he doesn't know about Taran'atar and me. Or maybe the ship is much worse off than it looks, and he's already judged it a lost cause.*

The last thought had troubled her . . . until she saw the first red-uniformed Jem'Hadar, then another, and another. She counted five in all, a figure Taran'atar confirmed when he unshrouded beside her, saying that there were strong indications that a larger group of soldiers was encamped some distance off. *That settles it,*

Ro thought. *You don't post guards around something unless it has some value. The ship is still viable.* The only questions now were how soon would Locken want it recovered, and could they take out the five guards without alerting any others?

And, of course, had Dax and Bashir really survived? Assuming they had, they'd probably been captured, taken to Locken's stronghold about fifteen klicks to the east. If they'd escaped into the forest, the Ingavi would have known about it.

"How do you think we should do this?" Ro asked.

By way of response, Taran'atar holstered his phaser and readied his throwing knives.

"You have got to be kidding," said Ro. "We could pick them off from here before they knew what hit them."

"Possibly," Taran'atar said. "But energy weapons are loud. Even if we got them all before they could return fire, which I think unlikely, the sound of our phasers alone would attract attention from the rest of their unit."

"Oh, and they won't shoot at you while you're throwing knives at them?"

"Watch and learn," Taran'atar said.

"I thought that was supposed to be your job," Ro said.

Then Taran'atar gave her a look that she could have sworn bordered on mild amusement, and was gone.

Ro shook her head and resumed watching the patrolling guards. She hadn't had the opportunity to get a good look at Locken's Jem'Hadar until now, but she was finding them to be an interesting contrast to the ones she'd fought in the war. These seemed younger somehow, as if they wanted very badly to be fierce, but weren't entirely certain how "fierce" was supposed to look.

While she waited for Taran'atar to make his move, she once again tried to make sense of something that had been nagging at her since they'd set out for the runabout. Ostensibly, Section 31 sent Bashir against Locken because they believed that while their rogue agent could withstand an all-out assault against Sindorin, they didn't think he'd respond to Bashir as a threat.

But according to the Ingavi, Locken had created no more than two hundred soldiers. Locken's resources and manpower were so limited, in fact, that he was using technological scraps to build spacecraft. His orbital weapons platform notwithstanding, it wouldn't take more than a few dozen well-targeted quantum torpedoes to reduce his ships to the wreckage they came from, and the entire southern continent to a lifeless wasteland. So why hadn't they done it? Was it that Locken was more powerful than she knew . . . or was Section 31 less powerful than everyone had assumed?

Only an hour past dawn, the sun was just now high enough in the sky to send a few stray beams slanting through the dense canopy. Ro saw that the two Ingavi that had come with her—Kel and one of his cousins—were doing their best not to be seen or heard while waiting for Taran'atar's plan to unfold. The rest of their party, about three hundred Ingavi armed with blowguns, slings, and spears, were camped a kilometer away awaiting word, downwind from the Jem'Hadar.

Ro wasn't sure what she would do with three hundred Ingavi, but she was dead set against throwing their lives away in a frontal assault. Taran'atar had agreed, and her confidence in him had risen considerably. *At least, until he decided to start throwing knives.*

"Do you see him?" Kel whispered.

Ro started to shake her head when, without warning Taran'atar was there in the guards' midst. He'd managed to find a spot in the center of the group where no one was looking, their attention all focused on the surrounding terrain. It was a sloppy mistake, very amateurish, and Ro wondered how much training these Jem'Hadar had received. They were bred for ferocity and strength, but there were other qualities—cunning and guile—that could only be gained through experience of the sort Taran'atar had.

Everything happened very quickly.

He was holding throwing knives in both hands and, with a terrifying grace and economy, he flung them at the opponents to his immediate right and left. The one to the left, closer by about three meters, was struck in the back of the head just below the base of the skull and crumpled to the ground without uttering a sound. The Jem'Hadar immediately to Taran'atar's right spun around just in time to see the second knife as it shot through his eye and pierced his brain. The soldier was dead before he hit the ground.

The other three guards were turning also, but Taran'atar had already planned his attack, had already visualized the deaths of these other Jem'Hadar. In his mind, Ro knew, they were already dead.

The soldier nearest him, less than two meters away, was raising his Federation phaser even as Taran'atar ran toward him, bringing down his *kar'takin* one-handed from its place behind his back. Ro winced as the blade bit deep, and Locken was short one more Jem'Hadar.

Taran'atar leaped into the air, spun to gain momentum, then threw his *kar'takin* at the acme of his arc. He landed lightly on all fours, rolled forward, and jumped up in front of a fourth Jem'Hadar just as the soldier was coming to terms with the fact that he had the *kar'-takin* buried in his chest. As the soldier fell over backward, Taran'atar drew his phaser with inhuman speed and pointed it at the last of the guards, who was staring at him, ten meters away, paralyzed. Seconds after it began, the battle was over.

"Leave," Taran'atar told his target. "Or die. It makes no difference to me."

Ro's eyes widened in disbelief and she found herself pointing her own phaser directly at the last guard.

The guard threw down a Breen disruptor, his only weapon, and ran into the forest.

Kel and his cousin followed Ro down and onto the battlefield as Taran'atar walked from body to body calmly collecting his weapons. "What the hell was that?"

This time Taran'atar didn't need to have the question rephrased. "I told Colonel Kira I would not kill if I didn't need to," he said, tugging his *kar'takin* free from its victim. "These Jem'Hadar are a disgrace, badly trained by other Jem'Hadar who were badly trained by a human. They fear death. That whelp was no threat, and he will be a living witness to what happened here so the others will know what they face. It will cause unease within the unit, and perhaps others as well. We can use that."

Kel and his cousin were stripping the dead soldiers of their weapons. "Leave the bodies," Taran'atar told them. "They will serve as a warning."

Ro shook her head, and began jogging toward the runabout, Taran'atar following. "I almost shot him myself. You took a big chance that I wouldn't."

"You told me you were once in the Maquis," Taran'atar said.

"That's right."

"And you were one of the few that neither the Cardassians nor the Dominion could kill."

"So?"

"That means you are a good soldier. I was not worried."

It was, Ro reflected, one of the strangest compliments she'd ever received. She shook her head again and started to check the runabout.

At first glance, the ship looked bad. It had gone down nose-first into the young trees and the bow was buried up to the viewport in a bog. Closer inspection, however, was more encouraging. There were no hull fractures, the warp nacelles were intact, and a careful examination of the terrain around the main hatch revealed that several people had walked into and then out of the ship. She keyed the door to open, and it responded. *Some power left, then.*

The interior was a mess, though Ro was relieved that there were no bodies aboard. Her initial assessment was looking more and more likely: Dax and Bashir were still alive and had been taken prisoner.

The deck was tilted forward at a precipitous angle and so thickly spattered with mud that it was difficult to keep her footing. She sat down in the pilot's seat and tried to access the onboard computer. She wasn't surprised to be rewarded with silence.

"All right," she muttered. "Then let's just spin the dabo wheel." Ro started tapping the power plant activation sequence, and a few key panels lit up. Speaking clearly and precisely, Ro said, "Computer, this is Lieutenant Ro. This is a priority-one command. Begin restart sequence on my mark. Authorization Ro-Epsilon-Seven-Five-One."

There was no immediate response from the computer, but a couple of standby lights on the main control panel went from red to yellow.

"Mark."

One of the engineering boards sparked and blew out. Somewhere in the mud under the runabout's bow something vented and the ship began shaking. Ro grimaced, expecting a burnout at any second. Instead, the rest of the runabout control cabin lit up. For the first half-dozen seconds, all the lights were red, but then, as the computer completed a cursory diagnostic, they flashed to yellow, some directly to green.

Ro patted the console fondly. "Good girl. Computer, how much time is needed to complete restart sequence?"

"Four minutes, fifty-five seconds."

"Are the main thrusters functional?"

"Affirmative."

"Antigravs?"

"Stern antigravity units are fully functional; bow antigravity unit has been damaged and must be considered unreliable."

"Okay," Ro said to herself. "So, we'll be using the main thrusters." She rose, then inched back up the mud-smeared deck to the main hatch, her mind now working on the next question—namely, now that they could go somewhere, where would they go? The Ingavi knew the location of Locken's stronghold, but was that necessarily the best destination? Wouldn't it be more sensible to go back to DS9 and get help? Just as she reached the hatch, it seemed to open of its own accord. The air shimmered and Taran'atar appeared.

"We are discovered," he said.

"Jem'Hadar?"

Taran'atar nodded. "Will the ship fly?"

"Yes, but we need four minutes. How many are coming?"

"Impossible to be certain. They are shrouded."

"Then how do you know they're coming?" Ro asked.

"They are loud. Assume at least twenty."

"Will we have four minutes before they arrive?"

Taran'atar took the safety off his phaser and set it on high. "I will get you four minutes," he said, then tapped his combadge. "Keep our link open. I will keep you posted."

Before Ro could say a word, Taran'atar was out the door. He shrouded three steps from the hatch and was gone, not a leaf or twig stirring. The Ingavi were nowhere to be found. Taran'atar must have sent them back to warn the others. "Computer, time to completion?"

"Two minutes, fifty-two seconds."

"Can we fire phasers?"

"Negative."

"Can we raise shields?"

"Negative."

Ro heaved a sigh, rubbed her eyes, now burning from exhaustion, and when she looked up, saw two Jem'Hadar suddenly appear in midair, one flying to the left, the other to the right, both of them trailing streamers of blood. Just as the bodies were dropping to the ground, Ro heard Taran'atar's voice through her combadge. "Shield your eyes," he said.

Just in time, she screwed her eyes shut and twisted her head to the side, but even with them closed, Ro saw a brilliant white flash. A second later there came a sharp crack and she felt a wave of intense heat on the exposed side of her face.

Voices cried out in agony, but only for a moment. When Ro opened her eyes again, there were four more bodies lying on the ground. Survivors had all unshrouded, the concentration needed to maintain their invisibility broken. She still couldn't see Taran'atar, but she heard his steady breathing through her combadge.

"Computer, how much longer?"

"Forty-five seconds."

She couldn't be sure that Taran'atar heard the computer over the sounds of battle, but she wanted to give him *some* warning, if possible. Leaving the hatch open, she climbed back down the slanted deck to the cockpit, slipping once and almost cracking her head on the engineering console. *Maybe fifteen seconds left,* she decided.

Checking her board, Ro decided that most of the main systems were back online, though she noted a couple of troubling red lights. Unfortunately, she didn't have time to check which systems were still out because the runabout was suddenly rocked by disruptor fire.

"Damage to port bulkhead," the computer announced. "Recommend raising shields."

"Raise shields!" Ro shouted, her hands dancing over the main board.

"Complying."

The runabout was rocked by another explosion, but since the ship didn't have a hole in the port bulkhead, she guessed the shields went up in time. Deciding her time was up, Ro eased power into the antigravs, but felt only the runabout's stern rise. Even if the bow antigravs were one hundred percent functional, the ship's nose was too deeply dug into the slope for the ship to rise horizontally. "Didn't think that would work. Time for something a little more dramatic."

Ro shut down the antigravs and the stern settled back onto the ground. As she strapped herself in, she instructed the computer to reroute power from the deflectors to the structural integrity field. She might be hit by another disruptor blast in the second and a half she needed to fire the fore thrusters, but it was a chance she had to take. It wasn't like she had any other options.

On the battlefield, Taran'atar crouched behind the largest of the young trees and waited for his opponents to finish shooting in random directions. He had just killed one by bouncing a rock off the underside of a tree bough so that it landed at the feet of one of his opponents. Three or four soldiers spun around at the sound and opened fire on their own man. Taran'atar shook his head, shamed by the idea that he might share genetic material with these amateurs.

His foes ceased fire and shrouded. Taran'atar waited, fixing his gaze on a narrow space between two saplings, then saw a blade of tall grass sway as if something invisible had brushed against it. Drawing a throwing knife from its sheath, he rose and smoothly threw the weapon into the gap. It halted in midair between the trees, the blade disappearing into a semicircle of amber-colored fluid. A Jem'Hadar fell forward, unshrouded in death, the knife embedded in his forehead.

Taran'atar heard the unit's First order his soldiers to move from cover and head for the runabout. *So, they aren't complete idiots after all.* They were doing what he would do if the situations were reversed—ignore the emplacement and advance to the main goal. Looking around, he saw leaves and blades of grass rustle and stir. Most of the remaining soldiers were within fifty meters of the runabout and he was at the edge of a clearing about halfway between them and their goal.

Someone became visible and opened fire. The runabout rocked.

Ro needed another ten, maybe fifteen seconds, but she wouldn't have them. . . .

Crouching low, Taran'atar ran to the center of the clearing, drawing his phaser as he ran. He'd studied the pattern of flattened grass, so even as his chest hit the ground and he skidded to a stop behind a large stump, he opened fire, aiming low. Two more Jem'Hadar unshrouded and fell to the ground screaming, cut off just below the knees. A third briefly solidified, staggered by a graze to his hip. He quickly reshrouded, but Taran'atar fired again before the soldier could either roll aside or drop to the ground. Another dead.

The ground rumbled and surged. Taran'atar felt the runabout's antigravs beat uselessly against the ground. He could have told Ro that wouldn't work. *Maybe this is a futile battle after all.* A volley of shots from several points around the glade hacked at the stump. Splinters raked the side of his face and it was only luck that kept him from losing an eye.

Taran'atar raised his head, fired five quick shots at random points around the glade, then ducked back down, covered his head with his forearms, rolled to the left, and tried to shroud. Something was wrong; he couldn't focus his will. Reaching up to his forehead, he found a large gash and a sliver of wood as big as his thumb. He felt no pain, but he knew shock would be coming on quickly. There was blood in his eyes now, but Taran'atar didn't need to see. He heard the run-about's thrusters roar and he felt heat on his face, but Taran'atar could not decide if it was the heat of blood or backblast.

He cleared his eyes and watched as the runabout tore itself out of the steaming earth, clods of dirt sliding down off the bow, vines clinging, as if the planet were reluctant to let it go. Then a half-dozen Jem'Hadar soldiers unshrouded around him, all of them pointing their weapons at his head.

The last vine snapped and the runabout rose rapidly into the air. Some shots hit the belly of the ship, but couldn't pierce the shields. "Computer," Ro called as she swung the runabout's nose around. "Activate transporter. Lock on to Taran'atar's signal."

"Cannot comply," the computer said. "Transporter is offline."

"What?" she yelled, then glanced at the status board. She cursed and saw that one of the red lights she hadn't had time to check was the transporter. "Can you reroute power?"

"Negative. Pattern buffers have been damaged. Risk to transportee would be unacceptable."

"Phasers?"

"Phaser banks have not had time to charge."

She was climbing fast—fifteen hundred meters—and decided it was time to level off. *And time to pick a direction, too*. Taran'atar was either dead now or captured. Bashir and Dax were probably prisoners. The Ingavi had seen her take off and must be wondering whether she was coming back. Locken's fighters would be deploying soon. If she landed someplace, they'd have a hard time scanning for her—the one good thing about Sindorin.

No choice? she wondered, and knew precious seconds were ticking away. More than anything, Ro hated feeling like she had no choice. It was a long way back to DS9, assuming she even made it out of the Badlands, much too long a way for her to stare at her reflection in the console and think about what might be happening on Sindorin. So there were choices, but only one good one.

Ro programmed in a new course and the bow of the *Euphrates* dipped back down toward the planet.

The cell seemed much smaller now. Objectively, Ezri knew, nothing had changed: same walls, same bunks, same sink, probably the same Jem'Hadar standing outside watching them, but everything was crowding in much closer now. Even so, Julian felt farther away than he ever had before.

He hadn't moved since they'd been brought back to the cell: on the lower bunk, his back to her, facing the wall. For a while, Ezri had tried to pretend he was asleep, but she could hear him breathe. In every couple, there's the one who falls asleep first, and though she suspected that Julian liked to think of himself as the bedclothes-tossing, careworn one, he was, in fact, the one who usually fell asleep first. Ezri knew what Julian sounded like when he was asleep and this wasn't it.

Before she had been joined with Dax, Ezri had learned enough about herself and the men she found attractive to know that it was best to let a relationship find its own level, not to be too demanding. She knew better than to push too hard with Julian, especially when it came to issues relating to his genetic enhancements.

And Julian, to his credit, had seemed to understand her circumstances, too. He knew the bare facts about her joining, but hadn't asked for a lot of details, obviously preferring to give her time to tell her story when she wanted. They were a peculiar couple and they knew it—two people who were simultaneously very experienced and surprisingly naive, especially where it came to matters of the heart.

And all that had been fine, she concluded, until the Jem'Hadar attack on the station. Somehow that tragedy had set Ezri on a personal voyage of self-discovery, one on which she was determined to learn her true potential as Dax's reluctant ninth host. The slow realization that she would take that journey had widened an already growing distance between her and Julian, and it wasn't until she'd almost lost him forever that they'd regained their equilibrium, each perhaps a little wiser and more sensitive to the needs of the other. They still took great comfort and great delight in their togetherness . . . but they had quietly agreed to move at a very cautious pace.

But now . . .

Something else had changed since this mission began, something that—for all her certainty that she'd come to understand the man who now shared her bed—was eluding her comprehension. Locken had spun such terrifying scenarios with a wink and smile, and Julian had listened as if on some level he could actually rationalize what the so-called Khan was proposing. And if that was true, did she really know him anymore?

Had she ever?

"Julian?" she called, her voice sounding a little sharper than she had intended.

He didn't answer right away and for a moment Ezri wondered if she had been wrong, if he *had* been asleep, but then, before she called again, he asked, "What is it?"

"I need to talk."

Julian sighed, then stirred on the bunk as though he wanted to get up, but didn't have the strength. "Wait a second," he said. "My arm's asleep." He slapped his hand against the wall to get the circulation going again, then rolled over slowly, taking his time to get his feet on the floor. Head hung low, Julian rubbed the bridge of his nose and asked, his tone low and weary, "What do you want to talk about?"

Ezri felt a tiny growl blossom at the back of her throat. "I want," she started, "I *need* to hear you say that Locken was wrong."

"About what?" Bashir asked irritably.

"About you," Ezri said. "About . . ." Her voice trailed off and Ezri found she wasn't exactly sure *what* she wanted to say, let alone what she wanted to hear. Then her mind latched on to the image of Locken's self-satisfied smile and she rallied. "About who you are," she said.

"Don't you mean," Julian asked, "about *what* I am?"

"That's not fair, Julian. That's not what I was thinking at all."

"No?" he asked. "It's what I was thinking. It's what I would be thinking if I were you." He stood, stretched, but refused to make eye contact with her. "Please don't pretend that it isn't," he said, his voice louder. "Because I really can't take it anymore, the pretending."

Sensing the rising tide of Julian's despair, Dax understood it wasn't her he was accusing of pretense, but himself. "Julian," she said softly. "No one has ever asked you to pretend . . ."

"Don't say it," Julian snapped. *"Everyone* has asked me to pretend. Even after you all discovered the truth about me, you all wanted me to keep being the same old Julian. It was all right for me to show off a little bit, but that was all. It was fine just as long as I didn't remind anyone of what I *really* am or what *they* really are."

"And that is?" Ezri asked.

Bashir inhaled deeply, then let it out slowly, obviously struggling to rein himself in. His voice calmer, he said, "I don't know exactly."

"Or you don't want to say. Go ahead, Julian. If you can think it, you can say it."

The lines around his eyes tightened, but then he relaxed the grip he held on himself. "A beginning," he said slowly. "And an ending, perhaps. I'm a doctor, Ezri, a very, very good doctor. I've studied the issue very carefully and I've come to some conclusions. The frightening thing is that I think others have, too, but are afraid to say anything about it."

"Julian, I'm not following."

Bashir sighed. "Have you ever read a paper on human physiology, published a couple of hundred years ago by Tanok of Vulcan? He was an ethnologist who lived on Earth for fifty years during the twenty-second century. Tanok observed that human evolution had plateaued, that our cranial capacity and efficiency of neuronal activity had effectively reached its maximum unless we began to manipulate our genetic code."

"I know about Tanok," Dax said. "He deliberately published his paper only on Vulcan—and in a privately circulated journal—because he knew how the humans would react. This was less than two hundred years after Khan was deposed and he and his genetic supermen fled Earth."

"True," Julian said. "But Tanok also said that he thought the humans would eventually calm down and see that while Khan's methods might have been too extreme, the basic concept was sound. And he posed the same question Locken did: What if Khan had won? How different would the quadrant, the galaxy, be today? What would *humanity* be today? And can we really know that it might not be a better place?"

"Julian," said Ezri, "I can't believe I'm hearing this." At first, she had thought Julian was engaging in some intellectual brinkmanship, trotting out arguments he knew Locken might use to see if she could poke holes in them. Now she wasn't so sure.

"You can't believe what you're *hearing?*" he said, his voice rising. "I can just barely believe I'm finally *saying* it. Do you have any idea how many nights I've lain awake thinking about these things?" Julian spun around and faced the cell door, though he didn't appear to be actually seeing anything, so deeply was he burrowing down into himself. "Do you want to know something else about me, Ezri? I don't have to sleep very much. Did you know that? But I've always felt like I had to pretend, like I had to go to bed when everyone else did, wake up when everyone else did, complain about being tired because everyone else does. . . . But the cruel truth is that I lay there every night, willing myself to sleep, but finding my thoughts wandering. In the pit of the night, in my darkest moments, I *have* thought all those things Locken said: I *could* cure all of the Federation's ills. I *have* wasted my life pretending to be less than I am because the society I live in considers my very existence to be illegal, even immoral. It's all true, Ezri, every word, and I'm tired of lying."

Then Julian turned and, with a single, well-placed blow, struck the steel brace that held the bed on the wall. The brace cracked and the upper bunk sagged forward.

Ezri was a good enough counselor to recognize a soul unburdening itself of long-denied emotions, but she was also frightened by the unexpected burst of violence. More, she was stung by the discovery that her lover had for months been literally lying next to her, silently seething and keeping such a secret. She felt guilty and not a little embarrassed. With a struggle, she set aside the shame, rose and moved toward Julian, hoping to offer comfort. But before she could close the distance, he was there—Locken—standing in the doorway. It was almost as if he had been waiting for those words to come out of Julian's mouth.

"Of course you are, Julian," he said. "And now the question is simply this: Will you allow yourself to act on those thoughts now that the opportunity has come to do something for the common good?"

"The common good?" Ezri asked, the snarl rising in her again. "Just what would *you* know about the common good?"

But neither Locken nor Julian was listening to her. Julian was standing at the cell door, his eyes locked on their captor. "What about Ezri?" he asked.

Locken glanced at her, then returned his gaze to Julian. "She may join us if she likes," Locken said, "but she has to cooperate."

"Cooperate?" Ezri scoffed. "Cooperate? Like I would *ever* join your new order, your elite minority . . ."

Locken grinned, delighted. "What a very amusing attitude," he said, "coming from a joined Trill." Then he turned away from her, completely dismissing her from his thoughts. To Julian, he said, "So, what's it going to be? What's your answer?"

Julian looked at him, then turned to Ezri and studied her expression. She sensed uncertainty and confusion and though she wanted to be steadfast and supportive, she felt herself responding with outrage: *Damn you, Julian! How dare you not know what to do?* Julian nodded, as if confirming a conclusion he had come to during an inner argument, then straightened his back and lifted his shoulders, as if a great weight had just been lifted. He looked at Locken and said, "My answer is yes."

Exuding triumph, Locken pulled out his control unit and pointed it at the cell. The forcefield faded and Bashir stepped out into the hallway, then half-turned toward Ezri. He said "Ezri, you'll understand someday . . ." but stopped when her fist connected with his jaw. It was a poorly timed punch. She didn't have a chance to wind up and the angle was all wrong. Ezri doubted that it would even leave a mark. He grabbed her arm, immobilized her with a gentle twist of her wrist, then twisted her around so that she was back inside the cell, her back to Locken.

"You son of a—" she started, but he lifted his hand and covered her mouth superhumanly fast, silencing her.

"Don't fight me, Ezri. You'll see I'm right . . . soon." He took his hand off her mouth and gave her a small shove so that she stumbled back onto the lower bunk. She stared at him with loathing, her lips curled back over her clenched teeth.

"It's all right, Julian," Locken said gently, favoring her with smile. "Maybe she'll come around. She seems very bright. And spirited. That counts for a lot." A touch on his control unit, and the forcefield was back up. Locken turned and started down the hall.

"Yes," Bashir said sadly. "It does." Then he too turned away, following Locken.

Ezri listened as the footsteps grew fainter, her body shaking as she heard the double hiss of the hall's security door opening and closing. Then she turned and curled up on the bunk, facing the wall, her body racked with sobs. She raised her hands to her mouth as if to stifle her cries, and then, feeling certain she was safe from any surveillance devices . . . she spat out the object Julian had shoved into her mouth.

She kept up the pretense of the crying as she turned it over in her hands, recognizing it instantly as the primary circuitry module for a Starfleet communicator. The Jem'Hadar had taken Julian's, so this one must be hers. He must have found it on the floor of the runabout, probably cracked open just before they had been captured by the Jem'Hadar. Freed of its combadge casing, the circuitry module was small enough to conceal easily, inside his cheek, even in his hair. He must have been working on it the entire time he'd been lying in his bunk. The questions were, what had he been working on it *with* and what had he been trying to do?

She discreetly felt around the edge of the bunk pressed against the wall and found what she'd hoped for—a small shard of metal, undoubtedly from some damaged part of the runabout's control cabin.

So, Julian had been working on a plan. *Too bad he couldn't tell me what it was.* But then, lying down on the bunk, trying to look as dejected as possible, she decided that she would be able to figure it out. After all, she knew him better than anyone.

Chapter Fifteen

Vaughn decided to take his evening meal at Quark's, on the balcony level. The place had been fairly subdued when he'd walked in, which fit his mood perfectly, but by the time he was finished with his *hasperat,* a reasonably rowdy round of socializing had begun on the main floor.

Somehow, Quark had tapped into the SCE's surveillance feed of the work on Empok Nor and he was dumping the pictures into several monitors he'd installed around the bar. His stated reason was so that everyone could keep an eye on the work as it progressed, though it was obvious from the amount of interest displayed by the crowd that there was some heavy wagering going on. Vaughn only hoped that the Starfleet engineers were betting *against* one or the other station blowing up.

Though he had been ignoring most of the action, when he pushed his plate away Vaughn looked up from the report he'd been working on and glanced at the monitor nearest his table. The EVA crews had been working all day on the delicate job of aligning and inserting the new reactor core into Deep Space 9, and a collective cheer went up in the bar as the final connections were made. Tomorrow the task of repairing and restarting the six fusion reactors would begin, but that was tomorrow. For now it was enough for the crew to be able to celebrate this clear glimmer of light at the end of a very dark tunnel.

The commander was less than encouraged to hear that Quark was giving odds that even after everything was hooked up, the new core still wouldn't work. A chill ran down Vaughn's back and he tried to pretend that it was entirely attributable to the problems they were having with the heating plant and nothing whatsoever to do with his age. He sipped the very passable bock beer (where did Quark *get* this stuff?), and the hoppy aroma reminded him of something, but he couldn't remember exactly what.

Below him, the off duty engineers and other crewmen were all doing whatever they felt was necessary to fight off the chill. Some were talking animatedly, most were imbibing insulating beverages, and not a few appeared to be on the verge of attempting to share some body heat. Prynn Tenmei was at the center of one of the latter groups at a table, ringed by a platoon of SCE engineers, all of them either impressed with her knowledge of large-scale fusion reactors or dazzled by her smile or, most likely, a little of both. Tenmei was amused by their attention—that much was obvious—but Vaughn could see by the tilt of her head that not a single one of them was going to make a ding in her shields.

Vaughn raised his mug in mock salute and said, "Good luck, lads. You're going to need it." Then, he drained the last half-inch of his beer and set the mug down on the table. Before the bottom of the mug had a chance to make a damp ring on the tabletop, it was lifted off and replaced by a full one.

Without looking up, Vaughn said, "Hullo, Quark. I didn't ask for another drink."

"I know," Quark said. "But you looked like you were about ready. A good bartender knows these things."

Vaughn smiled ruefully and accepted the drink. "Thanks. Put it on my tab."

"Oh, it's there already." Quark, well-practiced in determining the focus of barroom stares, studied the angle of Vaughn's chin, checked the cant of his brow, and correctly triangulated on the top of Tenmei's head. "Come on, Commander," he said. "Don't do this to yourself. I sympathize, but it's not worth it—getting fixated like that—and I know whereof I speak. Not that I fault your taste. I've had a chance to observe Ensign Tenmei myself and there's definitely something special about that one."

"Quark . . ." Vaughn said, taking the mug and sipping off the head. "That's enough."

"No, really, I understand. And she's your conn officer, too, isn't she? That must be hard, working in close quarters that way." Quark wiped up an invisible speck of dirt. "But, listen, this is what you have to do: You have to get her off your mind. If you start obsessing, that leads to nothing but trouble. The sleepless nights, the gray days, the restraining orders . . ."

"Please, Quark," Vaughn said. "I'm asking you to stop now."

"But I have an idea," Quark continued. "A visit to the

holosuite. I can make you a reservation right now so you'll be the first one in when they reopen. I don't think you've had a chance yet to peruse my wide selection of Lonely Nights programs—"

"Quark," Vaughn said, slamming his mug down, beer slopping over the rim. He inhaled deeply, resigning himself to the fact that the truth was going to come out eventually. Why not now? "Prynn's my daughter."

Quark didn't respond for several seconds. Then, he picked up Vaughn's mug, wiped up the spilled beer, and set the mug down again. "On the house, Commander."

"Thank you, Quark."

"Well, *that's* going to cost me," Quark said to no one in particular as he descended the spiral stairwell. "And it started out to be such a pleasant evening, too." He had been doing that—talking to himself—a lot lately. "Because there's no one else to talk to," he decided, then realized he was doing it again.

Things had changed too much in the recent past for his taste. Kira had gone from being a zero on the fun scale to a negative number. Quark secretly blamed Odo, but he didn't feel comfortable voicing that opinion. Sure, they *said* there were no more changelings in the Alpha Quadrant, but who could be sure? And they might all be working for Odo now. Quark shuddered. It was all so unfair.

Threading his way back through the crowd, he tossed his tray behind the bar and dropped the empty beer glass into the recycler. He was frustrated; there was nothing to vent his embarrassment on. Even Frool—the only one of his waiters he'd been able to bribe into staying on during the core transfer—was too busy keeping after the engineers for Quark to subject him to the abuse he was contractually obligated to endure.

And the dabo girls were all busy, too. The Federation types weren't usually interested in gambling, but the whiff of danger in the air must have been making them feel lucky. It was still no substitute for the civilian freighter crews who'd been flooding the bar almost daily since the station had become the Cardassian relief checkpoint. But with the last such freighter for the next few days gone since this morning, relying on a smattering of Starfleet officers for most of his business was killing him.

"What's on your mind, Quark?"

Quark looked up, but saw no one.

"Over here, Quark."

He looked down the length of the bar and found himself staring into a pair of golden eyes set in a broad green face. He smiled his "neutral smile #7," usually reserved for persons unknown who appeared to be well dressed and were not holding a weapon to his head.

Looks like not all the civilians have left, after all. "Good evening, sir," he said, strolling toward the man. "If we've met, I don't believe I remember when. And there haven't been too many Orions around these days."

The small, dapper Orion grinned winningly. "We haven't met, sir," he said. "But your reputation precedes you."

Insincere flattery. I smell a business proposition. He pulled a glass from under the bar and set to polishing it. "You are too kind," he said. "What can I get for you, Mister . . . ?"

"Malic," the Orion said, and held out his hand to be shaken. Quark quickly catalogued the stones in the settings of Malic's rings and decided that whatever business he was currently in was doing pretty well. "And what I would like is to meet a businessman with an open mind."

Quark took Malic's hand and they shook. *You can tell so much about a person from a handshake.* For example, he decided, this deceptively small man could probably crush all of Quark's fingers into paste if he wanted. "I believe I might have one of those," Quark said. "For the right price."

Malic grinned and Quark was intrigued to see there was something shiny embedded in his rearmost molar, something that twinkled merrily and, more important, expensively. *There's something that you almost never see anymore,* he thought. *I do so like a pirate who pays attention to detail.*

Taran'atar had experienced many different flavors of pain. Almost twenty-one years ago, in his first campaign against a species called the v'Xaji, he had been burned across most of the left side of his body. It had been agonizing, beyond anything his training had prepared him for, and though he had found the flavor bitter, he had learned to take comfort in it, too. Pain, no matter how intense or disabling, told you one thing: *You are alive.* To a Jem'Hadar, being alive meant one thing: *You can still serve the Founders.* But, privately, Taran'atar had also decided it meant one other important thing: *I can still deal death.*

So, Taran'atar took the pain he felt now—this careless but precise agony—and embraced it. He made it a part of himself so he would not forget it. He inhaled once, slowly, and though he thought the pain might stop his hearts, he let it slowly sink down through his flesh and into his bones. He exhaled, then inhaled again, then caught the scent of blood—his blood—mingled with sweat.

He heard voices—two, no, three—and focused past the pounding in his ears. The first voice was saying, "His blood's not the right color."

"No, it's not," said another. "Not dark enough."

"That's dried blood you're looking at," said the third. "It might be the right color. Let's get some fresh." Something touched Taran'atar's chest and he felt a bolt of white light arc through his body. His arms and legs, he noted, were numb. That would be a problem later when it was time to escape. He tried to flex his toes, but wasn't sure if they were moving.

"I think he's awake," said the first voice.

"He's *been* awake," said the third. "Parts of him, anyway."

"Maybe he was being run by a handler. You saw the communications device he had. Maybe the one in the ship was telling him what to do."

"But look at his neck. He takes no white. How is that possible?"

"Keep your place," the third warned.

Taran'atar lifted his head and opened his eyes. He saw three Jem'Hadar, all wearing the red-and-silver uniforms of the Khan.

The third—no, the First—looked down at him curiously. "Awake again? Good. I was beginning to think we'd damaged you too much."

Again? This was strange. Taran'atar didn't recall being conscious since the battle in the glade, but a quick glance around the interrogation room made it obvious that he had been there for some time. There were implements strewn around, most of which had clearly been used. He recognized a few of them, had even seen one or two used in his time, though information extraction was a specialized field, one Taran'atar had never developed a taste for. There were some who seemed to derive satisfaction from it and he wondered if he had fallen into the hands of one of those.

"Not so damaged," Taran'atar rasped through cracked lips.

The First touched something to his side and Taran'atar felt his hearts spasm. He couldn't breathe for five, ten, twenty seconds and the blackness began to close in around him. When he regained consciousness, the First was standing very near to him wearing an expression of genuine concern. Taran'atar attempted to summon the strength to lift his head, but he couldn't control his neck muscles.

"Still there?" the First asked. "Impressive. I doubt any of my own men could take so much."

His breath coming out in ragged gasps, Taran'atar forced himself to look his torturer in the eyes. "You . . . are . . . fools," he muttered. "And your Khan . . ."

The two soldiers who had been standing behind the First drew their weapons and stepped toward Taran'atar, but the First held up his arm and signaled them to step back. The soldiers, he noticed, were glaring at him, but the First's expression was something closer to curiosity. "Go," he told his men. "Attempt to contact the Khan again and inform him that we have taken this prisoner."

The soldiers were confused. "We've already tried to

report to the Khan," one said. "We were told he was not receiving messengers tonight."

The First's eyes grew cold. "You are young, so I will excuse you this time—the only time. Do as I say. If the Khan will not receive you, leave word with the chief of guards, then return to barracks."

The two soldiers glanced at each other, but neither was prepared—or equipped—to argue. With one last curious look at Taran'atar, they turned and left.

He struggled to remain alert, but Taran'atar could feel his eyes fluttering, his vision dimming. Looking up, he saw the First leaning in close. "Do not take false hope," the First said. "You *will* die, but there are good deaths and bad deaths."

"I know that," Taran'atar managed, and would have liked to add, *better than you could ever know.* Instead, he asked, "What do you want?"

"What are you?"

"Exactly what I seem," Taran'atar managed. "A Jem'Hadar."

"You lie."

"You deny the evidence of your eyes? Scan me, if you have the technology. You will see I am exactly what I say. A Jem'Hadar of twenty-two years."

"I already have. The readings are not possible."

"So you deny your eyes, and your instruments," Taran'atar said.

The First grabbed at the knot of black hair behind Taran'atar's head and forced him to look up. "Do you know who I am? I am First. First among my men, and the First born of the Khan. Whatever you may be, you were not created by him."

"Very astute," Taran'atar said, intrigued despite his

agony. "Then how do you explain me? Either I am lying, as you say . . . or I am telling you the truth, in which case there must be other Jem'Hadar not of your Khan."

Taran'atar saw that he'd scored a hit. Suddenly the first leaned in closer. "Earlier, you spoke of the Founders. Do you remember?"

Surprise kept Taran'atar focused. Here was a Jem'Hadar *asking* him for information about the Founders. "I don't remember speaking of the Founders, but if you say I did, then I believe you."

"Who are they?" the First asked.

"The Founders are the givers of life and of purpose. They are the true creators of the Jem'Hadar. Your Khan . . . is not what you think he is. He has only corrupted the Founders' work."

The First seemed to consider this statement with some care for several seconds. "You seem very certain of this," he said. "How can you be sure what you have been told is true? Is it not possible that these Founders have lied to you? Perhaps they fear the Khan . . . which is as it should be."

"Then explain my age. I am not the first of my kind. The Founders have been creating Jem'Hadar for centuries. How many changes of season have you seen on this world? Do you truly believe that a life serving this human is all there is?"

The First shook his head. "You are misinformed. The Khan is not human. He is something else, the next step beyond humans. He was born to *rule* the other humans."

"So he says," Taran'atar agreed. "The human I came here with is the equal of your Khan in every way, perhaps even better, but he is not a ruler. He is a medic."

"Then obviously he is *not* the equal of the Khan," the First said. "Perhaps *he* is the fool."

"No," Taran'atar said. "He is no fool. I believe he *could* rule the humans if he wished to—some of them at any rate—but he chooses not to. He is a soldier of a sort, but he fights a different war. . . ." He barely understood his own words, but couldn't deny the truth he felt lay at the center of them.

The First stared at him as if he were mad or rambling from withdrawal, but then returned to his own topic as if impatient to be done. "But what are the Founders? Giants? Columns of shimmering light?"

"All of these things," Taran'atar replied, grateful to be able to return to the known. Here, at last, was a question he could answer without hesitation. "And more. They can be anything they wish. They are not trapped by flesh."

The First seemed interested. "Are they immortal?"

Taran'atar had to hesitate. He knew that the Founders could die, had even heard that Odo himself had once killed one of his own kind. He knew too that the Founders were ravaged by a plague not so long ago. And still, some Jem'Hadar had speculated that there were not truly any Founders at all, merely a single great being that could subdivide itself whenever and however it pleased, each of the parts having the knowledge of the whole. Did that mean if one Founder killed another, then he was killing a part of himself? The more he thought, the more he felt trapped by the First's questions, as much as he'd tried to trap the First in his own. "No," he conceded. "The Founders are not immortal."

The First listened without comment, waiting to see if

Taran'atar had anything to add, then said flatly, "The Khan is immortal."

"What proof of that do you have?"

"One does not ask a god for proof."

"Even if you have doubts?"

"I have no doubts," the First said. "It sounds rather as if *you* might have reason to doubt, but I do not. You say these Founders are gods, but they do not sound very godlike to me. They sound like mortals who have somehow tricked you into believing they created our kind."

The First turned to go, leaving his captive alone with his pain, but offered Taran'atar a final thought. "Whatever you are, whatever you may believe about your origins . . . it seems your gods have forsaken you."

Chapter Sixteen

Returning to Locken's quarters that evening, Bashir discovered within himself a peculiar prejudice: he found that he could not believe that anyone who could cook well was entirely, irredeemably evil. Locken's potato-leek soup was astonishingly piquant and he whipped together a lighter-than-air cheese soufflé with as little effort as it would cost Bashir to make toast. Bashir worked hard to beat back the envy he was feeling; he had never had the time to develop much in the way of culinary abilities. And the kitchen—it had seemed so small, but it was unbelievably well equipped.

"Where did you get all these utensils?" Bashir asked, looking at a rack of exotic kitchen tools. "The Dominion couldn't have left them all behind. Jem'Hadar don't need to eat and Vorta can barely taste."

"They're mine," Locken said, cheerily chopping potatoes. "I brought everything I could salvage from my home when I came here with Section 31. We were going to be here for a while and everyone is always happy to find a cook in their midst. The plan was that I would cook for everyone . . . which I did. It's how I managed to take them prisoner. A little extra dash of something in the morning omelets."

"So they're all still here?" Bashir asked, slightly surprised. He had imagined all the Section 31 agents were dead.

"In stasis," Locken said, scraping up potato chunks with his knife and dropping them into a pot of boiling water. "Less trouble that way."

"But long-term stasis can be . . ."

". . . Very detrimental. Yes, I know. Don't worry. I've worked out some of the kinks in that. They should be fine for a while longer."

Bashir sat at the kitchen table, watching the chef work. There were four chairs at the table, but only one placemat when they came in. Locken had taken an absurd amount of pleasure in pulling out another place setting and putting it down before Bashir. The food preparation had been almost like performance art and Locken's ongoing banter had been upbeat and witty. It was all so civilized, sad, and desperate that Bashir felt like he was going to scream.

"I'm impressed," Bashir said. "Not only have you worked out the cloning process, but you've had time to do other work, too."

"Oh, I did the work on stasis a long time ago," Locken replied. "I just couldn't publish it because . . . well, you know."

"Professional jealousy. Didn't want to draw too much attention to yourself. Yes," Bashir said, drawing a breath and releasing a genuine sigh. "I understand."

"Of course, all that will be different now. Think of it, Julian. Someday, years from now, maybe decades from now, we'll look back on this night and remember it as the beginning of a Golden Age."

"We could make sure it's made into a holiday."

Locken laughed. "You're joking. I know you're joking, but maybe someday you'll say that and you'll be serious. Or maybe that's the sort of thing we should leave to others . . ."

"Maybe we should," Bashir said. "It would be presumptuous to begin declaring galactic holidays. There are a few obstacles between . . . us and our goals."

"A few," Locken agreed, rinsing his hands at the tap. "Would it make you feel better if we discussed some?"

"It might," Bashir agreed, then paused as if pondering. "For example—and I'm sure you've already thought about this—there's the problem of sheer numbers. Even the Dominion, with their dozens of hatcheries, weren't able to defeat the Federation. Now, granted, they're weakened and we'll be able to outthink them on most fronts, but you're only turning out a handful of Jem'Hadar a week . . ."

"Which will soon change," Locken agreed, "especially now that we're working together, but you're right. This is a key factor—but one I've been preparing for." He checked the timer on the oven, then covered the soup pot and lowered the heat. "We have enough time for this," he said, beckoning Bashir to the door. "Come with me."

In the main room, Locken pulled out his control unit and used it to activate the computer console and a large holographic display tank. He clicked through several layers of security, entering passwords too quickly for Bashir to follow. Finally, colors swirled inside the holotank and an image formed: a protein model, accompanied by streams of data. "You recognize this," Locken said.

Bashir studied the model and the data for several seconds, then realized what he was looking at and a cold shudder went down his back. "A prion," he said. "But not like any I've ever seen."

Locken grinned with satisfaction. "It gave me trouble. I admit it. But I'm a pretty good cook. I'd never done work like this before, but once you get the knack, it's a great deal like making a good soufflé: mostly just following the recipe, but there's artistry and luck involved, too."

"You made this?" Bashir asked, genuinely awed despite himself. "It's astonishing." He wanted to add, ". . . and insane," but he dared not. He had to find out what the—and there was no other expression for what Locken was—mad genius had in mind. "If I understand correctly what you've done . . ."

"And you do, of course."

". . . then this could infect almost every form of humanoid life in the quadrant."

"As long as it has a central nervous system," Locken explained. "There are one or two intelligent species it might not affect, but they're inconsequential in the long run."

Bashir continued to stare at the rotating image, at once impressed and appalled. This chain of proteins, he realized, could transform the brain of almost any creature in the quadrant into a mushy pastelike consistency. "How is it transmitted?"

"Airborne, waterborne, through sexual contact," Locken said smugly. "It's versatile."

"But your Jem'Hadar are immune?" Bashir guessed. "And you, too, I assume?"

"Of course. And since your arrival I've taken care to make sure you are, too. I haven't tested it extensively, but I didn't think I would have to. It's the beauty of simple things; they're foolproof. But, just in case," Locken smiled, "I have a planet picked out already— the Romulan protectorate in the Orias system." He touched a control on his handset and another section of wall slid open to reveal yet another computer console. A large monitor lit up, presenting a medium-range shot of a missile-launching platform with a single completed gantry and two others under construction. Several Jem'Hadar soldiers stood around the gantries, weapons drawn and alert, while in the background a trio dressed in protective armor were busy fueling a medium-size missile. "I had to cobble the missile together out of components my Jem'Hadar salvaged from the ships and outposts we raided," Locken explained.

"Outposts?" Bashir asked.

"Nothing very large," Locken said. "I suspect they were secret bases set up by the Romulan Empire in case the Federation began to flex its muscles. Probably the Empire hasn't said anything to the Federation about the attacks, though I'm sure it has left them feeling very suspicious."

"And you plan to fire one of their own missiles at the Romulans?"

"Modified missiles," Locken agreed. "Yes. There will be some parts on the missile that they may find afterward that will make them suspect the Federation."

"But there won't be enough evidence to make them act immediately."

Locken smiled. "Julian, I can see you have a gift for this sort of thing. No, not immediately, but the Romulans *will* begin to arm themselves. They'll begin to prepare. And then, assuming my prion weapon is as effective as I know it will be, shortly after the first launch, we'll begin a full-scale assault. We'll have at least six gantries completed by then and I have plans to outfit my ships with similar devices. I suspect I'll be able to drive the Romulans from the entire sector within a week."

"Drive?" Bashir asked skeptically.

Locken smiled, then almost giggled. "Excuse the euphemism. All right. They'll be dead. Most of them, in any case. A few will escape, but not for long. I engineered the prion to lie dormant for a short time in certain genotypes—just long enough for survivors to get home and spread it around a bit. It won't really matter, though, because by then the war will have begun."

"A conflict between the Romulans and the Federation," Bashir concluded. "And soon after, the Klingons will be drawn into it. Then, possibly the Breen, at which point the entire Alpha Quadrant will become engulfed. And when they're finished savaging each other, the genetically enhanced humans will step in, the New Federation will rise out of the ashes of the old, and the quadrant will be united at last."

"I couldn't have put it better myself," Locken said, beaming.

Bashir thought about trying to smile, but he was afraid the best he would be able to do was a grimace, so he gave up the attempt. "And the timetable for all this is . . . ?"

Locken brightened even more, if that were possible. "Didn't I say? Tomorrow we launch the first missile.

Now, you'll have to excuse me. I think the soup is over-boiling." Locken slipped the control unit back onto his belt and ran for the kitchen. Bashir stayed behind for several seconds and studied the console, but then hurried after. After all, it wouldn't do to look too interested.

Ezri knew that on some level she should be insulted that the Jem'Hadar guard wasn't standing right outside the cell door anymore—obviously, she presented no *real* threat—but she was too busy working with the combadge module to let it bother her. Much. She had been fairly certain *what* she had to do, but not exactly sure *how* to do it. In the end, she had consulted Jadzia's memories and learned that her predecessor not only knew the techniques, but had what amounted to a fascination for this kind of technological trickery. Ezri wondered if Julian knew this and had counted on it.

The metal shard wasn't the ideal choice for altering the combadge's circuitry, but she kept at it and eventually found the settings she needed. And then, there was the *other* problem, the question of what to do once she managed to get her cell open. Only one idea suggested itself—not a great one, but the best she could come up with under the circumstances.

She jiggled the circuit's broadcast cluster with the shard until she found the correct frequency. The cell's forcefield flickered, then stabilized. Ezri swore and tickled the frequency key again. The forcefield emitters surged; then the door flared and collapsed.

The temptation was to leap up and make a run for it, but Ezri sat tight. Seconds later, the guard was there, glaring, disruptor drawn. When he saw her, he pointed his weapon at her head. She expected him to be smiling for some reason, but then she understood that this wasn't fun for him; it was his job. It was his job to stop her from leaving the cell however possible. And it was her job to escape. Simple.

Ezri jiggled the tool and the signal cut off. The force-field emitters snapped back on. The guard was standing in the threshold, and as the forcefield closed around him, every muscle in his body—including his trigger finger—spasmed. His arm jerked and the shot singed the air just above Ezri's head. The Jem'Hadar pitched forward, dropped onto the floor, and curled into a ball at Ezri's feet as the forcefield emitters shorted out and the field collapsed for the last time.

Ezri rose, walked quickly to the door, then prodded the Jem'Hadar with her foot. He didn't move. She stripped him of his weapons and communicator, then crept down the corridor.

After twenty meters of careful prowling she found an unmarked door. Opening it carefully, Ezri found a maintenance room that was obviously meant, among other things, to service the air-duct system. She opened a grate, climbed inside, and began to move as silently as she could, unable to suppress a wicked grin as she crept through the dark.

"Do these Founders then not give you the white?" asked the First.

Taran'atar's mind felt clearer and he wondered if it was because the First had administered some kind of drug while he had been unconscious. "They *created* the white," he said. "And, yes, they do. Your Khan merely stole the formula and re-created it. Badly, I might add."

"Badly?"

"Your soldiers, First, are either very weak or badly trained. I killed ten of them myself. No single soldier should be able to kill ten Jem'Hadar."

The First frowned and it seemed for a moment that he was about to strike the prisoner, but then restrained himself. "Thirteen," he said.

Taran'atar did not understand him. "Thirteen?"

"You killed thirteen. Your grenade landed in the midst of three soldiers. None of them had the sense to pick it up and throw it back."

Taran'atar felt a strange desire to make some sort of comment—either an expression of regret or a point of advice—but he refrained. It would not be well received and he knew that his life still hung by a thin thread. This soldier, this First, had come back to talk to him not because he felt Taran'atar had any valuable information to contribute, but because something they had discussed earlier had cut deep and was now festering. Though he was not a true Jem'Hadar, this First seemed to have some worthwhile qualities. He might grow up to be a respectable soldier someday.

"Then how do you take the white?" the First said, continuing his earlier line of inquiry. "You have a shunt, but we found no evidence of a tube in your possessions. And you have been here many, many hours. Explain this."

"I am not like most Jem'Hadar. What you obtain from white my body can produce naturally."

The First's turmoil was growing by the moment. He suddenly drew his disruptor and placed the weapon at Taran'atar's temple. "I should kill you. You have no useful information and the time I spend speaking with you might be better used training the soldiers who still remain under my command." He flicked a switch on the weapon and Taran'atar heard the charge build. The First watched his face. Then, slowly, he lowered the weapon and said, "But you have courage. I'll grant you that. And some of the things you've said . . ." He walked back to where he had been standing and holstered his weapon.

Turning, he pointed at the tube that pumped white into his throat. "You say you do not need this. Is that true?"

"It is true."

"Is that how Jem'Hadar are meant to exist?"

Taran'atar hesitated. Once again the First had surprised him, raising a question that stirred the Elder's own growing uncertainty. "I don't know," he said, the words tearing at his throat like poison. "A Jem'Hadar lives only to serve the Founders and I have served them well and yet, *and yet,* as soon as they discovered my flaw they sent me *here,* to this blighted corner of the galaxy. I am a *deviant.* I am unfit to live among my kind and so I must die here among you weaklings and traitors. It is what I *deserve.*"

The First listened dispassionately until Taran'atar finished his diatribe. Then, he reached up as if to touch the tube, though he could not seem to bring himself to do it. "Yes," he said. "I see. You are correct about one thing: Your Founders and my Khan are very different. The Founders made you so that you hate the fact that you do not need the white, while my Khan . . ." Struggling mightily, the First managed to wrap his fingers around the tube and looked almost as if he would tear it from the shunt, but Taran'atar knew he would not, *could* not. Instead, panting heavily, he snarled, ". . . he made me well enough to make me willing to do *any-*

thing for him, but not so well that I look upon this chain . . ." He pointed at the tube. ". . . as a benediction."

Stepping close, putting his face in Taran'atar's, the First hissed, "I am not a soldier. I am not a servant. I am a *slave*, but at least I know it. *Why don't you?*"

Chapter Seventeen

"We don't have much time to talk, Joseph," Kasidy Yates said to her father-in-law. The image on the viewscreen snapped and popped as the signal faded, then grew stronger. "They're taking the subspace net down all across the province later this afternoon to put in some new equipment."

Joseph Sisko scowled. "Well, they can just wait until we're finished," he said. "I've been trying to get through all day."

"I understand," Kasidy sighed. "It's harder here than it was on the station. Sometimes, it's easy to take for granted how efficient the Federation is."

"All right, all right," Joseph grumbled. "I guess I just thought that all this 'wife of the Emissary' business would have given you some sort of . . . I don't know . . . special status."

"It *does*," Kasidy exclaimed. "More than I know what to do with. Do you have any idea how many people have come to my door over the past couple of days just asking if they can help out? And they're all so earnest and polite, I can't turn them away! I've had furniture movers, kitchen cleaners, garden weeders."

"Sounds all right to me," Joseph said, something approximating a smile crossing his lips. "The kitchen-cleaning part, at any rate. Besides, you should take it easy." The picture cleared up and Kasidy took a moment to study Joseph's face and saw her fears confirmed: there were lines of weariness around his eyes and mouth that had grown more pronounced since Ben's disappearance. It was the ravaged look of a parent who'd come to believe he'd lost his child, despite Kasidy's conviction that her husband, Joseph's son, would someday return.

"Joseph, I'm in the middle of my second trimester—the best part of being pregnant according to my doctor—and I've never felt better. I *want* to do things. In fact," she laughed, "I'm feeling pretty broody."

Joseph's smile broadened and it took years off his face. "I remember that," he said. "When my second wife got to that phase. There weren't enough hours in the day to do everything she wanted. I was grateful to go to the restaurant every day where I didn't have to work so hard."

"Well," she said, smiling back, "things will be better when Jake returns. He's good at handling the visitors. He has a gift for putting people at ease."

"Ah, he gets that from me. Never was one of his father's strengths . . ." Then, Joseph's expression went sober again. "Well, where is he? Not back on the station again, I hope. I'd much rather he stayed there with you on Bajor."

Kasidy stared at the monitor, confused. What could Joseph mean? Jake was on Earth. He'd left . . . how long ago? Two weeks. Could they be teasing her? But, no, that wasn't like Joseph. He would never joke about something like that. She said, "What do you mean? He's there with you, isn't he?"

Joseph's smile slipped away and even with the poor connection, Kasidy could see the blood drain out of his face. "What? No . . . Of course not. What made you think he was here?"

"He *told* me he was going there," she said almost angrily. The surges of hormones came on that way sometimes; she occasionally found herself growing misty and weepy over strange things—a dew-covered spiderweb in the garden or a hand-thrown clay bowl that Ben had used to stir together a batch of mole sauce. Kasidy reined in her emotions and said, "Wait. Maybe we're talking about the same thing and getting ourselves confused. Two weeks ago, Jake took a ship from DS9 straight to Earth."

Joseph's lips moved for several seconds and Kasidy began to think that the signal was breaking down, but then she realized he was having trouble forming words. He clutched his chest and sat down, the camera automatically tracking. *Good Lord, no,* she thought. *Please, not now. Not when I'm so far away.* But then he seemed to take hold of himself and said, "I . . . I swear to you, Kasidy, Jake never called, never told me that he was coming here. Two weeks ago?"

Kasidy nodded. "But if he didn't go there, then where could he have gone? And why would he have lied?"

"He wouldn't have . . . Jake would never lie to you . . . Unless . . ."

"Unless what?"

"Unless he was going to do something he knew we wouldn't want him to do."

Kasidy felt herself grow light-headed and had to lean over so she wouldn't faint. When she looked up again, she looked into the old man's eyes and knew that whatever she said next would only make him look older and more fragile. "Joseph . . . where can he be?"

Ezri stifled a sneeze, wiped her eyes against her sleeve, and desperately wished that she had an antihistamine. Why was it, she wondered, that in all the holonovels and two-dees of her youth, whenever the plucky young heroine had to clamber through ventilation shafts, she never seemed to get dirty? Ventilation shafts, she had discovered, were *filthy* places. And dark. And small. And things *lived* in them, the sorts of things that usually tried to get away from you, but sometimes grew confused and lost their way and came back *to* you.

She guessed she'd been sitting still and trying not to make any noise for more than two hours. Enough was enough. Either they had discovered what she had done and were on her trail, or the other, more intriguing possibility had come to pass—the one she had devised once she'd figured out where the ketracel-white distillery was located. One way or another, it was time to get out of the air ducts.

But there were problems.

The first was that she no longer had any idea where she was. Ezri was fairly certain that the duct was sloping downhill and had been for quite a distance. She had, she realized, been unconsciously braking with knees and palms after every switchback. She must be quite a way below the holding cells by now.

The other problem was that Ezri was afraid to push open a grate without first checking out what might be below, which meant shining the palm beacon she'd found into a dark room. The other option was simply dropping down into the darkness without checking first, an idea that held even less appeal than staying in the ducts. Sooner or later, she would have to do *something,* but, for now, crawling along in the dusty darkness was an acceptable alternative to making a decision.

Wait.

She backed up. Something had caught her eye in the dark. *There.* A flash. Red. Ezri reached out toward it and found a slightly open louvered grate. She poked at it and the louvers opened wider, creaking slightly, but there was no alarming noise from beneath her, so she assumed she was all right. For now. Lights, most of them very small. Control panels and lab equipment. There were no overhead lights, but the panels were casting enough glow that she could see the floor, not *too* far beneath her. The question was whether or not the room was safe. Nothing seemed to be moving, but Jem'Hadar could shroud themselves and stay *very* quiet if they so chose. But no, it seemed unlikely that a Jem'Hadar would be waiting shrouded in a dark laboratory.

She pushed on the grate and was satisfied to discover it was on a hinge. No large piece of metal crashing to the floor, at least. Moving slowly, listening for anything, Ezri lowered herself through the opening and let herself dangle at arm's length before releasing her grip.

"You're alone, Ezri," she said, trying to settle herself. Her words echoed strangely and she amended her original estimate of the size of the room. Either it was bigger than she had thought or she had spent too much time in the air ducts.

"Lights?" she called, but nothing happened. "Computer?" No response. Maybe that was for the best. No computer monitoring, at least, or it might be authorization-code-protected. Ezri had a vague idea about tapping into Locken's main computer and trying to cause some trouble, but she knew that her chances of accomplishing that were fairly slim. Locken—or Section 31 or the Dominion before them—were probably ultra-paranoid about security. She had managed to perform her earlier piece of skullduggery only by tapping into Audrid's extensive knowledge of humanoid biochemistry, Jadzia's scientific acumen, and her own recent research into Starfleet's Jem'Hadar database, when she'd been trying to gain some insight into Kitana'klan.

She flicked on her lamp and played the beam over the control panels. The consoles and equipment looked like the sort of thing that she would see in a sickbay: sequence analyzers, tissue regenerators, even a small surgical bay. Ezri frowned. Why situate a medical facility so far away from the living quarters? It didn't make sense.

She continued to pan the light over the consoles, but not so slowly or methodically now. She had an idea what she was looking for now and, moments later, found it against the far wall.

Stasis tubes. Two banks of four. Seven were active.

Ezri felt the hairs on the nape of her neck stand up.

What would Locken want with stasis tubes? It wasn't a happy thought. It obviously wasn't Federation technology and she didn't like the idea of trying to figure out Dominion control systems. And it was possible that whoever was inside the tubes had a very good reason for being there—sick or injured beyond the abilities of the facility to heal. Or they might be Jem'Hadar. This was less likely, though. Why would Locken keep Jem'Hadar in stasis? Unless they were really *bad* Jem'Hadar. She brushed aside the thought. Anyone Locken would want kept out of the way would be her ally, even if only in the short run.

"Logs," she said. "There have to be log files."

The main workstation was a stand-alone, with dedicated memory and processing units. That spelled the end of any lingering plans for crashing the system, but Ezri let the idea pass unmourned. She was more interested in finding out what Locken had been doing in this room.

There was no security on the system, not even a password. Locken had made no attempt to conceal his activities, which made sense to Ezri in retrospect. He was too arrogant to believe anyone would breach his security. There was one directory labeled "Stasis," with seven files, named consecutively: "Subject 1," "Subject 2," "Subject 3" . . . No names, no identifying marks. They might have been petri dishes filled with mold.

Another directory was labeled "Failures," with many, many more files, some of them arranged into subdirectories. After a cursory review of both sets of files, Ezri concluded that the Failures had been the lucky ones: they were dead.

Not all the test subjects had been humans. At least one of the Section 31 agents had been a Betazoid and another appeared to have been an Andorian, though it was difficult to say because of the poor quality of the recordings. The subject's skin was blue, but he was hairless and didn't have antennae, though there were small, dark patches on the skull where antennae might once have been.

There were others: a pair of Romulans that must have come from the pirated starship; three small, furry beings that didn't belong to any species Ezri knew; a Cardassian who screamed into the camera until he passed out or died. Each holoclip was preceded by several pages of notes and formulas, but Ezri could only guess at the connection between them. Had Locken been testing a mutagen, a nerve gas, a spectrum of radiation, possibly all of the above? There was no way to know. She ran a search and found that there were over seven hundred individual clips, though there was no way to know how many subjects the number represented.

There was a detached, clinical tone about the proceedings, but there was something even worse underneath it all, something that made Ezri want to shut everything off, crawl back into the snug, safe air vents. Beneath the clinical veneer, there lurked the horrifying spectacle of an emotionally arrested young boy taking a shivering pleasure in pulling the legs off bugs.

She did not know why Locken had put these seven individuals into stasis and she wasn't sure she wanted to dig deep enough into his "work" to find out now. Neither could she be sure that it was within the power of Federation science to restore them. Ezri wavered for a moment, wondering whether she should try to see if there was some way to cut power to the tubes and terminate the poor, damned monsters Locken had created.

But, no, she decided. It wasn't her call to make. When all this was over, she would bring back help. But dealing with Locken would have to come first.

As quickly as she could, she climbed back into the air duct, eager to put herself as far from Locken's chamber of horrors as she could.

*　*　*

*Security Officer's Log. I'm leaving this record
in case I don't survive the assault on Locken's
stronghold.*

*It's still a few hours before dawn and we're
camped out approximately two kilometers east-
southeast of Locken's compound. We plan to leave
as soon as the Ingavi have eaten and made whatever other preparations—physical or spiritual—
they need to make. It occurs to me that I know
almost nothing about Ingavi theology, whether
they're ancestor worshipers, monotheists, athe-
ists, or something else entirely.*

*I'm guessing there are about fifteen hundred
Ingavi left, down from about five thousand when I
was here last. That's an unbelievably high mor-
tality rate and it's possible there are too few of
them left for them to survive here on Sindorin,
even if Locken and the Jem'Hadar left today. I
don't even know what else to say about that.*

*Last night, we had an army of about three hun-
dred. This morning, I counted one hundred sixty.
The rest have seen what was going to happen and
melted away into the forest. Wise, wise Ingavi . . .*

*They were watching me just a little while ago,
waiting to see what I do to prepare myself. When I
pulled out this tricorder, they left me alone. This,
they must think, is what I do, and I suppose
they're right. This is what I always did just before
going on a mission with the Maquis. Everyone did
it—left a will or, at least, a list of things you
wanted divided up among your friends. I would
do that now, but who would I leave anything to?
All my friends from the Maquis are gone and*

there's no one back on Deep Space 9 that I feel any compulsion . . .

Well, wait, yes there is. Whoever finds this, please tell Colonel Kira to search the mainframe in the security office very carefully. I found some things in it that she might find useful someday. Oh, and if anyone finds my . . . my things, please give the fractal blade to Taran'atar. He's the only person I know who might appreciate it.

I'm going to attack Locken's fortress with about one hundred sixty Ingavi, most of whom are armed with slings, blowguns, and spears. A few of them have phasers and disruptors. It's not much . . . hell, it's not anything *really, but if we can slow down Locken even a little, it might give Bashir and Dax a chance, assuming they're still alive. And if we can help them, maybe it will help the Ingavi. If you're Starfleet, try to find the Ingavi and help them. They might not make it easy— they don't owe us any trust—but do what you can.*

One last request. If I'm found dead . . . please, take my bones back to Bajor.

This is Lieutenant Ro Laren, chief security officer of Starbase Deep Space 9, over and out.

"This is going much too well," Ro whispered to Kel. The Ingavi, hanging upside down from a vine at that moment and looking over Ro's shoulder, shrugged, then suggested that Ro might not want to say anything that would endanger their good fortune. "There are always ears willing to listen to complaints of too much luck. What would you like us to do next?"

They were within seven hundred meters of the outer

wall of the compound and, as anticipated, they had encountered opposition, but the Jem'Hadar they had fought were nothing like the soldiers Taran'atar had combatted.

"How many soldiers have we killed so far?"

"Eight."

"Then we missed one. They usually patrol in three groups of three. He's either still on patrol or he's heard us and gone back to the base for reinforcements."

Kel asked, "If the latter, then why haven't we been attacked?"

Ro shook her head. "I don't know. Something strange is happening. How many Jem'Hadar have your people managed to defeat in the past?"

Kel hooted sardonically. "One or two. Maybe. No one ever stayed long enough to check. Believe me, we are as aware as you are that there is something wrong here."

"Could it be a trap?" Ro asked.

"Baiting a trap with one or two trained soldiers, maybe—but *eight?* Unless this Khan has bred thousands upon thousands—and we would know it if he had—there is something wrong with them. My people say they fight as if in a dream . . . if Jem'Hadar do dream."

"They don't," Ro said, running another scan of the forest before them. The missing ninth soldier was bothering her. "You can't dream if you don't sleep."

From above, there came a soft hiss and Kel scampered up the vine he had been hanging from. Looking up, Ro barely made out a pair of figures huddled together exchanging words.

Moments later, Kel dropped down again and the

other Ingavi climbed higher into the treetops. "We found him," Kel reported. "The ninth Jem'Hadar."

"And?"

"He was asleep."

"What?"

"He was asleep. Standing at guard, gun drawn, with his eyes closed. When my soldiers approached him, his eyes opened, but by then it was too late. Even at the last, he did not seem to understand what was happening."

Ro was baffled, but she didn't want to waste the opportunity. "All right, they'll notice the guards not reporting in soon enough. We can't assume this stupor is going to last. Tell your people we may still have a fight on our hands."

"I'll ask everyone to move up, then," Kel said, already heading back up the vine. "See you soon."

What a polite army I have, Ro thought. *"I'll ask everyone to move up."* She laughed quietly, the first real laugh Ro remembered having in days. She fished her binoculars out of her bag and trained them on the forest even though they weren't much use in the dense foliage. Even the infrared setting was flummoxed by the shifting bands of hot and cool air being pushed around by the treetop breezes.

"What the hell is going on here?" Ro asked herself. And why couldn't she shake the feeling that Bashir was somehow behind it all?

"Bashir," Locken whispered through clenched teeth, stalking down the corridor from the main lab to his quarters. "It must be Bashir." Too many things were going wrong all at the same time. First, even as he was preparing the new cloning chambers, came word that the Trill had escaped. The security logs showed that the

241

forcefield had been opened with some kind of electromagnetic pulse. And now there was something wrong with his Jem'Hadar, something to do with the white. The tests showed traces of a foreign substance, tainting it, making the soldiers sluggish. There was the puzzle of how the Trill had managed to get into the lab and Locken cursed himself for not taking internal security more seriously. Clearly he had underestimated Dax and Bashir both.

At least he had been suspicious enough to keep Bashir in his personal suite of rooms. If he had been allowed into the laboratory, there was no telling what kind of damage he might have done. The computers in his quarters, especially the units that controlled the missile launch mechanism, were protected by the most complex encryption programs he could conceive. Bashir might be clever, but he was no match for Locken's genius with coding.

And yet . . .

Locken stopped at the next check station and inspected the two Jem'Hadar who were on guard duty. One had the same glazed, numb expression he had seen on many of the other soldiers, but the second seemed alert, even eager. "You," Locken said. "You're feeling all right?"

The Jem'Hadar responded promptly. "Ready to serve, my Khan."

Locken nodded, noting the sputtering tube in the soldier's neck. Maybe the contaminant hadn't dispersed evenly through the white supply. Some of his men might still be as healthy as this one. He would find out after he'd dealt with the good doctor. "Come with me," he said, and the Jem'Hadar fell in smartly behind him. "We're going to my quarters. There will be a human there. Don't kill him until I order you to do so. Understood?"

"Understood."

Locken found Bashir precisely where he expected to find him: stooping over the master command console. His hands were flying over the controls, his brow furrowed with frustration.

"Stand away, Julian," Locken ordered.

Bashir's hands froze, but he didn't step away from the console.

"Soldier," Locken snapped. "Aim your weapon. If he doesn't move in three seconds, shoot him." The Jem'Hadar's rifle rose instantly and was pointed unwaveringly at Bashir's head.

Bashir lifted his hands off the console and took two steps back. "Over against the wall," Locken said. Bashir complied. It was hard to read his expression and that worried Locken, so he moved to the command console, entered his codes, and ran a quick diagnostic on the missile firing system. While the diagnostic ran, he checked the command system for viruses or other less elegant forms of sabotage.

Both checks reported finding nothing amiss. The command system was clean and the missile delivery system had not been tampered with. Locken almost laughed. Bashir must have had less time to work than Locken had assumed, or, possibly, he wasn't quite as clever as Locken had once suspected. "That was really foolish, Julian," he said. "All you've succeeded in doing is killing the inhabitants of the Orias system a little sooner." He keyed the launch code and activated the firing sequence. "I was going to do this after we had some breakfast, maybe a glass or two of ambrosia, but, well, sometimes it's best to do things without ceremony."

Locken punched up the exterior cameras and turned them toward the missile silo. The top of the silo opened, and, seconds later, a slim, matte black shape came forth on a point of blue-white flame that cut through the night sky. It rose swiftly, gained speed at an astonishing rate, then disappeared into the east.

"Honestly," Locken said. "I expected better of you. If you insisted on being my nemesis instead of my ally, the least you could have done was make it *interesting*. This was hardly worth getting out of bed for." He shrugged. "Well, at least we have the hunt for your little pet slug-girl to look forward to. Seeing as she managed to accomplish more than you did just by poisoning my Jem'Hadar . . ."

The barb did not seem to sting Bashir as much as he had expected. In fact, despite the implicit threat to someone Locken knew full well was dear to Julian, his captive looked not just unperturbed, but positively pleased with himself.

"I have to admit," Bashir said, "that the encryption on the missile console was more than I could handle . . ."

Locken nodded, graciously accepting the compliment.

". . . but it was surprisingly easy to alter the orbit of the weapons platform."

It seemed to Locken that the universe became frozen in amber. His muscles, his memory, his mind, all were immobilized for exactly the span of time it required for everything, *everything* he had been planning to begin to tip forward, to crumble, to topple into the void that had just opened beneath his feet. There came a voice—

whining, cajoling, exhorting—*why hadn't he been a little quicker, a little more clever, a little tougher . . .*

He was five again and there was the ring of faces standing around him, the boys who had taunted him for being slow, for being stupid. And here again was the desire to hurt them, to make them pay for what they said, except . . . except . . . he hadn't known how to do it . . . He *was* slow. He *was* stupid . . .

. . . And then time, stretched as far as it could, snapped back again. He looked down at his hands and saw that they were moving over the console, flying, his fingers a blur of motion, checking the sensors, checking the telemetry of the weapons platform, sending the disable code, but, no, somehow Bashir, damn him, had anticipated every move. The platform wouldn't do what he asked, though it *did* allow him to see Sindorin with its onboard cameras. Here came the missile, arcing up silently from the planet's surface, its blue-white flame bright against the black of space, unfettered, unstoppable, and then there came a dazzling flash of ruby light.

Then there was nothing, not even a trail of fragments.

Locken imagined what he hadn't been able to see: an explosion that consumed the missile and its biological payload, a chain reaction of blown power systems that was, even now, ripping his weapons platform apart. Locken stared at the monitor, stared and waited for some kind of meaning to emerge, but there was nothing. It was only space, only the void, only an abyss.

Behind him, he heard Bashir say, "It's over, Locken."

Locken composed himself and turned toward Bashir. He willed himself to remain calm, then slowly reached up and turned off the blank monitor. "You don't know what you're talking about, Julian. This was nothing. A minor setback, at best. I admit it—this stings, but that's all it is. A bug bite. I'll scratch it and by the time I'm finished, I'll have a new missile and a new payload. The Romulans on Orias III will live to see a couple more sunrises." He turned to look at Bashir. "But that won't mean anything to you, Julian. You won't be here to see it."

Bashir sighed. "Maybe," he said. "But I expect you won't be far behind me. You really don't get it, do you? You think you're so bloody intelligent, that you're always pulling everyone else's strings, but you haven't seen that you're really the puppet. This whole war—this decision to 'unite the Alpha Quadrant'—it wasn't *your* idea."

He stared at Locken as if waiting for comprehension to dawn, but Locken only stared at him blankly. Bashir shook his head, massaged the bridge of his nose, then continued. "During your time with Section 31, did you ever meet a man named Cole?"

Locken felt off-balance and found that he could not refuse to answer. "No. Who is he? And why should I care?"

"He's the one who sent me to stop you," Bashir said, then confidently walked back into the living area. Locken wondered if Bashir was going to try to make a run for it, then decided if he did, he would let him have a bit of a head start. It would make things more interesting. Bashir stopped in front of the small table that held the holo of the medical staff at the New Beijing Pediatric Center and pointed at the figure of Murdoch, Locken's friend and mentor. "That's him."

"You're lying," Locken said, a little too quickly.

"Am I?" Bashir asked. "Consider this: The Dominion was supposed to have obtained erroneous intelligence that New Beijing was producing biogenic weapons. But where did that information come from? I've been thinking about that," he said. "I've had a lot of free time on my hands lately, and here's what I believe: Section 31 wanted you badly. They desperately wanted an enhanced agent and since I'd already turned them down, they turned to you."

Locken felt himself begin to snarl, but then realized that Bashir was trying to make him angry, trying to make him make a mistake. He glanced to the right and saw that his Jem'Hadar was still tracking Bashir with his weapon, awaiting the kill order. Locken grinned.

"So, they assigned Cole to New Beijing," Bashir continued. "He obviously had some kind of medical training, enough at least to fool you and the others. As Dr. Murdoch, Cole had time to assess you and the colony. When he finished his assessment, he conceived a plan. He fed information to the Dominion that would guarantee they'd come in with weapons blazing, then made sure that the colony's defenses were disabled before he found a deep enough hole to crawl into until his ride home arrived."

"You don't—you can't—know if *any* of this is true."

"No, I don't," Bashir agreed. "But it all does fit, doesn't it? Even you can see that. Even you can see that Section 31 sacrificed five thousand men, women, and children—Federation lives—just so they could convince *you* to join their little crusade. They wanted that fantastic mind of yours working for them; it didn't matter how they got it. And all they had to do was let you think it was *your* crusade."

"No . . ." Locken said hoarsely.

"Yes," Bashir replied, his tone now quiet, even sympathetic. "You said it yourself: New Beijing changed everything. As much as you might have thought about it, you never would have done anything like this before. Think about it, Ethan: a missile . . . a *disease-laden* missile. Genetically engineered soldiers. What have you become? You were a *doctor.*" He let the words hang in the air for several seconds, then concluded, "But now you're their creature, their monster. . . . And I've been looking so hard to pry into your head, to try to *think* like you so I could stop you, that I almost convinced myself I was *like* you." Bashir rubbed the cuff of his sleeve over his eyes and Locken was surprised to see that his eyes were wet with tears.

"I want you to listen to me now, Ethan," Bashir continued. "It's still not too late. You wanted us to work together, and we can still do that. We could stop them, the two of us, bring Section 31 to justice. We can make sure they never again . . ."

Though Bashir could not have known it by any outward sign, Locken quickly and coolly processed all the possible outcomes that could be borne out of the option of joining forces with the Federation and crushing Section 31. It was a tantalizing prospect and offered, if nothing else, the twin pleasures of companionship and revenge. If he went with Julian, he would, Locken knew, have to undergo some form of discipline and punishment, but he also knew that Starfleet would not be permitted to parade him before a public tribunal. Word would never be allowed to leak out either about Section 31 or the attacks on the Romulans. He would be allowed to pursue vengeance and then, probably, be put somewhere out of the way. He might even be allowed to continue his research, to find new ways to help children, which was, in the end, the thing he wanted most to do. . . .

But Locken knew too that they would never, *ever* leave him alone. Already, he felt their gaze on him, their prying eyes, their meddlesome, ever-vigilant cow-eyed scrutiny. He closed his eyes and felt the blank, uncomprehending stares, and, worse, the tiny, smug smiles for the would-be conqueror. Something inside him crumbled and withered. It was more than he could stand; he deserved better.

But he didn't know how to say any of it, so instead he let the fear and anger speak for him. "The quadrant," he said, "the *galaxy,* still needs order. When people learn what I've been doing here, they'll flock to my cause. I'll deal with Section 31 in my own good time."

Bashir looked up at his flag, Khan Singh's flag, the merged sun and moon symbol dominating one wall of the room, and sighed. "Maybe you're right. Maybe you *are* just like Khan, after all." He caught Locken's gaze with his own and for the first time, Locken felt the power of the fury Bashir had been holding in check. "A deluded failure."

Locken flushed with loathing and finally turned to the Jem'Hadar guard, giving the order through clenched teeth: "Kill him."

The Jem'Hadar didn't move.

Locken screamed at him. "I gave you an order, guard!"

The guard turned to look Locken in the eyes. "My name," he said, "is Taran'atar."

One hundred meters from Locken's front door, it finally turned into a real fight. Either someone had roused the troops or all the wide-awake Jem'Hadar were just inside the front doors. Whichever it was, the bulk of the Ingavi troops were pinned down in the lee of a low hill. They were keeping their heads low and that meant the majority of the shots weren't dangerous, but every tenth or fifteenth bolt came at just the right angle and Ro heard an Ingavi die. She knew it was only a matter of minutes before the Jem'Hadar shrouded themselves, moved out to better positions, and caught them in a cross fire.

One way or another, she had to make a choice soon: charge or fall back.

The Ingavi could still melt back into the forest, though she knew it would spell their doom. If Locken and his Jem'Hadar won today, even if they never took control of the Alpha Quadrant, they *would* control Sindorin long enough to wipe out the Ingavi. She turned and looked at Kel, who was huddled down by her side, working hard to be as small a target as possible.

"What do you think?" she shouted. To their left, an Ingavi broke and ran for the edge of the forest, but was cut down before he had gone ten meters.

"I think," Kel said, grimacing, "that we may die soon, whether we flee or fight."

"I'm afraid I agree."

"So," he said, gripping the stock of his phaser more tightly, "we might as well die fighting."

Ro nodded in agreement and checked the charge on her phaser.

"You do not understand me, Ro Laren," Kel said. I am saying that the *Ingavi* should stay and fight, not you. We are not your people, and this fight is not yours. If we are distracting the soldiers, you might stand a chance to escape in your ship and warn your brothers and sisters, might you not?"

Ro was surprised by the idea. She had been preparing to die. She thought about the recording she'd made and realized that she had been hopelessly optimistic when she thought someone might find it before Locken had been defeated. This was his home base; no one would be able to make it down to the surface. It might be important that she make it back to the Federation with the information she had gathered . . . which was exactly what? That Locken was a genuine threat? And what would make that more obvious than *not* returning?

But this was all just rationalization. Ro Laren was too brutally honest with herself to continue in this vein. She wanted to stay because she felt she owed these people a debt. Someone had to try to make things right. She held out her empty hand and after looking at it curiously for several seconds, Kel took it and they pressed their palms together. "In my culture," she explained, "this means we have made a pact."

"In mine," Kel said, "it means you have agreed to watch over my children while I go look for something to eat."

Ro considered it and finally said, "All right. Good enough. Now, go over there and find out how many of your cousins will attack the gate with us."

Kel nodded and crept away. Seconds later, a bolt creased the turf where he had been sitting.

They must be using tricorders now, Ro thought. *We don't have much time. . . .*

Chapter Eighteen

Locken ran.

He was fast, much faster than Bashir could have expected, faster even than he himself was, and it made him wonder if Locken had made some additional enhancements to himself. Nerve and motor-system tweaking, though illegal on Federation worlds, were far from unknown.

Bashir watched as Taran'atar raised his disruptor and coolly tracked Locken as he sped across the room, but before the Jem'Hadar could fire, Bashir barked, "No! Don't!" Taran'atar jerked his arm up and the energy bolt sizzled across the lab to shatter one of the large picture windows overlooking the lawn. The Khan never looked back, but bolted through the door, disappearing from sight.

"Why did you tell me to do that?" the Jem'Hadar asked.

"Because I want him alive."

Taran'atar moved to the doorway, then glanced outside to make sure Locken wasn't waiting in ambush. "But he's insane," Taran'atar remarked.

"Yes," Bashir agreed, following Taran'atar down the hall. "But it may be treatable. He was . . . I think he might once have been a great healer. I owe it to him to try . . ." Immediately in front of them, two small panels opened in the ceiling and a pair of lightly armored fighting drones dropped down.

Taran'atar calmly sighted first one, then the other, and blasted them out of the air before either had a chance to lock on to their targets. Then, before they moved again, he checked the rest of the corridor's ceiling and walls for traps. "This will slow us down," he said. "We'll have to check every corridor before we can move. We could go faster if I knew his likely goal."

Bashir pondered, then answered, "The barracks. No, wait. The lab. He said Ezri poisoned the white."

"Someone assuredly did." The thought seemed to remind Taran'atar of something. He tore at the tube of white on his neck and tossed it on the floor. Bashir saw that it was a fake, rigged to loop the flow so that it only appeared to be working. "The other Jem'Hadar have become slow, semiconscious."

"That makes sense. I suspect she probably concocted a powerful sedative and added it to the reservoir. That means Locken will head to the distillery and barricade himself inside with as many soldiers as he can, then see if he can cure them."

Taran'atar nodded. "Then we must hurry."

"I agree. It won't take him long to figure out what Ezri did to the white. It can't have been too complicated. . . ."

"No, you misunderstand," Taran'atar said, moving quickly, but alert for traps. He was favoring one side, Bashir noticed. "If you want him alive, we must find him before any other Jem'Hadar do, especially the First."

Bashir retraced the route to the reinforced double doors. "We have to find another way in," he said. "Perhaps the ventilation ducts . . ." Before he could finish, Taran'atar had entered a passcode into the security system.

"Inside information" was all he would say.

As they turned the next corner, another pair of security drones dropped from a shadowy corner. One succeeded in firing before Taran'atar could destroy it and the wall above his head exploded into shards of molten metal. He dropped to one knee, gulped air, and groaned. Bashir knelt beside the Jem'Hadar and tried to steady him with a hand to his back. When he pulled it away, he noticed it was damp with blood.

"You're hurt," the doctor said.

"It can wait," Taran'atar hissed. He pushed himself away from the wall, wavered once from side to side, then straightened. Pointing down the hall, he asked, "That way?"

"Yes, that way," Bashir nodded. "One way or another, let's end this."

Crouching low, Taran'atar peered around the corner that led to the lab door, disruptor at the ready. Bashir stood behind him wishing he had some kind of weapon—a club or even just a sharp stick to fend off attackers—but then he almost laughed. *If whoever we're going to fight gets past this Jem'Hadar, how long could I possibly last? Better to go forward unarmed,* he decided. *It will help me resist the temptation to do something stupid.*

Then Bashir was distracted by an unexpected sound: Taran'atar grunting in a tone that sounded like satisfaction.

"What is it?" Bashir whispered.

Taran'atar straightened, groaned slightly, then cupped his hand over the side where Bashir had seen the blood stain. *Broken ribs,* Bashir decided. *Possibly a collapsed lung.* "Come and see," Taran'atar said, beckoning to Bashir.

In huge letters, someone had painted the word FALSE across the lab door. "The situation is worse than I thought," Taran'atar commented.

Bashir examined the "paint" more carefully. "Is this blood?" he asked.

Taran'atar leaned forward and his nostrils flared. "Yes," he said. "Locken's Jem'Hadar are coming out of their stupors. They're beginning to mutilate themselves. Soon, they'll begin to fight. I've seen this before. . . ."

"Then we have to hurry," Bashir said, stepping forward and tapping the entrance controls. Just as the doors parted, Taran'atar leaped forward and shoved the doctor to the ground. Multiple disruptor shots erupted from inside the lab. Taran'atar kept Bashir covered with his body until the first volley was over, then dragged him out of the line of fire. His ears ringing, Bashir realized how stupid he had been. There might be as many as two hundred enraged Jem'Hadar ranging throughout the complex. Bumbling into a room was an invitation to be shot.

One of the disruptor bolts must have destroyed the door mechanism, because it remained ajar. Bashir could hear cries from within, a chorus of Jem'Hadar soldiers bellowing, "False! Faaallllsssssse!"

But as pathetic as were these groans of the lost and fallen, more pitiful still was the single voice raised against them. Locken was trying to sound commanding, but there was, to Bashir's ears, more than a little desperation in his every word. Determined to know what was happening despite the danger, Bashir dropped onto all fours and carefully peered around the corner.

He could see Locken's head above the throng of Jem'Hadar, so he must have been balanced on the narrow platform the cloning tubes were resting on. Bashir couldn't get an exact count from his vantage point, but he thought there must have been almost two dozen Jem'Hadar in the room, most of them milling about randomly, not looking where they were walking. Bashir could see their eyes and they were dull, heavily lidded, dead, but still there was a palpable feeling of dreadful expectation. The room was literally a powder keg and it would only be a matter of time until something touched a light to the fuse.

Perhaps Locken would even do it himself.

Only one of the Jem'Hadar did not move. He stood stock-still before Locken, studying his face and demeanor. Bashir guessed from the bit of collar brass he could see that this must be a First, perhaps even the same one who had freed Taran'atar. As if to confirm the doctor's suspicions, the Jem'Hadar held up his hand and made a complex gesture. The others froze in place.

"Yes," the First said softly, as if he were piecing together the syllogism as he spoke each word. "Perhaps you are our god. But if you are, then you must be a weak god, because you have had to use the white to keep us faithful." He paused and seemed to collect his thoughts. "And if you are weak and we are your creatures, then we are weak, too." A throaty growl rumbled through the room. The First raised his hand again and the growl died away. "But we will not be weak now," he continued. "We are Jem'Hadar. *True* Jem'Hadar!" And a shout went up, a roar from every throat.

Bashir looked at Locken and saw in his face the first pencil-line crack in the façade. The corner of his eye twitched and there came from his throat a sound somewhere between a whine of terror and a cry of defiance.

"We are *strong*," the First concluded. "So you cannot be our god. You . . . are . . . *false!*"

With this, Locken reached into his pocket and drew a hand phaser. He moved deliberately, without haste, and pointed it at the First's head. It was, Bashir realized, either because he did not expect anyone to defy him or because he no longer cared. As he lifted his arm, Locken said simply, "I am your Khan . . . ," as if it would explain everything.

Two dozen disruptors came up. There was a massive *thrum* as they fired in concert. The Jem'Hadar, for reasons known only to them, continued to fire long after Locken had been reduced to atoms. The incubation tubes ruptured and the gestational fluids boiled away in the intense heat.

When he opened his eyes, Bashir realized that Taran'atar must have pulled him away from the door. There before him were two pairs of booted feet. One pair belonged to Taran'atar. The other belonged to the First.

"He's dead?" Taran'atar asked.

"Yes," the First replied.

"Good," Taran'atar said.

Angry, Bashir surged to his feet. He knew he would probably regret saying what he was preparing to say, but he could not countenance their callous attitude. A man had just died, after all. He might have been insane, but he had also been brilliant and, if not a god, then certainly a creator. Bashir was prepared to say all these things and more. He wanted the Jem'Hadar to feel as humbled and ashamed as he himself felt for his part in the tragedy—because surely there was some element of tragedy in this situation—but then he saw their eyes.

Bashir had studied Jem'Hadar anatomy closely enough to know that their faces didn't have the flexibility of some of the thinner-skinned humanoid species, so it was frequently difficult to "read" their expressions. But in the First's eyes he saw the truth. He saw a grim acknowledgment that the universe was without foundation. After all, if God could be killed, what other horrors might be possible?

Bashir clamped his jaw shut and looked back into the room. . . .

The Jem'Hadar who had been in the lab—the same soldiers who had been gripped by a killing frenzy only seconds before—were once again become passive, like sleepwalkers. The First and Taran'atar stared at the group, then looked at each other only long enough to nod, a suspicion confirmed. Bashir was about to ask him what this meant when he heard a loud crash behind him.

Bashir spun around, but, surprisingly, neither of the Jem'Hadar reacted. A grate fell out of the ceiling, and, seconds later, two legs dangled in the gap. Ezri Dax dropped to the ground, absorbed the impact with a roll, then came up on her feet. Her hands, face, and uniform were filthy, covered with the dust, dirt, and mold that accumulate in ventilation shafts and out-of-the-way corners, but, at that moment, she was the most welcome sight Bashir could have imagined.

Bashir helped Ezri to her feet and saw that though her face was almost gray with soot, her eyes shone bright with pleasure. Bashir embraced her so fiercely that she yelped. "Sorry," he muttered into her hair, then wrapped his arms around her more tenderly. Even as he enjoyed the feel of her warm body molding into his, Bashir was stabbed by a pang of guilt: why hadn't he been more concerned about her over the past several hours? For all he had known, she might have been lying in a dungeon or trapped in a narrow ventilation shaft or even dead, shot by a Jem'Hadar soldier who was standing at the wrong place at the wrong time. He released her, held her at arm's length, and began to ask, "Are you—?"

"I'm fine, Julian," she said, smiling. "Fine. Don't worry. How are you? And what was all that weapons fire? It sounded like it was right here."

"In the lab," Bashir said, glancing behind him at the still open door. "Things haven't gone exactly like . . ." He stopped. "I'm afraid . . ." He became frustrated with his inability to form a coherent thought. *Shock,* he thought. *I'm in shock,* and realized that the only thing he really wanted to do was wrap his arms around Ezri and sleep for three or four days. She seemed to read the thought on his face; without speaking, she pulled his head down onto her shoulder and rubbed the back of his neck. Bashir closed his eyes and inhaled deeply. She smelled of sweat and grease and mold, but yet, underneath all that, he still could find the essence of Ezri. He let it sweep through his senses and, briefly, Julian Bashir was comforted.

"I'm sorry," she whispered. "Truly sorry . . . for you. But not for him, Julian. Not for him."

He pulled away from Ezri and saw that she was weeping, but not, he thought, from sorrow, but anger.

"If you had seen . . ." she whispered, her voice cracking. "If you had seen some of things he did . . ."

Bashir pulled the cuff of his sleeve up over the heel of his hand and wiped away her tears, taking several layers of dirt with it. "It's all right," he said softly. "I understand. It's all right. I don't think . . . I don't think anyone could have helped him. Not even me."

"Hey," a voice said from the other end of the hall. "Break it up, you two. I'm getting embarrassed just watching you."

Ezri spun around and Bashir looked up. It was Ro looking, if possible, even more weary and begrimed than Ezri, but smiling, obviously relieved to find her companions alive and well.

"Ro!" Ezri cried, and threw her arms around the Bajoran's neck, almost dragging her to the ground. This turned out to be a mistake. Suddenly, half a dozen small green-furred humanoids appeared from out of the shadows behind Ro, each of them hefting an energy rifle of some kind. Behind him, Bashir heard Taran'atar and the First stir. From all around him there came the unmistakable sound of weapon chambers beginning to charge.

"Ro," Bashir said evenly. "Please tell me these are friends of yours."

"Doctor," Ro said, then swallowed dryly, "these are my friends, the Ingavi." She turned around and waved her hands down, speaking softly and quickly in clicks and long, guttural fricatives. Without his combadge, Bashir couldn't make out what she was saying, but the response was reassuring. The Ingavi lowered their weapons and shuffled back into the shadows. Ro flicked a look over her shoulder at Ezri. "Don't do that again," she said.

"Right," Ezri said. "Noted."

Obviously deciding it would only be appropriate to respond in kind, Taran'atar pointed at the lab door and he and the First slipped inside. It was still ominously quiet within, but Bashir sensed that the two Jem'Hadar knew this would not last much longer.

When Ro returned, she was escorted by one of the aliens who moved, Bashir thought, with a jaunty nonchalance. "This is Kel," Ro said. "He's the leader of these Ingavi. Most of the others are outside watching the perimeter."

"And the Ingavi are . . . natives of this world?" Bashir asked.

"It's a long story, Doctor. I'll try to explain later. But they deserve our help if only because of what they've done for me today."

"All right," Bashir said, and that seemed to settle things. The little Ingavi hunkered down on his heels, phaser rifle on his lap, eyes locked on the open lab door.

"So, what's been happening?" Ro asked.

Ezri launched into her tale. "After I broke out of our cell, I wasn't sure at first what I could do. I found the air duct and started nosing around. Eventually I found the white distillery and got inspired to do a little creative chemistry. After that, I spent most of my time avoiding Jem'Hadar patrols. It wasn't much fun the first few hours, but then the tainted white began to affect them and it got easier. Sometime after that, the shooting started." Turning to Bashir, she said, "I figured you would be here—one way or another."

Then Ro took up the tale of what had happened since she and Taran'atar had beamed off the runabout. Bashir was beginning to feel like too much time was slipping away, but he was soon caught up in her tale. "By the time we got within fifty meters of their main emplacement," Ro recounted, "at least half the Ingavi had either been shot or forced to retreat. Then the firing let up. Nobody dared to move until one of our snipers picked off a Jem'Hadar at the gate. When we got to the gate, we discovered he was the only one there. It didn't make any sense, but we weren't going to pass up the opportunity, so we kept moving. All we found was dead Jem'Hadar, all of them obviously shot by *other* Jem'Hadar." She looked at Dax with a curious combination of respect and apprehension. "What did you *do* to them?"

"More than I intended, obviously," Dax said. "I just wanted to knock them out. . . ."

"You couldn't have known," Bashir said. "Ketracel-white is a tricky bit of chemistry, one of the reasons it's impossible to replicate. Any impurity will eventually lead to aberrant behavior, eventually escalating into uncontrolled violence. If I can access Locken's records, I should be able to—"

Suddenly, Bashir became aware that Taran'atar was standing directly behind him. *How long has he been there?* he wondered.

"I do not think you will have time to perform tests," he said. "We must leave here soon or we will very likely die along with the Khan."

"Leave? What do you mean?" Bashir asked. "We have to download records, find evidence . . ."

From the lab, there came a deep, snarling yell, then the crash of something large and delicate crashing to the ground. Bashir saw the First's back in the narrow gap, then his face when he turned around. "Close this door," he ordered Taran'atar. "Now." Taran'atar rushed, gripped its edge and began to push in concert with the First. Before they could budge it more than a centimeter, Bashir heard a disruptor discharge and the First had to turn around. "Jem'Hadar!" he shouted. "Stand at attention!" The noise within died. Jem'Hadar conditioning died hard. The First turned back to the door and spoke quietly to Taran'atar. "The need grows strong in them . . . in all of us."

"But we can fix the white," Bashir said.

"No," the First said. "It's too late for that . . ." A tremor ran through his body.

Taran'atar grabbed his shoulder through the narrow space. Already, the Jem'Hadar inside were beginning to stir again. "Give them a good death," Taran'atar said.

The First nodded. Gripping the stock of his disruptor, he shook himself as if to turn away from the door. Without another word, Taran'atar finished shoving the door shut.

Moments later, from within the lab came sounds of death.

Chapter Nineteen

Taran'atar turned to the others. "We must go."

"The runabout is only about a half hour from here on foot," Ro said.

Ezri stared at her in surprise. "It survived the crash?" she asked.

Ro nodded. "She's tough. If we can get off planet, she'll get us home."

"No," Bashir said suddenly. They all looked at him. "We're not finished. We have to get his data. It's the evidence we need to expose Thirty-One. And the only place left now is his quarters." Bashir broke into a run.

Taran'atar and Ro looked at Ezri as if she were responsible for explaining Julian's behavior. "We have to stay with him," she said. "He's not armed."

"He's not *thinking*," Ro added.

"No," Ezri corrected her. "He's thinking too much. He almost can't help it." Something large and metallic crashed against the lab door and the floor vibrated underfoot. "Let's go."

In Locken's quarters, Bashir had already beaten the encryption codes on Locken's log files, but now he was furiously yanking open cabinets and cupboards and tossing their contents out onto the floor.

"Dammit!" he yelled. "Nothing!"

"What are you looking for?"

"A tricorder. A memory solid. Something I can record this data on!"

Ro opened her pack and pulled out a tricorder. "Here," she said, tossing it to Bashir.

Once Bashir found the correct frequency, he quickly developed a search strategy that discarded extraneous material while flagging files with key words and terms. An expert searcher would have required two hours to complete such a task, but Julian was finished in minutes, after which he was downloading the relevant data as quickly as the tricorder would allow.

The immediate task addressed, he began to browse through some of the other directories until he found a schematic of the entire complex. Ezri saw Julian's brow wrinkle. Something was bothering him. Wiping her hands, she walked toward him and saw that he was studying a corner of the compound where power lines and plumbing were leading into a seemingly empty space.

"What could that be?" she asked.

"I don't know," Julian said. "But I have some ideas, and they all bother me."

"Only one way to find out for sure," she said. "Want me to come with you? I know where all the entrances to the ductwork are just in case we have to avoid pursuit."

Julian smiled. "Wedged into a small, dark space with you? What more could I ask for?"

Ezri snorted. "You *are* feeling better, aren't you? Well, believe me, it's not nearly as interesting as all that. You can hear things moving around in those vents. Every once in a while, you surprise one—"

"Now you're just trying to impress me," Julian said. "Whatever we do, we have to do it quickly." He called to Ro and said, "When this is finished, call me, then head for the runabout. There's something we want to go check."

"I don't think it's a good idea for us to separate now," Ro protested. "Especially if the Jem'Hadar break loose."

"Locken might have left something behind. Possibly more Jem'Hadar cloning tubes. If we don't shut them down, there's no telling what they'll do after we're gone. We wouldn't want anything to happen to your native friends."

Ro surrendered. "All right. We'll leave when the download finishes. Take this with you," she said, handing the doctor her phaser rifle. "Watch your back. I have a feeling this place has a few more surprises left."

"You know," Ezri said as they made their way back toward the main lab, "that was quite an act you put on back in the cell. You almost had me convinced."

Bashir stopped and leaned against a wall and rubbed his eyes. "I had you convinced," he said, sighing, "because I wasn't lying. Not entirely. Don't misunderstand—I would never have joined him, Ezri. But those sleepless nights—they *do* happen and they scare the hell out of me. I just don't know how narrow the line is between what I am—" He glanced down the shadowy hall in the direction of Locken's lab. "—and what he was." They stood staring into the darkness and listening to the ominous silence. "What would it take, I wonder, for me to cross that line?"

Ezri reached up and touched his cheek. "Nothing that I can think of," she said reassuringly. "You're not him, Julian. You never will be."

Bashir grasped her hand with his, then pulled her toward him for a gentle kiss on the lips. He smiled and said, "Let's finish up this mission. I want to go home with you."

"That is the best idea I've heard in days," Ezri replied.

Bashir counted off a dozen paces and they found themselves facing a blank wall. "Nothing here," he said. "Nothing obvious, anyway." He laid his fingertips on the wall, then paced back and forth, feeling for some kind of bump or imperfection. He checked the seams to see if there was a raised area, then the joints between wall and floor. "Still nothing," he said.

"Might be voice-activated," Ezri said. "Or more likely, that control unit he carried everywhere."

"Hmmm," Bashir hummed. "Good point. Well, I'm not going into the lab to retrieve it, so it looks like we do this the hard way. Let's go back around that corner," he said, pointing back toward the intersection.

He set the weapon for moderate impact—he wanted to damage the wall without bringing the roof down on their heads—and fired. The wall cracked, but did not shatter. With the second shot, chunks of plasteel crumbled and fell onto the floor. The third shot blasted away large pieces. They coughed and waved their hands in front of their faces until the dust settled and they could see well enough to pick their way through the debris.

Three meters from the wall, Bashir said, "Stop," and pointed down. Something in the dark sparked and writhed. "Power lines."

Ezri pointed at the floor. "And some kind of liquid. You must have hit the plumbing. Not a good combination."

Without a tricorder, it was impossible to check whether they could proceed without danger, so they stood together for several seconds considering options until Ezri slapped her forehead and yelled, "Computer! Lights!"

A trio of fixtures flickered on and they could dimly see what was inside the room.

"More cloning tubes," Ezri said. "More Jem'Hadar."

A chill crawled down his spine. "No," he said. "Not Jem'Hadar." No longer thinking about the possibility of electrocution, he stepped lightly through the rubble, then climbed through the hole in the wall. Moments later, he heard Ezri climb in behind him, then a gasp, then a Klingon curse that would have made old Martok blush.

"When did he have time to do this?" she asked. "We've only been here two days!"

There were four cloning chambers, all of them full. The tube closest to the hole in the wall was cracked, obviously the source of the fluid on the floor. The body was slumped against the inside of the tube, the front of the head pressed flat against the glass. It was a young face, unlined by care or worry, but there was no question who it was.

It was him—Bashir.

He was immobilized, transfixed with shame and a sick kind of wonder. Ezri seemed compelled to peer into each tube. Stepping carefully, almost reverently around the cracked tube, she stared into the somehow unformed faces of the other three clones, each younger than the last, the smallest obviously no more than three years old.

"Oh, no—" she groaned.

Bashir seemed to snap out of the trance he was in and turned toward her. "What—what is it?"

"Julian—He must have been—Locken did some genetic manipulation—this one—is a female."

Bashir almost doubled over, staggered by the almost physical power of his revulsion. He leaned against the wall and felt his legs go numb.

"But, *why?*" Ezri asked. "What was he thinking?" But she already knew, Bashir thought. It was obvious. Cloning was a reliable technique, but nothing worked better than nature.

"Breeding stock," Bashir whispered. "For the new, better Federation." As he said the words, he felt the disgust well up inside his gut, threatening to detonate inside him, to destroy him. There was only one thing he could do. He said, "Get away from there, Ezri."

"What?"

"Get away." He hefted the phaser rifle.

"But, Julian—this is evidence. We can *use* this."

"It's not evidence, Ezri," Bashir said. "It's atrocity."

And she must have seen something in his eyes—something bitter and unwavering—because she didn't say another word, but crept back out over the rubble and stood beside him. When he pressed the trigger, he thought he heard a scream and some distant part of his mind wondered if it could be one of the clones. Was that even possible? He thought he heard the same noise every time he fired, as each phaser bolt cut through plastic and metal, plumbing and electrical conduit, as the tubes exploded, as flesh burned, and fluid boiled away.

It was only much later—when he realized how raw his throat was—that he realized it had been him.

When they stumbled back out into the hall, Bashir and Ezri were surprised to find a Jem'Hadar waiting for them, disruptor drawn, but not raised. Bashir hefted his own weapon, but he knew that if the soldier were to attack, they were as good as dead.

"Why are you still here?" the Jem'Hadar asked, and then Bashir and Ezri simultaneously exhaled. They recognized the voice; it was the First.

"We were taking care of some last-minute business," Bashir said coolly. "What about you? Were you successful? Did you complete your mission?"

"I have done my duty," the First said, glancing back at the lab. "But I have had communication from another squad, one that was on patrol and was not affected by the tainted white. There is something happening outside and I must go to them."

Bashir's mind raced. What could be happening now? Could it be the natives Ro had brought? No, that didn't seem likely. They were obviously not interested in confronting Jem'Hadar if it wasn't necessary. He quickly considered all the other possibilities and realized there was only one likely candidate. "Come with me," he said to the First. "I think I know what's going on."

When they reached Locken's quarters and the doors parted before them, Ro was struggling with the computer console.

"Doctor!" Ro called. "Get over here! Something's wrong." She was frantically working the controls. With a quick glance, Bashir saw that something was happening to the data stored in Locken's computer. The tricorder indicated that they were disintegrating at a precipitous rate.

"A virus?" he asked. "Did we set off a defense mechanism?"

"That's what I thought at first and I spent five minutes running virus-protection routines. I thought it was going after backups first and I had time, but that was just a mask. Meanwhile, most of the primary files were being slagged while it ran these phony displays." She punched in a series of commands. "It *looks* like a virus, but it's really a targeted EM pulse weapon. Someone outside, close, or the damned thing wouldn't work."

Suddenly, Ro's tricorder alarm sounded and she turned away from the console. "Damn!" she shouted, and reached for the tricorder just as its power coupling blew out. She jerked her hand away, grunted in pain, then ran for the kitchen, where she began running water over her fingers. Bashir ran to follow her, but was stopped by the sight of the tricorder. It was a blob of molten metal and plastic swimming with bits of gleaming circuitry.

Before Bashir could inspect Ro's injury, Taran'atar called, "Look here," and pointed at the surveillance monitor. At first, Bashir couldn't make sense of what he was seeing. His first thought was that he was looking at the rays of dawn, but then he caught sight of small animals and birds breaking cover. Through the heavy shadows and bright lights, he saw a sapling, then two larger trees crash to the ground. Then came the men, most of them wearing camouflage or night suits, though a few of them were carrying phaser rifles with searchlights.

A cluster of Ingavi burst from cover and ran at the soldiers. The men with phasers turned toward them and began firing, cutting them down with almost casual ease. There was no sound, but Bashir could hear the little aliens screaming in his mind.

Bashir knew who the newcomers were. He'd done what they asked of him; now they were moving in to finish the job. And that meant wiping out any evidence that they'd ever been to Sindorin. And any witnesses.

Bashir sensed Ro and Kel come up behind him. The Ingavi cried aloud when he saw the images on the screen, then ran for the door. Ro called out to him, "Kel! Wait! We can help."

"No," Taran'atar said. "We can't. It isn't a battle we can win. This mission is over."

"I'm not talking about winning," Ro said. "I'm talking about keeping a promise."

Kel had little patience for their debate, but Bashir sensed that he understood and sympathized with the conflict raging inside Ro. Fighting his desire to join his comrades, he stayed long enough to say, "You have already kept your promise, Ro. You have freed us from the Jem'Hadar. It was much more than we could have hoped for." He pointed the muzzle of his rifle at the monitor. "Do not make the mistake of believing it is your responsibility to resolve this. Not *everything* is your responsibility. The weight of so much guilt would crush you."

And then he was gone.

Ro tried to grab her weapon from Bashir, but she was no match for him with her burned hand. "Doctor," she said. "I'm begging you . . ."

Bashir shook his head. "No," he said. "Taran'atar's right. We have to go. If we stay . . ."

"If we stay," Ro spat back, "we die. But if we go, the Ingavi will die. Maybe not all of them, maybe not immediately, but they can't survive much longer if we don't *do* something." She lurched toward the door, but Taran'atar put his hand on her shoulder, not restraining her, only reminding her of his presence. Ro seemed to sag within herself.

"How," he asked Bashir, "do we get out of here?"

Bashir mentally scanned the complex's layout and had begun to plan an escape route when he was distracted by the flash of disruptor fire. But something was different. "Look here," he said calling to the First, pointing at the monitor. "This is disruptor fire, isn't it?"

The First barely glanced at the images. "My soldiers," he said. "They must be the ones who called me earlier. I've lost contact with them." He checked the grid coordinates on the surveillance feed. "Who are they?" he asked, referring to the humans with phasers.

"They're Locken's accomplices," said Dax, who had been silently watching the Jem'Hadar for the past several minutes. "They're the ones responsible for all this."

The First gritted his teeth. "Then," he snarled, "I will gather my soldiers and we will greet our makers appropriately." He glanced at Bashir, but then spoke to Taran'atar. "There is a transporter pad in the room at the other end of this corridor. You can use it to get to your ship. Go now."

Taran'atar nodded once, but the First wasn't even thinking about him anymore. As they ran down the corridor, Bashir heard the sounds of phaser fire slashing through walls and doors. The Section 31 operatives didn't seem to be encountering any resistance, though he suspected that would change as soon as the First reached his men.

They'd monitored events from inside the plasma storms as best they could. Cloaked surveillance probes had recorded some very interesting images on most of the frequencies in the EM spectrum, detailed enough that they knew the moment Locken was dead, but not the exact circumstances, save that somehow Bashir had turned the would-be Khan's own Jem'Hadar against him. But once the kill was confirmed, Cole gave the order to deploy.

He took off his night-vision lenses and glanced around to get a better look at the spot he had staked out as his observation post. The sun had just barely climbed over the top of the tree line and he would have to switch to the standard binoculars now. *The worst part about dawn operations,* he reflected, *is that sooner or later you have to see everything that was done under cover of darkness.* There were bodies everywhere, most of them Jem'Hadar, but some of the local ape creatures, too. A few of his men had gone down, but not many, and well within acceptable losses.

But Cole knew some things about this rain forest. It wouldn't be long before things started to smell bad. And there were scavengers crawling over some of the bodies. These would disappear as soon as the sun came up, but then the insects would begin to appear and they would lay eggs and the eggs would turn into larvae and then the larvae would begin squirming—

Cole was glad he would be gone within the hour. He was here to make sure the cleanup operation was well under way, but he had no intention of staying for the whole thing.

One of his runners ran up beside him and waited to be acknowledged. Cole made him wait for a few seconds, then spoke without turning. "Yes?"

"Sir, sensors report a Starfleet runabout lifting off to the northwest of us. You gave orders to be alerted if we picked up on anything like that."

"Right. I did, didn't I?" He picked up a pair of standard-issue binoculars and studied the battlefield—no, the killing field. Cole shook his head in wonder at how careless Sloan had been to let Bashir get away. He would have been an astonishingly effective field agent. Not that he didn't have other uses . . . Well, that explained where the locals got phaser rifles. He wondered how many of Bashir's team were making it off alive.

"Orders, sir?" the runner asked.

Cole lowered his binoculars, and stared into the northwest sky, almost convincing himself he could spot the fleeing runabout with his naked eyes. "Let it go," he said.

"Sir?"

"Let it go." He studied the front of the compound and wondered how many quantum torpedoes it would take to level the place once they had cleaned out the useful bits.

The *Euphrates* would, as Ro had said, get them home, but she wasn't the same ship she had been when she left DS9. Ezri was fairly sure she could get them out of the Badlands, but if they ran into any major plasma-storm activity, it would be a near thing. Once clear of the Badlands, they would activate the distress beacon and head for home at a conservative pace.

Julian was in the back treating Taran'atar's wounds,

which were already healing at an astonishing rate. According to his readings, Taran'atar had suffered a punctured lung, but it was completely healed now.

Ro was back in the aft compartment. She wanted to be alone.

And then there was Julian. She had seen him in some black moods, but nothing like this. In his eyes, the fact that they had probably just saved the quadrant from months or years of struggle and strife didn't mean anything. The only thing that mattered was that he hadn't been able to slay his dragon. Section 31 was still out there, still three steps ahead of all of them.

The sensor alarm blipped and Ezri glanced at the readout. The short-range sensors had begun to act up shortly after liftoff and she was tempted to just shut them down, but she was worried about encountering another orbital weapons platform. She checked the display and found—what? A sensor ghost of some kind. She reset the master grid and the ghost disappeared.

Steering to starboard, giving a plasma plume a very wide berth, she wondered why so many of their missions didn't have happy endings.

Chapter Twenty

"Deep Space 9, this is the *Euphrates*. Come in, Deep Space 9." Ro waited for several seconds for a response, then repeated the message.

"Are you sure the transmitter is working?" Ezri asked.

Ro stared at her, expressionless. "Would you like to try?" she asked.

Ezri smiled guiltily. "No, sorry. Go ahead. I'm just getting worried."

"We're all worried," Bashir said from the engineering station behind them. "But there's no way to be sure whether the scanning problem resides in the runabout's systems or in the diagnostic programs. Everything *looks* like it's working, but we could be transmitting on the wrong frequency . . ."

"Or the station's comm system could be offline," Ro added.

"But shouldn't we be able to pick up one of the patrolling starships?" Ezri asked.

"There may be subspace interference," Ro suggested. She didn't elaborate; she didn't need to. Everyone aboard knew that only a massive explosion was capable of causing that much interference—the kind of explosion no one wanted to think about.

"Can we get any more speed out of this thing?" Bashir asked.

Ro shook her head. "Without knowing whether the diagnostic programs are functioning properly—and I'll say again that I don't think they are—then, no. Warp two is the maximum and we're taking a big chance there. If it were up to me, we'd drop to impulse and send out a distress call."

Bashir didn't want to admit it, but he knew that what Ro was suggesting was not only proper protocol, but the sensible thing to do. The problem was he didn't feel like being sensible—he wanted to go home. "Best speed, Lieutenant," he said, rising from his chair. It was his turn to get some sleep. "But do whatever you think is best."

"Yes, sir," Ro said flatly, and it was clear from her tone that if they had done what she thought best they would still be on Sindorin. *A problem to deal with after I've had some sleep,* Bashir decided.

Bashir was so weary that when he lay down he thought for a moment that Ezri had suddenly doubled the gravity, but then realized, *No, it's only my body surrendering.* He closed his eyes and a gruff voice asked, *"So, what did you learn, Doctor?"*

Bashir struggled feebly to open his eyes, but it was too late, his system had been too abused. He couldn't rouse himself and he couldn't refuse to answer. *What did I learn? I learned that it's always possible to feel more alone than you thought you could ever feel.*

And from up out of the dark came the approving voice of Sloan. *"Excellent, Doctor. You've learned your lesson well."*

"Julian, you have to come see this."

Bashir's eyes snapped open. He didn't remember closing them, which was unusual for him because most of the time sleep was an elusive thing. He tried to sit up, but his arms felt numb, his legs rubbery. "What? Yes. . . . Coming." His mouth felt like a dried-up tennis ball and his eyelids were grating over the surface of his eyeballs. He had been dreaming about . . . something disturbing. What? Oh, the clones . . . just before he had triggered the phaser, the clones had come to life and pressed their faces against the tubes. . . .

He stumbled to the cockpit and felt the runabout shudder as they switched over from warp engines to impulse. "What's happening?" he asked, his eyes still not clear. "Where are we?"

But then he looked out through the main viewport and he knew where they were. It hung there—a glistening jewel, an ornament against the night—Deep Space 9. Nog had done his job: all the lights were on, much brighter even than usual, blazing so brilliantly that the stars themselves seemed dim.

Ezri, seated in the copilot's chair, reached up, took his hand, and said, "We're home, Julian."

Ro repeated, *"We're* home," and it was clear that the betrayal of the Ingavi was still foremost on her mind. Bashir felt it, too, but didn't begrudge himself the wave of relief that swept through him.

"Can we contact them?" he asked.

"No," Ezri said. "It's definitely our subspace transmitter. The diagnostic program sorted it out while you were asleep. It also said we were safe to go to warp four, so we got back a lot faster than we had expected."

Bashir did the calculations. "So I was asleep . . . ten hours?"

"Twelve," Ro said. "The rest of us took turns. We figured you needed the sleep."

He didn't know how to respond, so he said only, "Thank you," and gripped Ezri's hand more tightly. A shadow crossed between them and the station and he looked up. Directly above them, a Klingon attack cruiser shed its cloak.

"They're challenging us," Ro said.

"Come to a halt," Bashir said. "And release the emergency beacon. They'll figure it out."

Ro did as he asked, and several minutes later the attack cruiser grappled the *Euphrates* with its tractor beam and set them down on a runabout pad. Suddenly her combadge—the only one to survive the mission—chirped for attention. "Ops to Lieutenant Ro."

"Ro here. Go ahead, Nog."

"Lieutenant? Is everyone all right? I have no other combadge signals from your team."

"We're all okay, Nog."

"That's a relief. Colonel Kira would like you all to report to her office directly."

"Of course she would," Ro said quietly.

"So," Nog continued, "doesn't the station look great?"

Even Ro smiled a little at that. "Yeah, Nog," she said softly. "It sure does."

"That's a hell of a story," Kira said when the companions finished delivering their report. "My only question is: How much of this can you tell to Starfleet Command?"

The question seemed to surprise Dax, but Bashir understood what she was asking. "I think we can tell Admiral Ross most of the tale," he replied. "Though I expect he'll have to edit it heavily before Starfleet shares it with any other Federation worlds. I'd like to be able to tell the Romulans *something* about their missing ships. But the part about what happened on New Beijing . . ."

"That'll never come out," Kira sighed. "On the bright side, now that we know what was done, Starfleet can take steps to ensure that such a thing never happens again."

Ro sat stone-faced, arms crossed over her chest. "I can't help but notice," she said, "that none of you has said a word about the Ingavi. What are we going to do about them?" She looked from face to face. "Colonel? Doctor? Any thoughts? Do you even *care?*"

"You're being unfair," Dax said. "Of course we care. And it's not like we didn't accomplish anything. If we hadn't gone to Sindorin, probably all the Ingavi would be dead by now."

"Most of the Ingavi probably *are* dead by now," Ro muttered.

"That's enough," Kira snapped. "This is hard enough without everyone sniping at each other." She turned to Ro, modulating her tone. "You're welcome to make your thoughts on the subject clear in your formal report, but otherwise I think that's the end of the topic for now. We'll do what we can."

"Right," Ro said. "When things cool off. When the Romulans stop searching the area for the missing ships. When no one will have any reason to suspect anything terrible has happened on Sindorin." She leaned forward and slapped the top of Kira's desk with the flat of her hand. "When they're all dead."

"Ro . . ." Dax began, but Kira signaled for her to be silent.

Unable to listen to any more, Ro rose from her seat without asking leave. "I'm going back to my office to check on some things. Sir."

"When you get there," Kira said, "contact Commander Vaughn. He left me a message saying you should get in touch with him. He's on Empok Nor with one of the engineering teams."

"Where *is* Empok Nor?" Bashir asked.

"Nog towed it into orbit of Cajara."

Cajara. The Bajoran system's seventh planet, Bashir recalled. *Currently on same side of the sun as DS9. A short trip by runabout.*

Ro sighed, picked up her travel-stained bag, and headed for the door.

As soon as she left, Bashir rose. "Well, you'll have to excuse me, too."

"No, wait. Stay right there," Kira said, pointing Bashir back into his seat. "I already know what you're thinking."

Bashir sagged back into his chair. "What am I thinking?" he asked.

Kira folded her arms. "One: You're thinking that you utterly failed because you weren't able to bring back the evidence you wanted in order to expose Section 31 and bring it to justice."

Bashir smiled wanly.

"And, two," Kira continued, "you're pondering ways you could slip back to Sindorin while no one is looking and save the Ingavi. 'It should be simple,' you're thinking. 'I'm ever so much smarter than everyone else.

And, oh, while I'm there, I'll look around for some more evidence that I can someday use to crush Section 31. And, no, I don't need to bother telling the colonel because she would just try to tell me I'm being an idiot.'"

Bashir's smile turned into a weary grin. "You've been listening at my door," he said. "That's pretty good, though I'm not nearly that humble."

Kira almost smiled in return. "I've ordered ops to keep a close eye on all outgoing traffic. I already have one missing person; I don't want another." Then, she filled in Dax, Bashir and Taran'atar on the situation regarding Jake Sisko.

When she finished, Dax rose and said, "I'm going to call Kasidy. She must be frantic."

"She seemed all right when I spoke with her," Kira replied.

Dax shrugged. "And she probably was at the time. But the hormones kick in at unexpected times. Pregnancy, you know. I remember—"

Kira nodded, also remembering. "All right. Thank you, Ezri. Yes, please call her and tell her we'll come down to Bajor to see her as soon as possible."

Dax nodded and left.

Bashir rose to follow, but before he could leave Kira stopped him and said, "I know this must have been difficult for you, Julian. So let me just say thank you. If you have trouble sleeping tonight, think about how many people you saved on this mission."

Bashir nodded gratefully and said, "You're getting good at this command thing, Nerys. That almost makes me feel better. It almost helps me forget the ones I *didn't* save."

"I don't want you to forget them, Julian," Kira said. "I just want you to forgive yourself for not being the superhuman you sometimes think you are."

Bashir locked eyes with her for several seconds, unblinking, then bowed his head, the tension that he had been holding in his shoulders and neck melting away. Finally, he nodded, and with a heartfelt "Thank you, Nerys," he left.

That left only the colonel and Taran'atar.

He had been sitting in the corner, in the seat farthest from her desk, and though he had not said a word during the debriefing unless asked a direct question, Kira had sensed his interest in the proceedings.

Even after Bashir had left, he did not speak for some time, but only stared at her from beneath his brow. She waited for him to speak, but finally decided that Jem'Hadar weren't accustomed to speaking first. "Dr. Bashir said that the mission would have failed without your assistance," she said. "Thank you for that. It must have been difficult for you to be here so short a time, and already finding yourself having to face other Jam'Hadar in combat, twice now."

"These were not the first times Jem'Hadar have fought Jem'Hadar. They will not be the last."

Kira mentally filed that statement for later consideration. "The doctor also said that you were badly injured and that some of the injuries might not have been battle-related. Again, if that was the case, I appreciate how you might have suffered. I know a little bit about torture—"

"How to take it or how to give it?" Taran'atar asked.

Kira hesitated. "I don't think I want to answer that question," she finally replied. "Let's just leave it at that."

"All right," Taran'atar replied. "We will."

When he did not rise to leave, Kira asked, "Is there anything else we can do for you right now? Do you want to send a message back to the Dominion? I could arrange it if you like."

"I was not instructed to make reports, so I will not. The Founders will contact me when they wish—if they wish."

Again, he did not rise to leave, so Kira asked again, "Something else?"

Taran'atar inhaled deeply, then slowly released it. She could see that he was trying to make up his mind about something, but she resolved to wait it out in silence. At last, he leaned forward in his chair, balled up one fist, and cupped it with his other hand. He said, "Lieutenant Ro told me that she has never met anyone who has as much faith in her gods as you. Is this so?"

Kira was more than a little surprised to find out that Ro had any opinions about anyone's spiritual life, let alone Kira's own, but for the sake of discussion, she decided to agree. "It's hard to measure such things, but, yes, I believe my faith is very strong."

"How did it get to be so strong?" Taran'atar asked. "How can you . . . not doubt?"

Kira leaned back in her chair. She hadn't been prepared for a theological discussion today, especially not with a Jem'Hadar. She resolved to cuff Odo the next time she saw him . . .

. . . if she ever saw him again.

But she said, "I do doubt. Every day, I doubt everything. I doubt that I'm doing this job right. I doubt that I'm a good and decent person. I even doubt that we'll all be here tomorrow. I doubt, and doubt, and doubt. But through it all, I draw strength from the idea that the

Prophets are weaving a tapestry in which my life is a thread, and that my faith helps bring me closer to understanding my part in the whole. It's become my belief of late that the Prophets have no use for blind devotion. They want us—their people—to question our beliefs every day, because the only way our faith can grow stronger is by having it challenged." Kira stopped then, slightly embarrassed. "Does any of this make sense?" she asked.

Taran'atar mulled it over. "This," he said at length, "is all very paradoxical."

Kira shrugged. "At best," she said, "it's paradoxical. On its bad days, it's just complete nonsense."

The Jem'Hadar grunted his assent.

"If nothing else," she concluded, "have faith in Odo. I know I do."

He looked up at her then and the glaze of confusion in his eyes seemed to lift and he nodded. "Then perhaps that," he said, "will be our common ground."

The corpse of Empok Nor was growing cool; and though several of DS9's emergency generators had been transferred over to keep the chill out of a few sections, Vaughn found something sad about it, but he seemed to be the only one who did. Perhaps it was a function of having seen so much death over the years. *Old people,* he reflected, *think about death more.* Well, nothing profound there. *They also think about being cold more,* he decided, and zipped his coat up to the neck and flipped up the collar.

It was one of the old-issue Starfleet field coats, probably one of the best garments the quartermaster's office had ever issued, and Vaughn, like most officers who had been cadets eighty years ago, had held on to his. They were sturdy, had deep pockets, and the heating cells were well placed.

Vaughn was standing at the docking port in one of the station's lower pylons, watching the stars through the airlock viewport. He appreciated that about Cardassian station design, being able to actually *see* the ship approaching the dock rather than relying on a monitor or a holotank. He was thinking about the term "mothball." Many, many years ago, he had looked the word up in one of the older editions of the *Oxford Dictionary of Terran Languages* and had been surprised to find that it had something to do with a substance that was stored with clothing to kill insect larvae. The definition still made him shake his head and smile in wonderment; what a wonderfully flexible language Late English had been.

"Mothballed," he said aloud, letting the word roll over his tongue. How long would it be before someone somewhere decided it was time to mothball *him?* He glanced out the viewport at the huge docking ring above him and decided, *Well, a little longer, anyway.*

Someone was coming up behind him. It was in itself unusual enough that Vaughn hadn't heard the approach. There were only two or three possibilities for who it might be. One of the three would have killed him by now. The second . . . well, he knew it couldn't be her, because he always knew *exactly where she was.*

"Dr. Bashir," Vaughn said without turning. "What can I do for you?"

Bashir stopped walking, obviously puzzled. Vaughn heard him take a deep breath, then release it slowly. *He's angry,* Vaughn decided, *but trying to keep it under control. Almost doing it, too.*

"I need to ask you some questions," Bashir said, obviously struggling to remain polite. "And I'd like some straight answers, please." Then he added, "For once."

Vaughn turned around to look at the doctor, then leaned back against the airlock portal. "Of course, Doctor."

Bashir closed the distance between them, then stopped, set his feet as if he was expecting Vaughn to throw a punch at him. "You knew what was going to happen."

Vaughn cocked his head to one side. "That's not a question."

Bashir sighed and began to turn around to leave.

Vaughn held up his hands. "All right, all right. Sorry. Evasion is a difficult habit to give up. The answer is, no, I didn't know exactly what was going to happen. I had suspicions. I know how Thirty-One works, Doctor, and there's always more than one meaning to anything they say." He pulled his combadge off the front of his uniform and held it up for Bashir to see. Then he curled his fingers around it, shook his fist in the air, and opened his palm. The combadge was gone. "And always remember," he added, "whatever it is they let you see, no matter how interesting it might be, they're only letting you see it so you won't pay attention to something else." He held out his other hand and showed Bashir a combadge. Bashir shrugged and then Vaughn pointed at the front of the doctor's uniform. His own combadge was gone.

Bashir held out his hand and Vaughn dropped the combadge into it. "Section 31 needed Locken out of the way. And while they most likely could have mustered a force capable of reducing him, his Jem'Hadar, and the hatchery to ashes, they would have lost what they were really after all along."

"His data," Bashir guessed.

"Yes," said Vaughn. "But the only way to accomplish both goals, get rid of Locken and obtain his data, was to put someone on the inside, something Section 31 couldn't do. Cole needed you to do it for him. Once you took care of him, their job would be simpler. They got what they wanted, and they covered their tracks. Section 31's first principle is to protect the secret of their existence. Any other motivation they might espouse is secondary and serves only to reinforce the first principle. It may have been different once, but not anymore. It's their greatest strength and their greatest weakness."

Bashir studied Vaughn carefully. "Are you telling me, then, that you *aren't* one of them? Another Starfleet officer on a short leash—"

Vaughn's eyes narrowed dangerously. "I'm not on anybody's leash, Doctor. And I've *never* worked for Thirty-One."

Bashir saw the truth then, and the revelation left him breathless. "You've been fighting them, too."

"Longer than you've been alive," Vaughn said. He turned to look out the viewport again. "I think, Doctor, that you've always been and always will be a bit of a romantic. Your latest romantic fantasy is this idea that you're the solitary opponent to this gigantic conspiracy. It feeds your ego."

Bashir began to protest, but Vaughn waved him to silence. "There's nothing wrong with having an ego, Doctor," he said. "It's a necessity if you're going to survive this. The truth is that there are only a few of us. The other much sadder truth is that the only ones among us who have survived opposing Thirty-One are the ones who are patient, and who can think even more moves ahead than they do."

"A lot of good any of that did the Ingavi," Bashir muttered.

In response, Vaughn tapped a command code into the companel on the wall. He pointed up to Empok Nor's docking ring, where an odd-looking, blocky starship suddenly decloaked.

"What the hell is that?" Bashir asked.

"That, Doctor, is a mobile environment simulator—a holoship, for want of a better word. The only one of its kind, in fact. It was custom-built in secret and illegally equipped with a cloaking device. It's a relic from a failed Section 31 operation in the Briar Patch last year. Thirty-One was never implicated, unfortunately. The blame went instead to a single rogue admiral, now dead, who was working with the Son'a. But those of us who have made it our business to oppose Thirty-One knew perfectly well who and what was pulling his strings.

"After the operation failed, the holoship was officially confiscated by Starfleet Command and destroyed." A small smile made its way into Vaughn's beard. "At least, that's what the paperwork says."

"Are you telling me you stole it out from under the noses of Starfleet Command *and* Section 31? But why?"

Vaughn shrugged. "For a rainy day. The idea of using one of Section 31's own instruments against them appealed to me. This one was designed specifically to relocate a small colony—in secret."

The last piece clicked into place for Bashir, and

he started laughing. "You got the Ingavi off Sindorin!"

Vaughn nodded. "Most of them. As many as we could find in the time we had. And I didn't do it personally. But as I said . . . you aren't alone."

"Ezri mentioned that we picked up a sensor ghost while leaving the planet."

"Nothing is perfect, Doctor," Vaughn said. "Not even one of *my* plans. You'll learn that as we work together."

Bashir suddenly smiled, a roguish, almost boyish grin. He looked like he might climb through the airlock without an e-suit to get to the ship. "But—Ro! You have to tell her! She was devastated!"

"She's already up there," Vaughn explained. "Trying to make it clear what happened. With only mixed results, I'm afraid. They're pretty shocked by this whole affair, though she seems to be getting a lot of help from one in particular."

"Is it Kel?" Bashir asked, delighted. "He made it?"

"I didn't catch the name, Doctor. All I can tell you is that whoever he is, he seemed very pleased with himself."

"It's Kel!" Bashir shouted, delighted. "I have to tell Ezri! I have to explain it to Kira! Otherwise, she'll start making plans—"

"The colonel knows," Vaughn said. "We couldn't have done this without her looking the other way at the proper time. And as for Lieutenant Dax—I think you should wait."

"Wait? Wait for what?"

"Wait until you've gone over there and started doing some medical assessments on our guests. Then, you help me explain that they're to be resettled on Ingav—which, incidentally, is a Federation protectorate these days. And then . . ." He clapped Bashir on the shoulder. "Then you come back to DS9 with me and I'll make you a cup of good twig tea, and together, *together,* we'll begin to make plans."

About the Authors

David Weddle was an Executive Story Editor on the television series *Star Trek: Deep Space Nine.*

Jeffrey Lang is the author of "Dead Man's Hand," a short story in the critically acclaimed anthology *The Lives of Dax,* and *Immortal Coil,* a *Star Trek: The Next Generation*® novel that will be published in 2002. He lives in Wynnewood, Pennsylvania, with his wife and son and is one amazingly fortunate guy.

Look for STAR TREK fiction from Pocket Books

Star Trek®: The Original Series

Star Trek: The Next Generation®

Star Trek®: New Frontier

Star Trek®: Invasion!

#1 • *First Strike* • Diane Carey
#2 • *The Soldiers of Fear* • Dean Wesley Smith & Kristine Kathryn Rusch
#3 • *Time's Enemy* • L.A. Graf
#4 • *The Final Fury* • Dafydd ab Hugh
Invasion! Omnibus • various

Star Trek®: Day of Honor

#1 • *Ancient Blood* • Diane Carey
#2 • *Armageddon Sky* • L.A. Graf
#3 • *Her Klingon Soul* • Michael Jan Friedman
#4 • *Treaty's Law* • Dean Wesley Smith & Kristine Kathryn Rusch
The Television Episode • Michael Jan Friedman
Day of Honor Omnibus • various

Star Trek®: The Captain's Table

#1 • *War Dragons* • L.A. Graf
#2 • *Dujonian's Hoard* • Michael Jan Friedman
#3 • *The Mist* • Dean Wesley Smith & Kristine Kathryn Rusch
#4 • *Fire Ship* • Diane Carey
#5 • *Once Burned* • Peter David
#6 • *Where Sea Meets Sky* • Jerry Oltion
The Captain's Table Omnibus • various

Star Trek®: The Dominion War

#1 • *Behind Enemy Lines* • John Vornholt
#2 • *Call to Arms...* • Diane Carey
#3 • *Tunnel Through the Stars* • John Vornholt
#4 • *...Sacrifice of Angels* • Diane Carey

Star Trek®: The Badlands

#1 • Susan Wright
#2 • Susan Wright

Star Trek®: Dark Passions

#1 • Susan Wright
#2 • Susan Wright

Star Trek®: Section 31

Cloak • S. D. Perry
Rogue • Andy Mangels & Michael A. Martin
Abyss • Dean Weddle & Jeffrey Lang
Shadow • Dean Wesley Smith & Kristine Kathryn Rusch

Star Trek® Books available in Trade Paperback

Omnibus Editions
   Invasion! Omnibus • various
   Day of Honor Omnibus • various
   The Captain's Table Omnibus • various
   Star Trek: Odyssey • William Shatner with Judith and Garfield Reeves-
      Stevens

Other Books
   Legends of the Ferengi • Ira Steven Behr & Robert Hewitt Wolfe
   Strange New Worlds, vols. I, II, III, and IV • Dean Wesley Smith, ed.
   Adventures in Time and Space • Mary P. Taylor
   Captain Proton: Defender of the Earth • D.W. "Prof" Smith
   New Worlds, New Civilizations • Michael Jan Friedman
   The Lives of Dax • Marco Palmieri, ed.
   The Klingon Hamlet • Wil'yam Shex'pir
   Enterprise Logs • Carol Greenburg, ed.

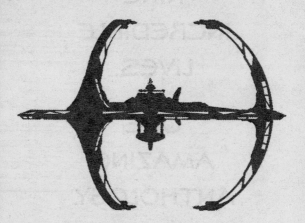